LOVE'S VERDICT

Reviewers Love the Lone Star Law Series

Outside the Law

"This is by far the best book of the series, and Ms. Taite has saved the best for last. Each book features a romance, and the main characters, Tanner Cohen and Sydney Braswell, are well rounded, lovable, and their chemistry is sizzling…The book found the perfect balance between romance and thriller with a surprising twist at the end. Very entertaining read. Overall, a very good end of this series. Recommended for both romance and thriller fans. 4.5 stars."—*Lez Review Books*

Letter of the Law

"Fiery clashes and lots of chemistry, you betcha!"—*The Romantic Reader Blog*

Above the Law

"[R]eaders who enjoyed the first installment will find this a worthy second act."—*Publishers Weekly*

"Ms Taite delivered and then some, all the while adding more questions, Tease! I like the mystery and intrigue in this story. It has many 'sit on the edge of your seat' scenes of excitement and dread (like watch out kind of thing) and drama…well done indeed!"—*Prism Book Alliance*

Lay Down the Law

"Recognized for the pithy realism of her characters and settings drawn from a Texas legal milieu, Taite pays homage to the prime-time soap opera *Dallas* in pairing a cartel-busting U.S. Attorney, Peyton Davis, with a charity-minded oil heiress, Lily Gantry."—*Publishers Weekly*

"Suspenseful, intriguingly tense, and with a great developing love story, this book is delightfully solid on all fronts. This gets my A-1 recommendation!"—*Rainbow Book Reviews*

"This book is AMAZING!!! The setting, the scenery, the people, the plot, wow."—*Prism Book Alliance*

Praise for the Luca Bennett Mystery Series

Switchblade

"I enjoyed the book and it was a fun read—mystery, action, humor, and a bit of romance. Who could ask for more? If you've read and enjoyed Taite's legal novels, you'll like this. If you've read and enjoyed the two other books in this series, this one will definitely satisfy your Luca fix and I highly recommend picking it up. Highly recommended."
—*C-spot Reviews*

"Dallas's intrepid female bounty hunter, Luca Bennett, is back in another adventure. Fantastic! Between her many friends and lovers, her interesting family, her fly by the seat of her pants lifestyle, and a whole host of detractors, there is rarely a dull moment."—*Rainbow Book Reviews*

Battle Axe

"This second book is satisfying, substantial, and slick. Plus, it has heart and love coupled with Luca's array of weapons and a badass verbal repertoire…I cannot imagine anyone not having a great time riding shotgun through all of Luca's escapades. I recommend hopping on Luca's bandwagon and having a blast."—*Rainbow Book Reviews*

"Taite breathes life into her characters with elemental finesse…A great read, told in the vein of a good old detective-type novel filled with criminal elements, thugs, and mobsters that will entertain and amuse."—*Lambda Literary*

Slingshot

"The mean streets of lesbian literature finally have the hardboiled bounty hunter they deserve. It's a slingshot of a ride, bad guys and hot women rolled into one page-turning package. I'm looking forward to Luca Bennett's next adventure."—*J. M. Redmann, author of the Micky Knight mystery series*

Praise for Carsen Taite

A More Perfect Union

"Readers looking for a mix of intrigue and romance set against a political backdrop will want to pick up Taite's latest novel."—*Romantic Times Book Review*

"This is a fabulously written tightly woven political/military intrigue with a large helping of romance. I enjoyed every minute and was on the edge of my seat the whole time. This one is a great read! Carsen Taite never disappoints!"—*The Romantic Reader Blog*

Sidebar

"*Sidebar* is a love story with a refreshing twist. It's a mystery and a bit of a thriller, with an ethical dilemma and some subterfuge thrown in for good measure. The combination gives us a fast-paced read, which includes courtroom and personal drama, an appealing love story, and a more than satisfying ending."—*Lambda Literary*

"*Sidebar* is a sexy, fun, interesting book that's sure to delight, whether you're a longtime fan or this is your first time reading something by Carsen Taite. I definitely recommend it!"—*The Lesbian Review*

"This book has it all: two fantastic lead characters, an interesting plot, and that sizzling chemistry that great authors can make jump off the page. While all of Taite's books are fantastic, this one is on the next level. No critiques, no criticism, you only need to know one thing…this is a damn good book."—*The Romantic Reader Blog*

Without Justice

"Carsen Taite tells a great story. She is consistent in giving her readers a good if not great legal drama with characters who are insightful, well thought out and have good chemistry. You know when you pick up one of her books you are getting your money's worth time and time again. Consistency with a great legal drama is all but guaranteed." —*The Romantic Reader Blog*

"All in all a fantastic novel…Unequivocally 5 Stars…"—*Les Reveur*

"This is a great read, fast-paced, interesting and takes a slightly different tack from the normal crime/courtroom drama having a lawyer in the witness protection system whose case becomes the hidden centre of another crime."—*Lesbian Reading Room*

Reasonable Doubt

"I was drawn into the mystery plot line and quickly became enthralled with the book. It was suspenseful without being too intense but there were some great twists to keep me guessing. It's a very good book. I cannot wait to read the next in line that Ms. Taite has to offer."
—*Prism Book Alliance*

Courtship

"The political drama is just top-notch. The emotional and sexual tensions are intertwined with great timing and flair. I truly adored this book from beginning to end. Fantabulous!"—*Rainbow Book Reviews*

"Carsen Taite throws the reader head-on into the murky world of the political system where there are no rights or wrongs, just players attempting to broker the best deals regardless of who gets hurt in the process. The book is extremely well written and makes compelling reading. With twist and turns throughout, the reader doesn't know how the story will end."—*Lesbian Reading Room*

"Taite keeps the stakes high as two beautiful and brilliant women fueled by professional ambitions face daunting emotional choices... As backroom politics, secrets, betrayals, and threats race to be resolved without political damage to the president, the cat-and-mouse relationship game between Addison and Julia has the reader rooting for them. Taite prolongs the fever-pitch tension to the final pages. This pleasant read with intelligent heroines, snappy dialogue, and political suspense will satisfy Taite's devoted fans and new readers alike."
—*Publishers Weekly*

Rush

"A simply beautiful interplay of police procedural magic, murder, FBI presence, misguided protective cover-ups, and a superheated love affair...a Gold Star from me and major encouragement for all readers to dive right in and consume this story with gusto!"—*Rainbow Book Reviews*

Beyond Innocence

"As you would expect, sparks and legal writs fly. What I liked about this book were the shades of grey (no, not the smutty Shades of Grey)—both in the relationship as well as the cases."—*C-spot Reviews*

"Taite keeps you guessing with delicious delay until the very last minute...Taite's time in the courtroom lends *Beyond Innocence* a terrific verisimilitude someone not in the profession couldn't impart. And damned if she doesn't make practicing law interesting."
—*Out in Print*

The Best Defense

"Real life defense attorney Carsen Taite polishes her fifth work of lesbian fiction...with the realism she daily encounters in the office and in the courts. And that polish is something that makes *The Best Defense* shine as an excellent read."—*Out & About Newspaper*

Nothing but the Truth

"Author Taite is really a Dallas defense attorney herself, and it's obvious her viewpoint adds considerable realism to her story, making it especially riveting as a mystery. I give it four stars out of five."
—*Bob Lind, Echo Magazine*

"Taite has written an excellent courtroom drama with two interesting women leading the cast of characters. Taite herself is a practicing defense attorney, and her courtroom scenes are clearly based on real knowledge. This should be another winner for Taite."
—*Lambda Literary*

Do Not Disturb

"Taite's tale of sexual tension is entertaining in itself, but a number of secondary characters...add substantial color to romantic inevitability."
—*Richard Labonte, Book Marks*

It Should Be a Crime

"Law professor Morgan Bradley and her student Parker Casey are potential love interests, but throw in a high-profile murder trial, and you've got an entertaining book that can be read in one sitting. Taite also practices criminal law and she weaves her insider knowledge of the criminal justice system into the love story seamlessly and with excellent timing. I find romances lacking when the characters change completely upon falling in love, but this was not the case here. I look forward to reading more from Taite."—*Curve Magazine*

"This is just Taite's second novel...but it's as if she has bookshelves full of bestsellers under her belt."—*Gay List Daily*

By the Author

Truelesbianlove.com

It Should be a Crime

Do Not Disturb

Nothing but the Truth

The Best Defense

Beyond Innocence

Rush

Courtship

Reasonable Doubt

Without Justice

Sidebar

A More Perfect Union

Love's Verdict

The Luca Bennett Mystery Series

Slingshot

Battle Axe

Switchblade

Bow and Arrow (novella in *Girls with Guns*)

Lone Star Law Series

Lay Down the Law

Above the Law

Letter of the Law

Outside the Law

LOVE'S VERDICT

by

Carsen Taite

2018

Credits
Editor: Cindy Cresap
Production Design: Stacia Seaman
Cover Design by Sheri (hindsightgraphics@gmail.com)

Acknowledgments

When it comes to the finished product, a whole bunch of people make me look good. Thanks to the entire Bold Strokes Books family and:

Sheri for another amazing cover design.

Cindy Cresap for fierce edits delivered with a side of humor.

Len Barot and Sandy Lowe for making Bold Strokes Books a nurturing home where authors can thrive.

Paula Tighe for always being available when I want to brainstorm legal strategy.

VK Powell and Ashley Bartlett for their steadfast friendship and keen editorial eyes.

Georgia Beers for keeping me on track with our daily check-ins.

Love and thanks to my wife, Lainey, who brainstorms plot points and takes care of all the things while I'm holed up in my office writing or traveling to literary events around the country. None of my success would be possible without you.

And to all of my readers—your support fuels my inspiration and daily word counts. Thanks for taking this journey with me. Let's keep going—shall we?

To Lainey. I love that we aim for the top together.

Prologue

Carly stood in the entrance to the ballroom and searched for a safe place. A place to have one token drink and bide her time until she'd done her duty by appearing at the firm's annual ritual of no fun whatsoever.

"Hey, Pachett, you just get here?"

Damn. Carly managed a smile for Keith Worthington, but it was totally fake. Keith, one of the other associates at the firm, loved to give her a hard time about how little she enjoyed the firm's social functions. Unlike her, he lived for free cocktails and apps handed out by sleek cater waiters. Tonight he had a date on his arm—a tall, size zero blonde with a little too much Botox for her age—the perfect date for Keith since she wouldn't be fighting him for the free food.

Carly wouldn't mind these social events if they didn't happen so often, but it seemed like every month there was some after-hours drain on her time that had nothing to do with billable hours and everything to do with making small talk with people she wouldn't care to spend time with outside of the office. Keith loved the schmoozing. He'd been at the firm four years and already had his eye on a partnership spot to which Carly silently said, *get in line*. She was well into her fifth year at Sturges and Lloyd, and when Jane and Mark, the senior partners, decided to add a name to the partner roster, she expected to be at the top of the list. She didn't have a lot of hands-on litigation experience, but she excelled at negotiations and her win record on appeal was unparalleled. She'd earned her spot at the top. The only less-than-stellar feedback she got at year-end bonus time was that she would do well to loosen up a little, muck it up with clients to bring in more business. She'd assured them she would do her part, even if it killed her, which was why she'd decided to put in an appearance tonight at the firm's annual holiday gala.

"Where's the bar?" she asked Keith, who insisted on leading the way. She gave in, figuring it would save her being buttonholed by firm clients if she looked like she was with a group, even if the group was Keith and his flavor of the month. Her plan failed miserably as Keith stopped at every cluster of people along the way to show off his date, Mia. He'd announced she was a model so often that Carly could recite her resume of photo shoots, and by the time they made it to the bar, she needed a double. She ordered a vodka and soda and wandered over to the side of the bar to recover from way too much interaction until she could escape unnoticed.

The party was the perfect place to people watch. Jane and Mark worked the room like pros, sometimes apart, often together, tag-teaming their way through the throngs of guests, stopping long enough to make everyone feel personally welcome. When they made their way over to her, Carly braced for a talk about mingling with the other guests.

"Hi, Carly, are you having fun?" Jane asked while signaling to one of the tray-carrying waiters. She grabbed three glasses of champagne and handed one to Mark and one to her. Carly set down the now empty rocks glass and took the bubbly. She didn't care for champagne, but people didn't say no to Jane, and she'd learned which battles were worth fighting on her personal route to the top.

"Let's toast," Jane said. "To a new year full of new possibilities for the firm and for you, Carly."

Carly raised her glass and clinked each of theirs, suppressing a knowing smile. It was so like Jane not to say the words, but a partnership was in her reach. It had to be. She started to make some comment about how much she was looking forward to what the new year held, but a commotion at the door to the ballroom diverted their attention. A tall blond woman smiled at the doorman, who frowned in response. The blonde just smiled harder and clapped him on the shoulder in a friendly gesture, seemingly undeterred by his attempts to keep her from crashing the party. The blonde looked around the room, her gaze settling on Carly. Her smile was intoxicating, and despite Carly's best efforts at staying calm and cool, her body hummed as she basked in the stranger's attention.

Jane turned to Mark. "Did you know she was coming up for the party?"

"No. Probably didn't RSVP," Mark said. "You know how she hates to commit. I'll take care of it." Mark strode briskly to the door, and Carly kept watching, riveted as Mark swept the stranger into a hug and shrugged off the doorman, who stepped to the side to let them pass. Mark escorted the woman toward the bar, but it took them forever to make the trek because everyone they passed stopped to greet them. It quickly became clear Mark wasn't the one they were greeting.

"Who is she?" Carly asked, almost in a whisper to herself. Almost.

"That's Landon Holt, from the Austin office. She started just a few months before you."

Landon Holt. Carly rolled the name over in her mind. Of course she'd heard the name. The business of the Austin and Dallas offices intersected on occasion, and she'd met several of the partners and associates from Austin, but never Landon. Word was she never came to Dallas, and rumors swirled around the office as to why that was the case, but Carly didn't spend her valuable time paying attention to idle gossip.

As Landon made the rounds, Carly found it surprising Landon didn't spend much time in Dallas since she worked the room like she owned the place. She treated everyone to an intense smile, a lingering handshake, and fully focused attention. Landon talked and laughed and handled each interaction like it was the most important meeting she'd have that day, and for a moment Carly forgot her usual reticence about social events and wished she was on the receiving end of a Landon Holt encounter.

CHAPTER ONE

Eight months later

Carly stood in front of the courthouse waiting for the press conference to start, but unlike the rest of the attorneys representing football star Trevor Kincade, she made sure she was nowhere near the podium and as far away from the cameras as possible.

Trevor, sporting wavy sandy brown hair, caramel eyes, and a million-dollar smile, was flanked by his agent and the two named partners of Sturges and Lloyd, the premiere boutique law firm in Texas. Jane Sturges stepped to the podium and thanked the press for covering this important story.

"Today, justice was done. Federal District Judge Niven entered an order finding the evidence insufficient to support the unreasonable and unjustified ban imposed on Mr. Kincade by the NFL. Under Judge Niven's ruling, Mr. Kincade will be able to play without restriction at the start of the regular season, and he is grateful to the court and all of his loyal fans for believing in his character. We'll take your questions at this time."

Hands shot up throughout the crowd of reporters, and Carly watched in awe at the way Jane fielded their every question with ease. Jane had been the face of the case in court, but Carly had done all the research and written all the briefs to convince the judge to overturn the ban. She wasn't jealous of the attention. She preferred to work behind the scenes without the attendant client drama, but Carly couldn't help but feel a surge of pride knowing that this big win, drawing national press coverage, was due to her legal smarts.

After the press conference, Jane insisted Carly join them for a celebratory lunch. Three courses in, Carly was completely over the social aspect of the meal and engaged in a mental pep talk about how this kind of schmoozing was good for her career. Trevor sat directly across the table, persistently trying to engage her in conversation, while Keith, who'd only worked tangentially on the case, badgered him about inane football stats. Carly could almost get how every straight woman in Dallas found Trevor so appealing. For her part, she found him to be nice but of fairly average intelligence, which didn't really matter in his profession since he had an insane ability to run really fast and leap high into the air to catch footballs—trivia she'd picked up only since she'd started working on his case. Keith was acting like he wanted to switch teams and ask Trevor out on a date.

Carly had spent the last few weeks learning only what she needed to about the game of football. It wasn't that she wasn't sporty. She'd participated in several sports, like cycling, running, and rowing, but none of her activities involved long commercial breaks, six- to seven-figure incomes, and stadiums full of adoring fans, and she was cool with that since being in the limelight wasn't her favorite thing. Even this lunch, as innocuous as it seemed, was way more interaction with people than she usually preferred. She was happiest when she was hunkered down with a load of files, a puzzle to figure out, and briefs to write.

While Jane and Mark ordered dessert, Carly took the opportunity to go to the ladies' room. When she emerged from the stall to wash her hands, Trevor's agent, Shelby Cross, was at the counter, applying a fresh coat of lipstick to her otherwise impeccable face. Shelby caught her eye in the mirror and smiled, a fact Carly found surprising since Shelby had been fairly standoffish from the moment they'd met.

"Hey," Carly said, waving her hand under the sink in a futile attempt to trigger the motion detector that would set the water running.

"Here, try this one." Shelby eased away from the sink in front of her and Carly had no choice but to give it a go, and was relieved when the water started flowing. "Thanks."

"I guess it's me who should be thanking you," Shelby said, tucking her lipstick in her expensive-looking handbag. "If he'd wound up having to sit out the entire suspension, it would be hell for all of us."

Carly nodded, but she thought the sentiment was a bit overstated.

She'd worked as hard to win as anyone else and she was happy that her well-briefed arguments had won the day, but if they'd lost it wouldn't have been the end of the world. It was football, not saving the planet from destruction. "We had the law on our side."

"You and I both know that you can be in the right but still lose," Shelby said. "It's all about convincing the powers that be through whatever means necessary. Why do you think we pay y'all what we do?"

It was a rhetorical question laced with sarcasm, and Carly let it go unanswered. As a fifth-year associate with the firm, she took home a hefty salary plus bonuses, and she didn't need to mess that up by telling one of their highest profile clients they were being overcharged. Besides, she knew just how important this case was to the firm. Jane and Mark viewed landing this case as a gateway to even bigger things. The services of Sturges and Lloyd were already highly in demand when it came to criminal defense, but if they could get more cases involving administrative issues like Trevor's suspension, it would create an entirely new line of business.

Lunch lasted another hour, and Carly tried not to think about all the work piled up on her desk back at the office, which would be harder to wade through now that she was loaded up on Dom Perignon. When the bill finally came, Jane leaned over and whispered to her, "This win was all you. Don't go back to the office this afternoon. Go do something fun with the rest of your day. We insist."

It sounded like a trick, but the offer was tempting. She saw Keith watching their exchange, his eyes questioning, and she begged off. "I'll think about it," Carly said, knowing there was nothing to think about. Even if she took Jane up on her offer not to return to the office, she had a brief due on the Rogers case in two days and tons of research left to do to get it in shape.

Jane persisted. "Seriously, Carly. You make the rest of us look bad. Do it as a personal favor to me."

Well, when she put it that way. Carly ruminated. Fun for her would be putting the Rogers brief to bed, which spoke volumes about her life. But most of the files were on the network, and she could access them just as easily from home in her pajamas as she could at the office pretending to be sober. "Okay, fine."

Jane smiled and started to say something else, but a clatter of a commotion behind them captured their attention, and Jane's expression turned to the steely anger Carly had only seen when one of the associates missed a deadline or she was facing down an opponent in court. Carly turned to see what was going on and gasped at the sight of no less than five Dallas police officers surrounding their table. She whipped her head back around to speak to Jane, but Jane was on the move, placing her body between the wall of officers and the rest of their lunch party.

"Excuse me, officers," Jane said. "May I help you?"

"No, ma'am," one of the officers replied. "We're not here for you." He started toward the table again, but Jane, not to be deterred, moved into his path. "If you're here for someone at this table," she said, "then I need to know what's going on. I'm Jane Sturges, attorney for everyone sitting here."

The big guy in the lead sighed and handed her a folded slip of paper. "Arrest warrant."

While Jane scoured the paper, Carly glanced around the table. Other than Mark and Jane, who regularly skewered the police in court, there was only one other person worthy of such a big public display, but Trevor didn't look at all rattled to see a herd of police officers standing only inches away. Mark, finally catching on to the show, stood up and walked over to Jane and Carly, and asked in his trademark slow, easy drawl, "What's the problem, Officers?"

Carly chimed in. "They have a warrant."

"And it appears to be in order," Jane announced, handing it back to the lead officer. "Seriously, you couldn't have just called and asked us to turn him in? Did you bring the press in with you or are they waiting outside?"

The cop shrugged. Carly figured it wasn't his call anyway. Forgetting for a second—probably due to the champagne—she wasn't in charge, she spoke. "What's the charge?"

Jane shook her head. "Not here."

But the officer got the word out before she could stop him. "Murder."

"What the hell?" Mark said in an exaggerated whisper. "That's ridiculous."

"What do you need me to do?" Carly asked, feeling tremendously out of her element, but now completely sober.

Jane pulled her aside. "Go outside and see who's here from the press. Give them your card, tell them Trevor has just learned of the charges against him and he is innocent. Tell them you're not at liberty to discuss the case now, but they can call the firm later for details." She stared hard. "You got this?"

"Absolutely," Carly said with tons more confidence than she felt about stepping out from behind the scenes. She shot a look at Trevor. Shelby had moved to sit next to him and was whispering in his ear, no doubt preparing him for what was about to happen. Carly wanted to stick around and watch her client through this mess, but she had a job to do. She dug in her purse for a mint, lodged it in her cheek, and strode toward the front door. She had this.

❖

Landon, like everyone else in the Austin office of Sturges and Lloyd, watched the replay of the arrest of Trevor Kincade on the big screen in the conference room.

"There went my fantasy football season," Greg Paulson, the senior partner at the Austin office, said. "I guess he did harass that woman after all."

Landon punched him in the arm. "Shut up. You don't know jack about the guy, and he's our client."

"Like being our client means he's automatically not guilty. I've never met the guy. Have you?"

Landon shushed him as one of the reporters outside the restaurant where Trevor was being arrested started talking. "We're here with Carly Pachett, attorney for Trevor Kincade. Ms. Pachett, we just saw a group of police enter this restaurant and they tell us they have a warrant for Mr. Kincade's arrest. Can you provide any specifics about the situation?"

Carly pushed her glasses up her nose and frowned at the reporter. "No, Linda, I can't give you specifics about the case, but Mr. Kincade has volunteered to help law enforcement with their investigation."

"But aren't they here to arrest him?"

"I have no personal knowledge of that." Again with the glasses.

"Do you have any comment about the big win Mr. Kincade had in court this morning and what impact, if any, this new development will have on any appeals?"

Her response was cut off when a group of police officers escorting a very unhappy-looking Trevor burst through the doors. The press abandoned Pachett and ran after Trevor and the officers like they were chasing a first down.

"Who the hell is Carly Pachett?" Greg asked. "I thought Mark and Jane were handling Trevor's case."

"Who knows? Not my problem." Landon backed out of the conference room. She had plenty of real work to do, and the Dallas office would take care of the big shiny cases.

Back in her own office, Landon pulled out the case file for her hearing the next morning. What should've been a simple bond reduction hearing had turned into an examining trial on a new charge after her client said some pretty hair-raising things about the victim while talking to his girlfriend on the jailhouse phone. Clients never listened when Landon told them all those calls were recorded. Everything she ever told a client, from the moment they were arrested to the moment they were released, went through a filter that held back anything that didn't match what they wanted to hear. Now that this guy had complicated things, it was her job to try to smooth over the very pissed-off district attorney assigned to the case to keep him from filing a new case based on the threats made in the phone conversation.

A couple of hours later, the buzz of a text on her phone jarred her out of work.

Don't forget, you promised. Seven sharp.

Landon groaned, but she had promised and she didn't take promises lightly, even when they interfered with her usual routine. If she left now and went straight to the restaurant, she'd make it on time. Landon closed the file and packed up her desk. When she walked down the hall, she was surprised to see she wasn't the last one in the office. "Hey, Greg, you trying to show me up?"

"As if," he called out. "Jane and Mark asked me to pick up some slack after their day hit the skids with Trevor's arrest." He set the file down. "What's got you out the door before ten o'clock?"

"Just a thing. I'll be ready for the hearing tomorrow," Landon said, hoping he wouldn't pry. Greg exaggerated about the hours she kept, but it was true that she was almost always the last one to leave. "Just figured I'd mix it up a bit."

"Right." Greg looked like he wanted to say more, but settled with, "You know, you don't have anything to prove. Not to me, anyway."

"I better get going." Landon waved good-bye and took off before Greg could say or ask anything else. She'd known him since he'd been a professor at UT and she was a first year struggling her way through Constitutional Law. Greg had always had her back when it came to work, but their close relationship at the office didn't merit breaking her steadfast rule about not mixing business with her personal life.

Austin traffic was its usual snarl of madness, but a lead foot and quick moves had her at the valet stand just moments before seven. She tossed the valet the keys, grabbed the claim check, and crashed through the doors. "Tremont party?" she asked the hostess.

"Right this way."

It was seven straight up, but she was in the building, so that should count, right? She followed the hostess to the back of the restaurant, preparing her excuse for why she was slightly late. When they reached a door, the hostess stepped aside, and Landon gave her a questioning look, but before she could ask what was going on, the door swung open and a loud chorus of "Surprise!" flooded her ears.

She pushed into the room and was swept into a hug from her best friend, Kylie Tremont.

"Oh my God, you're actually surprised."

Landon shook her head. "Is this the 'emergency, I have to talk to you tonight and it can't wait' dinner you had planned for us?"

"Be nice. It's your birthday eve and I never thought I'd be able to pull this off without you finding out or coming up with an excuse why you couldn't make it. I even had to get your boss in on the deal to make sure you didn't get swept into some urgent case at the last minute. All your friends are here, so act like you're having a good time."

Landon looked around the room. A big cake, a buffet line, a bar, and lots of people—mostly Kylie's friends. Kylie had thrown a surprise party for her, the absolute very last thing she'd expected, and she wasn't entirely sure how she felt about it. "You shouldn't have."

"Perhaps by the end of the night you'll be saying that with the right tone, but for now have some fun." Kylie pushed a drink into her hand.

Landon stared at the drink. Kylie had been begging her to come out and play for weeks, but she'd pushed her aside with various excuses, all of which ended in words like *write a brief, file a motion,* or *court appearance.* Her fifth year at the firm was kind of make it or break it—either she wound up snagging a partnership slot or it was time to consider other options. She wasn't entirely sure what she wanted, but she didn't want to limit her choices, so work had become her girlfriend, her confidant, and the only thing she came home to at night. But one evening off wouldn't hurt, would it?

Three tequila shots later, she blew out the exaggerated amount of candles in one breath. Not bad for an almost thirty-year-old. While everyone grabbed a piece, Kylie pulled her aside. "Look at you, having fun in spite of yourself."

"You make it sound like I'm normally a dud."

"You didn't used to be."

"I didn't used to have a high-stress job. And I was younger. You may be able to party all night and go to work bright and early, but I require a little bit more recovery time nowadays."

"Now who's making you sound like a dud?" Kylie punched her in the arm. "Seriously, Landon, I'm not saying you have to party all the time, but you should check in with your friends now and then. We all have jobs too, but we find time to keep in touch."

Landon flinched. When her personal life had gone south, she'd immersed herself in work and lost any sense of balance. "You're right. I promise to be better. Thanks for pushing me to come out tonight."

"Sounds like you're saying good night, but the evening is still young. Promise me you won't duck out while everyone's face diving your cake?"

As if on cue, Landon's phone rang. Reflex had her looking at the screen before Kylie could grab it out of her hand, and then she held it out of reach when she saw the name on the display. Mouthing *I'm sorry*, she answered. "Holt here."

"Landon, it's Jane Sturges."

"Hi, Jane. Big day in Dallas today."

"Yes, it was. Are you up to speed?"

Jane's delivery was urgent and demanding, and Landon paused before answering. She recognized the tone and was certain there was a big ask coming. "I only know what I saw on the news. It wasn't much."

Jane sighed. "That's okay. I'm emailing you a copy of the arrest warrant affidavit. You can read it later tonight and email me your thoughts from the plane."

Tonight. Plane. Arrest warrant affidavit. Landon quickly digested the information. "Wait, what? Jane, I have a hearing in the morning and I'm at—"

"I'll talk to Greg and get him to cover. It's time for you to come back to Dallas where you belong. Aren't you tired of working behind the scenes? I'm talking possible partnership. You're booked on the ten a.m. flight tomorrow morning. See you at the office. Oh, and happy birthday."

And just like that, Jane hung up. Landon stood with the phone against her ear as the party swirled on around her. All these people, drinking, celebrating, like they didn't have a care in the world. Kylie stood at the bar a few feet away and raised a glass in a silent toast, but Landon was no longer sure what she was celebrating. Had Jane just dangled a partnership in front of her? In Dallas? She lowered the phone and stared at the screen. She should call her back and tell her she wasn't interested in moving, that she was happy plodding along as an associate with no real future.

Well, she might not be ready to move back, but the possibility of a partnership did excite her. She'd earned it, and if she had to go back to Dallas to get it, then that's what she'd do.

Her phone dinged to signal she had a new email and she saw a message from Southwest Airlines with her flight information. Kylie walked over with another drink. Landon shook her head. "Sorry, pal, but I've got to bug out."

"Let me guess. Emergency at work."

"Kind of." Landon decided telling Kylie about Dallas would only start a protracted conversation that would be a real downer for the evening.

"It's your birthday, Holt." Kylie pressed the drink into her hand. "These occasions come around once a year. Besides, I have someone I want you to meet. Do you really have to be somewhere tonight?"

Landon stared at the drink. If Greg was handling the hearing in the morning, all she needed to do was email him her notes, and she could do that from her phone. She could sleep off the effects of tonight on the morning flight. It was her birthday and she'd gone a long time without giving in to her friends' entreaties to socialize. She pointed at the drink in Kylie's hand. "Is that for me, because this is the only place I want to be tonight."

CHAPTER TWO

Carly penned in the final answer to the crossword puzzle while munching the last bite of her egg white and turkey bacon English muffin. She unfolded the paper and set it, front page up, to the side of her plate and skimmed the headlines while she sipped the rest of her coffee. The headline about Trevor's arrest took up most of the real estate on the front page, from the story of the arrest itself to sidebars about how the cloud hanging over him would affect the team's chances in the upcoming season. Not giving a whit about sports, she skipped the latter and focused on the lead article, homing in on one key phrase: "Kincade's attorney was tight-lipped, barely offering any information other than a 'no comment.'"

Of course they were talking about her. She couldn't decide if the article made her sound like she didn't know anything or if she was being prudent for keeping quiet until all the facts were out, but she had a feeling the reporter was knocking her for not sharing information. Jane never should've sent her to field the press on any case, let alone this one. Every day until it was over was going to be a media feeding frenzy.

Carly looked at her watch. She still had ten minutes before she usually left for the office, but if she left now, she'd be early, and she could use a few minutes alone in the office before everyone else arrived and the fallout from Trevor's arrest buried them all in urgent work. She gathered her dishes, rinsed them, and put them in the dishwasher. She brushed her teeth and examined herself in the mirror, taking time to brush her hair up into a French braid. She could use a haircut, but she'd have to make do for another week, until things settled down at the office. Satisfied that she was ready for anything the day might bring, she tucked her phone into her purse, gathered her briefcase, and stepped out the door. She'd just put the key in the deadbolt when a loud voice startled her out of her careful routine.

"Ms. Pachett, I have a piece of your mail."

Carly plastered a smile on her face and turned to her neighbor, Eugene Jasper, standing at the other end of the hallway, waving an envelope in the air. She sighed. Good thing she was running ahead of schedule since interactions with Mr. Jasper—she always returned his formality—were never quick. "Thank you, Mr. Jasper," she said, striding briskly down the hall toward him. "I guess the postman must've gotten our boxes confused again."

She stopped a couple of steps from him and held out her hand, but Jasper was not to be deterred so easily. He held the envelope just out of reach. "Nope," he said. "Not this time. They knocked on your door, but you weren't in. Guy didn't give up easy, and I came out to see what the racket was. He insisted someone had to sign or he'd take it away. I remember once a letter came my way that I had to sign for and it was from the lawyer who handled my great-aunt Beatrice's estate. Barely knew Beatrice, but I happened to recall how she always had a house with a pool—a big one, not one of those little, tiny things people try to squeeze into the backyards of their zero lot line houses—"

"Did you say you had a letter for me?" Carly interrupted. Although part of her was interested in what had ultimately happened with Aunt Beatrice's estate, Jasper ran long in the telling of any story and this one promised to be no different.

"Yes, yes, of course." Jasper glanced one more time at the letter before handing it over. "Hope it's not bad news."

Carly tucked the envelope into the side pocket of her briefcase and thanked him. "Have a great day," she called out as she hurried down the hall, not to be deterred by the sad look on his face. No doubt he'd expected her to bust it open and read it right there in front of him. She slid behind the wheel of her car and let it warm up while she fished the letter from her briefcase. Before she could open the envelope, the phone rang. *Jane*. Carly sent the call to the car's Bluetooth connection. "Good morning, Jane."

"Can you come in early?"

"On the way now."

"Excellent. Landon Holt is on her way up from Austin, and I'd like to have a complete dossier about the case ready for a meeting at noon so you can bring her up to speed."

Carly froze at the name, and a memory of Landon working the room at last year's holiday party surfaced. She'd left the event before meeting Landon in person, but the picture of her larger-than-life presence was fixed in her mind. Landon was one of those people who breezed into a room like she owned the place, oozing all kinds of confidence and charm—the kind of person who took over without even trying. Carly had been curious enough after the party to do a little research and had learned Landon was the only daughter of George Holt of Holt Industries, a multi-million-dollar conglomerate of businesses ranging from housewares to clothing lines. More likely than not, Landon's confidence came from growing up in a family where she had everything she wanted and more. Did Jane think Carly wasn't good enough to handle the work on Trevor's case on her own?

"Carly, did you get all that?"

Carly came back to earth at Jane's urgent tone. "Uh, yes. Put together a summary of everything we know so far about the murder case and include any salient details about the allegations that resulted in Trevor's suspension."

"And email her a copy of the arrest warrant affidavit," Jane said, not bothering to hide her impatience. "There's a copy on your desk. It's under seal, and as far as I know, the press doesn't have a copy yet. Let's keep it that way. Don't scan it, email it, or share with anyone outside of you, me, Mark, and Landon. Understood?"

"Yes, but—"

"And if you could pick up Landon at the airport, it would be a nice touch. Get the flight info from Rhonda. See you at noon."

Carly glanced at the screen in her car, but Jane had disconnected the call. She should be used to Jane's abrupt manner by now, but she wasn't and didn't think she ever would be. It especially irked her that she'd been demoted to the role of chauffeur. What was so special about Landon Holt that she couldn't be bothered to take a cab or an Uber like any other Sturges and Lloyd attorney arriving from the Austin office? Carly started to steam over it, but pushed the unproductive thoughts away. She spent the rest of the drive to the office summarizing the case file in her head, so it would be easier to get it done when she got to the office, but until she saw the arrest warrant affidavit, she'd be hard-pressed to paint a complete picture.

Less than ten minutes later, she pulled into the parking lot of the firm. Jane and Mark had both been partners in top tier big law firms in downtown Dallas before breaking away to start their own practice. Their first goal was to develop their own style, and they'd started by purchasing and refurbishing a two-story, vintage 1960s office building in Uptown with flat lines and geometric accents. Carly loved the location because she didn't have to fight the traffic and parking downtown, and clients loved the unique vibe of the retro space.

She'd no sooner pushed through the doors of the office than she was assailed by Jane's secretary, Rhonda. "Carly, here's the flight info for Landon. Jane said you volunteered to pick her up at Love Field. What a nice touch to welcome her to the Dallas office."

Carly bit back a response about how many billable hours her gesture of hospitality would entail, and accepted the piece of paper from Rhonda, who was uncharacteristically friendly this morning. "Thanks. Jane mentioned she'd left the arrest warrant for me to review."

"Yes, it's in your office. Top drawer on the right."

Carly hated that Rhonda had been in her desk drawers, not because she had anything to hide, but because she was careful to keep her office orderly. She refrained from saying anything. It was a few pieces of paper at most and unlikely to cause chaos. At least that's what she thought before she started reading it. Carly flipped through the pages and then started reading again from the beginning. The affidavit painted a grim picture of Trevor, but that's what these documents were intended to do. In addition to detailing the alleged harassment of Vanessa Meyers that led to his NFL suspension, it named her as the murder victim. Carly pulled out a legal pad and started listing the evidence.

Vanessa had taken a few days off from work to duck out of the public eye following the round-the-clock press exposure surrounding Trevor's suspension. When she failed to return to work as scheduled, her employer contacted her family, who used a key to access her house and found evidence of an altercation—smashed glass and overturned furniture—along with Vanessa Meyers's dead body and the thin length of rope that had been used to strangle her still circling her neck.

Carly made a note to get more details about the cord, and kept reading.

A neighbor told the police he'd heard yelling coming from her house earlier in the week. When he went outside to see what was going on, Vanessa was standing on her porch, alive and with no visible injuries. She told the neighbor it was just more of the Trevor Kincade drama but didn't volunteer any additional information and he hadn't asked. The neighbor had not been home at the time the medical examiner believed the murder had occurred.

The detective went on to detail how Trevor had been in town, not on the road to an away game, at the time of Vanessa's death. In addition, they'd found pieces of rope similar to the length that was found at the scene in Trevor's trash. Carly underlined her note about the rope. Not rock-solid evidence by any means, but when they tossed it in with Vanessa's allegations that Trevor had been sending her threatening messages, and what she'd told her neighbor about the argument at her house, the police had convinced a judge to issue a warrant for Trevor's arrest. Carly reread the detective's statements several times. He made several references to the pattern and practice of domestic abusers, and while he didn't come out and say it, Carly suspected he was talking about more than the threatening emails Trevor had been accused of sending to Vanessa or the argument they'd had about those emails.

She made a note and then shuffled through the rest of the papers attached to the affidavit. Copies of the emails, which she already had since they were subject of Trevor's suspension, and a search warrant for Trevor's house, served at the same time as the arrest warrant.

"Hey, whatcha doin'?"

Carly looked up to see Keith standing in her doorway. She casually lifted a file folder and placed it over the affidavit. "Just some research. You need something?"

His eyes roved over the interior of her office and then settled back on her desk. "Just checking in. Thought maybe you could help me with some ideas I have for pretrial motions in the Danziger case."

Carly recognized his code. He wanted her to volunteer to draft the motions and then hand them over so he could take credit. Under normal circumstances, she wouldn't mind helping him out. Jane was smart enough to know she'd done the writing, and Carly knew she'd do a much better job than Keith for the client. But she had enough of her own work to do today and she wanted Keith out of her office before he spotted the eyes-only documents and used the information to impress his pals.

"I'd love to help, but I'm under a deadline. I'll catch up with you later." She turned to her computer and started typing a random search into Lexis to signal the conversation was over. When she heard him leave, she pulled the affidavit back toward her and reread it twice. The cops had taken a bold move by arresting Trevor before they'd searched the house, and she wondered if they had other information they were keeping under wraps.

Whatever it was, it would have to wait because if she didn't leave now, she was going to be late to pick up Landon. Her initial annoyance about being called on to chauffeur had subsided into curiosity about meeting the infamous Landon Holt for the very first time. Would she live up to the hype?

Landon rolled over and reached for her buzzing phone, but instead she wound up fisting a handful of hair. Not hers. Her eyes flew open and she struggled to make sense of the tableau in her bed. Ivory skin, long limbs, and big bunches of red hair. The naked woman hadn't woken up despite the fact Landon's hand was still gripping her long tresses. Her deep slumber probably had something to do with the near-empty bottle of tequila on the nightstand.

Guess I had a good birthday in spite of myself. Landon reached her arms over her head and stretched, long and hard, as the memories of the evening before drifted back into her consciousness. She'd gotten over being mad at Kylie for the surprise and, after a few shots of Patron, settled into some fun. Red wasn't the first woman she'd danced with, but apparently she'd been the last, and visions of an evening spent doing gymnastics all around her bedroom made Landon smile. Most of the rest of the evening was a blur, for which she blamed the tequila. Good thing Greg was handling her hearing this morning.

Holy shit!

Landon lunged out of the bed, her mind racing. Greg was handling her hearing because she had a flight to catch. To Dallas. To work on the Trevor Kincade case. For a chance at a promotion. All the lingering effects of the tequila burned off, and she started calculating. It was eight o'clock. Fifteen minutes to shower and dress, another fifteen to pack, that was cutting it close, but even then it was unlikely she'd make it to the airport in time to catch the flight and no way would she have time to check a bag. She'd need to pack suits, lots of them, and she had no idea how long Jane planned on keeping her in Dallas before she could make a trip back.

Her car had a full tank and it was parked downstairs. If she hit the road by eight thirty, she could make it to Dallas by noon, which was within the margin of error for when she'd make it if she took the flight, waited at baggage claim, and caught a cab to the office.

"Hey, baby, come back to bed."

Landon glanced at the forgotten bedmate and factored in another five minutes for making nice and sending her on her way. Damn Kylie for getting her in this mess. She'd managed to stay focused on her work to the exclusion of everything else for a while now, but all it took was one night of abandon, and she was back in a mess. This was not going to happen in Dallas. She would stay completely focused on the prize and that prize was a partnership, one that she would earn all on her own.

Ten, not five, minutes later, Red was dressed and in the back seat of an Uber. Landon took a power shower and dressed for the road in slacks, a collared blouse, and driving flats. Traffic on I-35 was notorious on a regular day, but in her favor, most cars this time of day were headed toward Austin, not away from it, and she lived on the north end of the city. It was a perfect day to ride with the top down, but she wouldn't have time to correct the windswept look before she showed up at the office, so she kept the top on and her foot on the accelerator of her BMW M5, easily darting around the other traffic on the highway. Once she passed Waco, she settled into a rhythm and started to reflect on what lay ahead. She called ahead to book a room at the Crescent. It was close to the office and had all the creature comforts. After she finished the call, the screen on the dash scrolled through the other numbers in her contact list. She saw the number for Holt Industries go by and considered calling her father to tell him about the impending partnership. She dismissed the idea quickly. She wasn't going to Dallas for a reunion, she was going to work, and nothing would get in her way.

❖

"She's not here."

Carly listened to Rhonda on the other end of the phone tell her one more time that Jane expected her to bring Landon directly to the office. Carly was used to Jane's aversion to taking no for an answer, a trait that had rubbed off on Rhonda. She started to lay out her case about why she'd determined Landon wasn't at the airport, but decided it was pointless. She hung up the phone and wandered over to the baggage attendant one more time. "I'm guessing you haven't had anyone show up in response to the page?"

"No, ma'am. Are you sure your friend was on the flight?"

Carly didn't bother correcting her. "Actually, I'm not, but I appreciate you checking. Thanks."

Not that she needed it, but Carly had a picture of Landon on her phone from the firm's website. She'd arrived at the airport before the flight landed, but hadn't seen anyone matching Landon's description wandering from the gates. She supposed it was possible she'd missed her in the crowd and Landon had taken a cab. Probably just a miscommunication. Either way, if she didn't get back to the office soon, she'd be late for the meeting.

The office was a quick fifteen-minute drive from Love Field, and Carly pulled into the parking lot just moments before noon. She'd already prepared packets of information about the case for everyone and made sure there were sufficient copies before heading to the airport, so all she'd need to do before the meeting was grab a minute alone to review her notes and she'd be all set.

Her plans were thwarted by pastry. Russell, the firm's receptionist, accosted her the second she walked into the reception area.

"Kolaches!" he called like he was hawking the baked goods for extra cash. "You don't want to miss these." He punctuated the admonition by waving a white baker's box under her nose.

"I'm good," Carly answered although the loud rumble of her stomach betrayed her.

"Seriously, Car, they're from the Czech Stop. In West?" Russell shook his head. "None of this is registering, is it?"

Carly resisted telling him one more time not to shorten her name, and peered into the box where several rows of sweet rolls lined the interior. She looked back up at Russell. "Should it?"

"You need to get out more. West, Texas, home of one of Texas's oldest Czech settlements, and a must stop on the way to or from Austin, exit 353 to be precise. I never make the drive without stopping on the way there and back…"

He kept talking, but Carly had stopped paying attention after he said the word Austin. "Wait a minute. Who brought these?"

"Guilty as charged."

Carly whirled at the sound of the unfamiliar voice behind her and came face-to-face with the missing-in-action Landon Holt. She opened her mouth to give her a piece of her mind for not being at the airport, but stopped at the sight of her wide smile and stunningly gorgeous blue-gray eyes.

Landon stuck out her hand. "I'm Landon Holt, nice to meet you." She looked down at her hand which Carly had left hanging, and pointed at the box in Russell's hand. "You should have one of these. Or two. I risked the wrath of Jane getting them, so it would be a shame for them to go to waste." Landon reached into the box. "Sweet or savory?"

"You stood me up at the airport." Carly blurted out the non sequitur, instantly regretting her lack of control. While she fished around for something more intelligent to say, Landon cast a sideways glance at Russell, who merely raised his eyebrows while munching on one of the kolaches. Carly took a breath and tried again. "Jane asked me to pick you up at the airport. I was there. I waited. I even had you paged, but you never showed." She rolled her hand with each statement as if the physical action would jog Landon's memory.

"Oh, sorry. I decided to drive." She rocked back on her heels. "My bad. Guess I should've called, but I had no idea Jane was sending someone to pick me up. Please accept my apology with a kolache on the side." She flashed a big smile and waited for Carly to relent.

Caught in the tractor beam of light, Carly held out for about five seconds before muttering, "It's okay." Truce accomplished, she glanced at her watch, noting there was only three minutes before the meeting was supposed to start. Barely enough time for her to consult her notes. She edged away. "I have something I need to do."

"Before you go, can you let Jane and Mark know I'm here? And who should I talk to about getting a Coke?"

Carly started to ask if Landon thought she was a secretary, but instead she merely pointed at Russell and marched to her office, hoping Landon's stay in Dallas would be short-lived.

CHAPTER THREE

Landon avoided Carly's glare and waited until everyone else took their seats before sliding into one of the chairs around the table. How was she supposed to have known Carly was an attorney and a fifth-year associate at that? What self-respecting attorney volunteers to pick up one of their fellow employees at the airport?

Jane, seated at the head of the table, cleared her throat to draw attention to the front of the room. "Looks like we're all here, or most of us anyway. Carly, I assume you met Landon." She didn't wait for an answer before tossing packets onto the table. "Mark has his hands full with the Rogers case, so I've selected Carly and Landon to take point with me on this case. Carly will give us a full report in just a second, but I wanted to see if anyone has any comments about the information contained in the arrest warrant affidavit."

Landon looked around the table. Besides her, Carly, and Jane, there were a few other people she tagged as interns and first-year associates by the way they sat on the edge of their seats, eager to run errands at the slightest hint they might be useful in order to stand out from the crowd. Had she ever been like that? Maybe, for a millisecond, but it hadn't taken long for her to realize sucking up didn't necessarily equate to racking up billable hours, which was the only real way to get noticed. She'd done her part in that regard, and although the Austin office was viewed as the laid-back younger sister of the Sturges and Lloyd empire, she knew her annual billable hours put her at the top of the scale.

But she hadn't done it to rise in the ranks. Her immersion in her work was more about proving to herself she was capable, on her own, of top-notch legal work without any assistance from the pedigree that came with being a Holt. Jane's news that she was being considered for partner was icing on the cake, but now that it had been dangled in front of her, she wanted in. She waved a hand at Jane. "I noticed a couple of things."

Jane nodded and Landon pressed on. "Other than the strand of rope, no physical evidence is mentioned. The only thing that definitely points to Trevor is the bit about the neighbor who heard arguing, and Meyers said it was about 'Trevor Kincade drama.' Now she's dead, and boom, he must have done it. If there hadn't been a prior police report documenting their argument over whether or not he was sending her threats via email, and Trevor's recent headline-grabbing bid to contest his suspension, DPD may still have looked at him for this, but I doubt they would've made an arrest." She settled back in her chair and watched for the rest of the team's reaction to her summary.

Jane gave a low whistle. "Pretty good for as little time as you had to review the warrant."

"I had Siri read it to me in the car," Landon said, but her pride at making good use of her time was dampened when she heard Carly mutter, "Of course you did." Landon turned to her and said, "Excuse me?"

Carly looked around and then cleared her throat. "It's not that simple."

"Sure it is. You just load the document and ask her to read it out loud."

"No." Carly waved her hand in a dismissive gesture. "Yes, the evidence is weak on facts, but the circumstances all point to Trevor. Who had the most to lose if Vanessa Meyers kept pressing for his suspension? What are the chances someone else wanted her dead or that this was a random act of brutality? Do I believe the police jumped the gun by arresting him before all the facts were in? Yes, but they have time to develop more evidence before they present the case to a grand jury, and we need to make sure there's nothing else looming."

Jane nodded at Carly's words, and Landon wished she'd gotten a better night's sleep and hadn't been so cavalier, because Carly was right. "What does Trevor say about all this?" Landon asked.

"The NFL is looking at appealing the suspension and imposing a new one, and word from management is they plan to sideline him for now to keep the drama of the arrest from distracting the rest of the team. Trevor says the charge is ridiculous and wants to fast-track the trial so he can get back in the game," Jane said.

"That's insane," Carly blurted at the very same time Landon said, "That's brilliant."

"It is," Landon insisted. "Brilliant, I mean. The DA's office will be expecting delay after delay, especially since he's out on bond. They'll never see this coming." She reined in her enthusiasm when she saw Jane smiling. "What?"

"You two will be perfect for this."

Landon wasn't sure she wanted to know what "this" was, and she sure as hell wasn't as enthusiastic as Jane seemed to be at the prospect of working with Carly, stick-up-her-butt, Pachett, who disagreed with everything she said, but what else was she going to do? She was already here in Dallas and Jane had gotten her all whipped up at the prospect of a partnership. She supposed she could be a team player with just about anyone for that kind of reward. "When can we meet with Trevor?"

Jane nodded. "That's the spirit. Let's give him the day. The bond hearing was this morning, so he's still pretty worn out. In the meantime, I want you two to spearhead all the research you can find to justify getting early discovery, even before grand jury. Donna Wilhelm is the prosecutor on the case and the grand jury setting is in ten days. Let's try and win there first, and if that doesn't work, we'll ask for a speedy trial. And we need a private investigator. See if Skye Keaton is available to work with us to interview witnesses and see what she can dig up.

"Landon, Carly can fill you in on the grand jury procedure up here. Put together a packet and run it by me." She gestured to the first years sitting on the perimeter of the room. "Use whatever resources you need."

Landon remembered what it was like being a first-year associate whose job was to hustle for research assignments the more senior attorneys and partners didn't want to do in an attempt to rack up the necessary billable hours to stay on track for bonuses and promotions. The push to outshine the others hadn't been as strong at the Austin office, where things were a little more laid-back, but the pressure was still there, just below the surface. Resolved to making this work, she took a few more notes as Jane outlined more of her conversation with Trevor at the jail, and when Jane called the meeting done and the rest of the attorneys started to disperse, she hung around to ask about where she should office.

"Carly," Jane called out. "Can you stick around too? I'd like to talk to you and Landon for a moment."

Sounds serious, Landon thought, sliding back into her seat when Jane motioned Carly into the chair opposite hers. Landon assessed her new litigation partner. Carly took all her notes on an iPad with a keyboard case, and she'd hauled it back out and was poised to type up whatever new assignment Jane unloaded on them. Landon glanced down at her Montblanc fountain pen and Midori notebook. She enjoyed the convenience of technology as much as anyone else, but these simples tools were still her favorites. Tattered ends of tiny slips of paper notes edged past the aged and worn leather cover and the string holding it closed bulged against the girth of too much information. As if. She'd carried the coveted notebook all through law school, and it was as much a journal as it was a place to capture important assignments and research. Landon had always shrugged off the judgment of those who viewed her analog system as an inferior method. She'd found that the act of handwriting was the perfect method to remember key facts and ideas that would be lost quickly after she typed them into a software program. She released the string fastener and opened to a new page, poised to write down whatever Jane had to say.

"Both of you have shown a strong commitment to this firm and you both deserve to be rewarded for your efforts. This case is going to be very important for us since it's likely to produce headlines on a weekly, if not daily, basis until Trevor Kincade is either vindicated or convicted." Jane crossed her arms and let her gaze linger on each of them for a few seconds as if to impress upon them the gravity of what she was about to say.

Landon held her breath. This was the moment. Maybe Jane was about to make them both partners. She didn't know if Carly deserved it, but she knew she did and she could hardly wait to hear the words. Becoming a partner at Sturges and Lloyd would take the sting out of being back in Dallas. She glanced at Carly, who sat ramrod straight on the edge of her chair, her face fixed into an expression of rapt attention, and Landon wondered what dream this announcement would fulfill for her.

"We have one partnership slot this year," Jane announced. "We'll be announcing the new partner as soon as this case is resolved."

"Wait, what?" Landon bit down on her lip, wishing she'd kept her mouth shut, but now that the words were out, there was really no point in stopping. "Did you say one slot?"

Jane nodded, and Landon looked over at Carly, whose fast typing fingers had frozen over her mini-keyboard.

"It's a dead heat between you. You both have very different strengths, all essential for a successful law practice."

"I don't get it." Landon was frustrated at her inability to process Jane's announcement. "You're saying the partnership will go to one of us. Just one."

"Yes."

"And how are you going to decide?" Landon felt a rising anger she fought to tamp down.

"Trevor's case is the perfect test. You'll work on the case together. A good team will not only play off each other's strengths, but learn to become better on their own."

"You're kidding, right?" Landon didn't bother to hold back. "I ditched a good docket back in Austin to come here—something you know I didn't want to do—based on the promise of a partnership, but in reality, it's just some contest between me and…her." She jerked her chin at Carly, who wore the hint of a self-satisfied smile. *Figures.* Of course Carly thought she had the partnership in the bag, which was why she wasn't saying anything. She worked with Jane and Mark in this office every day.

You could have too. Landon shut down the voice and struggled to get her anger under control. "How do you plan to quantify our work?"

"Obviously, our assessment will be subjective, but I think you have a good idea about what we look for in a partner. Loyalty, dedication, hard-work, ingenuity." Jane rolled her hand in the air to signal she could go on and on. "What better way to measure success than performance on a high-profile case for one of our well-known clients?"

"But we'll be working toward the same goal."

"Yes, you will. It's a win for everyone." Jane stood to signal the meeting was over. Landon sat frozen in her seat, trying to process what had just happened, but Jane had moved on. "I'd like a preliminary plan for the grand jury on my desk tomorrow."

And then she was gone. Landon stared at the conference room door willing the last thirty minutes of her life to rewind. Hell, she'd like to rewind to last night, when she'd celebrated her birthday with tequila shots and a night of rowdy sex with Meg. Or was it May? Whatever. She should've ignored Jane's phone call and stayed in Austin where she might not have been a superstar, but she knew what to expect.

❖

"Did you know about this?"

Carly flinched at the press of a hand on her arm, but she schooled her features into a neutral expression and turned to see Landon standing behind her, looking completely out of sorts. No surprise there. Carly had met plenty of people like Landon in law school and after—people who got by on their looks and charm, often leaving the harder, smarter workers in the dust. She shrugged off Landon's touch, ignoring the surge of cold that sprang up in its place. "Know what?"

"That there was only one partnership spot."

She hadn't, but admitting that would put her a couple of steps behind. She was already feeling a bit off-kilter since Jane handpicked Landon to come to Dallas to work on this case. "I don't really focus on stuff like that. I figure if I do a good job, I'll get what I deserve."

Landon shook her head and grunted. "Nice sentiment. I feel kind of sorry for you if that's what you believe."

A shadow fell over Landon's eyes, and she seemed suddenly distant. Something was going on in there, but it wasn't Carly's job to figure it out. She started to edge away. "I have to make a call." She was two steps into her escape when Landon called out.

"Wait. Do you know where I'm supposed to office? And where can I find the files about the suspension? I think we should start with the allegations that led to his suspension and go from there."

Carly sighed as Jane's words played back in her head. Loyalty, dedication, hard work, ingenuity—all the things they looked for in a partner. Carly didn't have any loyalty to Landon, but she did have an allegiance to the firm and Trevor, and she was going to have to find a way to make this work if she wanted a chance at the partnership slot. "Come with me." She didn't wait for a response before she took off at a brisk pace until they arrived at Rhonda's desk.

"Rhonda, this is Landon Holt from the Austin office. She needs an office for the foreseeable future so she can help us out with the Kincade case." She'd barely finished her spiel before Rhonda was out of her chair pulling Landon into a big bear hug. Carly knew her jaw was hanging open, but she couldn't help it. She'd never seen Rhonda express affection toward anyone but Jane, and even then it was the kind of begrudging affection a drill sergeant shows for a just graduated recruit.

"Landon Holt," Rhonda exclaimed. "You look amazing. I guess Austin agrees with you."

"It's good," Landon said, meeting Carly's eyes over Rhonda's shoulder. Carly tried to read her expression without success, and she found a spot on the wall to occupy her attention, a distraction from the slow burn of Landon's steady gaze. She resolved to spend the next hour finding out everything she could about Landon. First rule: know your enemy.

"She can take the office next to yours," Rhonda said. "Why don't you two grab a late lunch and I'll stock the desk with supplies while you're out."

It wasn't a question, and Carly balked at the command. For one thing, when had Rhonda become so fast and loose with office supplies? Carly stocked her own office with her favorite pens because of Rhonda's stinginess. But the big thing was lunch. Rhonda knew Carly didn't do lunch, at least not in the way all the other attorneys at the firm did. To everyone else, it was an occasion to eat too much and sneak a drink in the middle of the day, but to her it was the perfect opportunity to rack up billable hours when the office was quiet. Besides, after Jane's bombshell, she'd completely lost her appetite.

"Lunch sounds great," Landon said, turning to Carly. "Do you have a favorite place?"

Damn. Carly felt Rhonda's eyes on her, daring her to be antisocial to the newest addition to the team. This whole vow of loyalty thing was beginning to wear thin, but she didn't want Rhonda to report to Jane that she'd snubbed her pet. "Actually, why don't you choose? Didn't you used to live in Dallas?"

The enthusiasm in Landon's expression dimmed for a moment, and Carly smiled brightly. There was some weakness here, and she was determined to find out what it was and make the most of it. Suddenly, her appetite returned full force.

"Let's go to Sammy's. That is unless you don't like barbecue."

"I love barbecue," Carly said, hiding her surprise at the choice. She'd expected something more posh. Landon gave off a carefree, rich girl vibe, which made sense since the Holt family owned half of Dallas. Which begged the question of why Landon was working in Austin in the first place. Carly mentally bookmarked that topic for further investigation.

"Great," said Landon. "I'll drive."

Carly ducked in her office to grab her purse and took a moment to stuff her case notes into her briefcase in hopes Rhonda would view that territory as off-limits. She could imagine Rhonda making a copy for her buddy Landon as part of her welcome to the office routine. Notes secure, Carly paused at the door, pulled her lipstick from her purse, and applied a quick coat. Second rule: look better than your enemy.

Landon drove a convertible, of course, and with a click of her remote, she lowered the top as they walked toward the car, insisting they take advantage of the unseasonably mild temperature. It took every ounce of Carly's strength not to ask her to put the top up. By the time they arrived at the restaurant, she was certain her hair looked like ravens had built a permanent home on top of her head. In contrast, Landon simply shook her head a few times, and her blond waves cascaded down her neck like she'd emerged from a salon. Score one for Austin.

Sammy's was a dive, but it was also a place to see and be seen. Tucked up against the sleek glass Federal Reserve building, the restaurant was a rustic contrast to the rest of the upscale downtown neighborhood, but people in suits gladly grabbed their trays and stood in the cafeteria-style line for slow-roasted brisket, ribs, and homemade sides. Carly's mouth watered at the sight of the ribs and the squash casserole, but in an attempt to avoid an afternoon food coma, she ordered lean brisket and a side salad with no dressing. Landon went all in.

"I'll have the rib platter with fried okra and squash casserole. And a slice of pecan pie if you have any left."

"Landon Holt, is that you?" the older woman behind the counter exclaimed. "Girl, you are a sight for sore eyes. Your daddy was in here just yesterday and I asked him how you were. He didn't say a word about you coming back home."

Carly watched the exchange and caught that same shadow fall over Landon's expression again. She was smiling, but judging by the tension in her shoulders, she was clearly uncomfortable. Was it something about the woman behind the counter or was it the mention of Landon's father?

"You know how it is," Landon said, "He was probably distracted by business. Besides, I'm just in town to work on a case. Not sure I'm back for good."

She took the dishes handed to her and started to walk toward Carly when the woman called out, "Well, you be sure to come back again before you go. It's good to see you looking so well."

After she paid the cashier, Carly started toward one of the tables inside.

"Do you mind if we eat outside?" Landon asked. "I could use the fresh air."

Carly refrained from pointing out they'd gotten a healthy dose of fresh air on the way over, and followed Landon to one of the picnic tables on the patio. After they'd settled in, Carly started cutting her meat while Landon dove into the ribs like a member of the Donner party.

She wiped some sauce off her chin and set down the well-cleaned rib bone. "I was starving. Guess I should've eaten some of the kolaches I brought to the office."

"They were a hit," Carly said dryly.

"I noticed you didn't touch them." Landon picked up another rib and pointed it at Carly's plate. "Are you on a diet or something?"

"I don't know that I'd call it a diet per se. I just try to eat like it's one of many meals and not my last."

"Ouch."

Her words had come out harsher than she'd intended, but Carly couldn't help it. She found Landon's facade of living life with total abandon annoying—driving with the top down, not even thinking about calling to say she was driving instead of flying, gorging on a massive plate of greasy, fattening food. How was she supposed to work with this person?

Get a grip. You're going to have to make it work. She fished around for a topic that would get Landon talking but wouldn't simultaneously drive her crazy. "You seem to know a lot of people in Dallas. How long has it been since you lived here?"

"A while." Landon shoveled into her fried okra. "How about you? Are you a native?"

"No." Carly considered leaving it at that. After all, it wasn't like Landon was sharing any personal details. But after a few beats of silence, Carly decided that maybe if she opened up a little, Landon might do the same. "I went to law school at Baylor. I interviewed with Jane and Mark the summer after graduation and moved up here after I took the bar."

"Good school."

"Yes, it is." Carly pushed her salad around the plate. "How about you? Where did you go to school?"

"UT Law School."

The statement was short and simple, but Landon's tone conveyed a level of annoyance Carly would never have associated with the carefree attitude she'd witnessed thus far. "Let me guess, you're a legacy."

"Not even. All the Holts go to Harvard. It's a thing." Landon picked up her fork and stabbed a stack of okra and shoved it toward Carly. "Try this. It's a vegetable, but I can guarantee it tastes a million times better than that pile of wimpy greens on your plate."

Carly filed Landon's cryptic answer away and scrunched her nose at the forkful of okra. The truth was it smelled divine. Fried food always did, which was why she stayed far away if she could help it. But here it was being force-fed to her. Telling herself that accepting one bite was a harmless way of breaking down the barrier between her and her opponent, she smiled, reached for the fork, and crunched down on the salty, crispy no longer a vegetable vegetable, barely holding back a moan.

"It's amazing, right?"

Carly nodded. The okra was delicious, but it was Landon's broad smile that caught her attention. She needed to watch that smile because it wasn't real. They were rivals, and she would do well to remember that only one of them was going to become partner, and no amount of crispy, delicious fried goodness or sexy smiles would deter her from her goal.

❖

Landon transferred the files to one arm and shoved the key card in the slot of her hotel room door for the fifth time. Finally, the little green light appeared and she pushed her way into the room. The king-sized bed with its half dozen pillows beckoned, but she had hours of work ahead before she could rest.

She picked up the phone and dialed room service, ordering a burger, fries, and a large pot of coffee. She'd spent the hours since lunch poring over the full case file and had made copies of the documents she wanted to review further while she did some online research here in the hotel. Rhonda had arranged for her to move to one of the hotel's executive condominiums tomorrow, but tonight she was grateful for the full service the main building had to offer. Landon had no idea how long the firm intended to pay for her digs, but she'd been too tired from the drive and the full day of work to ask. She had a ton of questions about being called back to Dallas, but today hadn't been the day for questions. It had been the day to size up her competition.

Carly Pachett was pretty, smart, and way too high-strung. Who eats a salad at a barbecue place? And she'd obviously been put out at riding around in a convertible, so much so that Landon had driven an extra few blocks out of the way just to prolong her agony, which she admitted now hadn't really been a nice thing to do. But being nice wasn't part of Mission Get the Partnership. It was time to put aside her natural instinct to make friends with everyone and step up to win this race. She cracked the files and resolved to win, no matter what the cost.

CHAPTER FOUR

The next day at eleven thirty a.m., Landon ducked past the press into the restaurant and was ushered to a private room. She pointed at the table, which was empty except for Jane. "Where is everyone?"

"You're late?"

She chose a seat on Jane's right side. "Sorry, I was reading a case on Lexis, and lost track of time." To her credit, it looked like she'd beaten Carly to the restaurant. Plus one in her column. "Where's Trevor?"

"I asked him to join us at noon, so we'd have time to talk before he arrived," Jane said. "I figured that would give you and Carly time to bring me up to speed on what you've learned about the case so far."

Landon looked across the table at the other empty seats. "I guess you'd like to wait until Carly gets here before we start?"

"Actually, she got here before I did. She just stepped out to call Trevor and let him know where we're meeting, but she's back now." Jane pointed toward the door.

Landon watched Carly walk toward them, her stride confident and her face impassive. The complete opposite of Landon's rushed entrance moments before. In fact, Carly's entire appearance was a stark contrast to hers. Carly's black suit was stiff, dark, and somber whereas Landon's light gray slacks and cornflower blue collared shirt was more laid-back and gave her a pop of color. Carly wore minimal jewelry—a simple silver chain around her neck, a plain silver band on her right ring finger, and a basic silver watch. Landon's watch was the latest design from Shinola, and she wore several rings, including a large lapis stone she'd purchased on a vacation in Santa Fe. She'd bet big money that Carly considered vacations frivolous.

"We don't have much time left," Jane said, "So let's get started. Landon, Carly was telling us some information she'd managed to unearth about possible extraneous offenses. Carly?"

Carly nodded at Jane and consulted her iPad. "We all know about the most recent case with Vanessa Meyers." She turned to Landon. "Vanessa told police that while Trevor was traveling during the off-season, she started getting emails from him, accusing her of cheating on him. The emails ramped up and words like *slut* and *whore* were tossed around. The last email, the one that caused the NFL to impose the suspension, told her to just break things off or there would be dire consequences. The email was sent from a computer in a hotel business center near the team's practice center. The league has taken a firm stance on actual violence recently, but threats without more was something else entirely. To avoid bad press, they took a hard line and suspended Trevor, but we won the first round by alleging they didn't have proof Trevor actually sent the emails."

"This is all in the file. Is there a reason you're repeating it?" Landon asked.

"Context. Something about the way the arrest warrant affidavit read made me think the police have reason to suspect Trevor has a history of threatening women. I contacted Skye and asked her to check Houston PD for any police reports that listed Trevor as either the complainant or defendant. She found two calls." Carly swiped to the next page on her iPad. "In the first one, Trevor called 911 because his girlfriend at the time, Jocelyn Aubrey, was behaving erratically, accusing him of being an ass for ghosting her. She'd been drinking, and the police offered to arrest her for public intoxication, but Trevor asked them not to and had someone drive her home. The second call, a month later, Jocelyn dialed 911when she opened her back door and found a pile of clothes burning on the steps. She told the police she recognized a shirt in the fire as one she'd left at Trevor's house when they'd been dating. The police questioned Trevor, but he said he knew nothing about it, and his alibi that he'd been traveling at the time checked out solid. Jocelyn didn't press the issue and no case was ever opened. Since they didn't make any arrests, there isn't much to the record, but there might be some portion of the report that we don't have access to."

"Sounds like a bad *Dateline* episode," Landon chimed in. When Jane frowned, she protested. "Everyone always looks at the boyfriend first, and even when there's no proof of any wrongdoing, a cloud of suspicion looms over them and follows wherever they go. But why wasn't any of this in the arrest warrant affidavit?"

Carly cleared her throat. "Probably because they didn't want to tip us off or distract the judge with sketchy facts. The bigger question is why Dallas hired him if they knew about all this."

"One word," Landon replied. "Touchdowns. Trevor is one of the best wide receivers in the league. He could sell fake stocks to little old ladies, and this team would have traded for him because they need a winning season."

"Investment fraud is a far cry from murder." Carly edged back in her chair as she delivered the words like she wanted to get as far from Landon as she could.

But Landon wasn't having it. She leaned forward. "He's not a murderer until they prove he did it. If you're going to start with the premise he did it, then they've won already."

"Hey," Jane said in a hissed whisper, "let's take it down a notch. First, when I said I wanted you two to work on this case, I meant you'd be working on the same side. Second, everything is on the table here—all theories and opinions are fair game. We don't rule anything out until we can rule everything out. Understood?"

Landon glanced at Carly and read her reluctance to agree. She was reluctant too. How was she supposed to work with someone who so clearly didn't get it? Did Carly even have any experience working on criminal cases? Landon made a mental note to extend her digging on this case into her trial partner's background, but for the moment, she made a strategic decision to step up. "I understand." She thrust a hand at Carly. "Let's make this work."

Carly looked at Landon's hand like she was holding a knife, but after an uncomfortable few seconds, she gripped it in her own. Her hands were warm and her grip was strong, both details that surprised Landon, and she let slip a slight smile that Carly almost returned. Before she could analyze whether their truce was real, Trevor walked up with a beautiful woman by his side. Landon's first thought was new girlfriend, bad optics, but she plastered a smile on her face.

Everyone at the table stood and greeted the new arrivals. When

Jane introduced the woman as Shelby Cross, Trevor's agent, Landon breathed a sigh of relief. Hopefully, Shelby was a helluva lot friendlier than Carly, otherwise there was going to be a whole lot of tension in the room. After an awkward moment where Landon had to snag the waiter to get him to bring another chair since obviously no one expected Trevor to show up with his agent in tow, they all ordered and settled in to talk about the case.

Jane started off. "Before we get into any details, Trevor, I have to tell you that anything you say to us is privileged and we can't be forced to reveal it unless you tell us about a crime you're about to commit—"

"As if," Shelby huffed. "Trevor is no criminal."

"Or if you tell us something in the presence of third parties who we do not represent." Jane finished her admonition with her eyes squarely on Shelby.

Trevor shook his head. "Shelby's been with me since the beginning. Anything you have to tell me, you can say in front of her."

"Actually, it's more a matter of *what* you have to tell us," Carly piped in. "If you tell us about incriminating evidence, then we can be forced to divulge the information if no reasonable expectation of privacy is assumed."

Shelby stared hard at Carly and then turned to Landon. "What about you? Do you speak English?"

Landon smiled one of her big, jury-winning smiles, and ignored the daggers Carly was shooting her way. "Absolutely." She went on to explain the privilege in layman's terms, and watched Shelby relax. "As long as we're discussing strategy and procedure or merely reviewing the evidence, it's perfectly fine for you to sit in." She turned to Trevor. "But if you decide you're about to blurt out some information that might implicate you, then by all means, let's clear the room."

"Not going to happen," Trevor said, with a reassuring glance at Shelby.

Pleased she had so quickly identified that the way to Trevor ran through his agent, Landon shot a look at Carly, who stared like she wanted to throat punch her. Landon may have been late to lunch, but she'd scored first in this round. She smirked at her competition. Bring it on.

❖

Carly glared at Landon, who was openly flirting with Shelby, and wished she had the ability to make people disappear. But she had no such power, and Shelby, and Trevor for that matter, were soaking up Landon's words like they were gospel. Two minutes ago, she'd said essentially the same thing that Landon was saying now, but apparently, Trevor and his agent were big on delivery and short on substance, and although she preferred to win on expertise alone, she filed that little note away. Two could play this game.

"I'm confident Trevor has nothing to hide," Shelby announced. "But if he wants me to leave, I will."

Everyone at the table looked between them, waiting for Trevor's decision. They didn't wait long. "I don't have any secrets," Trevor said, opening his arms wide. "Besides, I'd prefer Shelby hear everything firsthand so I don't have to try to remember it all. Regular season starts soon, and even if I'm riding the sidelines, I need to get my head in the game."

Carly watched Jane closely, but her expression remained neutral. Out of the corner of her eye, she saw Shelby duck her head. It was possible no one had discussed with Trevor that his team was unlikely to allow him to show up at the games while the cloud of the criminal investigation loomed, but maybe she was missing something. She wasn't about to be the one to bring up the unpleasant reality, so she kept quiet.

After they placed their orders, Jane dove in. "We have a lot to do to prepare for your case. The first step is the grand jury. I spoke with the prosecutor assigned to your case and she plans to present the case in the next two weeks."

"She?" Shelby asked.

"Yes," Jane replied. "Her name is Donna Wilhelm, and she's an experienced prosecutor in the family violence unit."

"What?"

"I don't get it," Shelby said. "Family violence?"

Carly's jaw nearly dropped as she watched Landon place a hand on Shelby's arm. "Don't get hung up on the name of her unit. She's a felony prosecutor who happens to work in the family violence unit. The DA's office considers it a crime of family violence whenever the victim had been dating the person they've accused of being responsible for the harm."

"Because the law says so," Carly blurted out, unable to help it. "There are special considerations in these types of cases which can enhance the punishment based on alleged prior acts of family violence." She ignored Landon's incredulous stare and pressed on. "That's why it's extremely important that we find out everything there is to know about Trevor's past. If there are any skeletons that might come jumping out, better we know up front so we can make plans to deal with them."

"And by skeletons," Jane said, "Carly means people who would say harmful things about Trevor to try to hurt his career or get him to pay hush money. Right, Carly?"

Not at all what she meant, but Jane's arched eyebrows signaled exactly what her reply should be. Fine, Jane was the boss, and Carly would defer to her lead. "Exactly." She turned to Trevor. "Like the false allegations that got you suspended." She started talking faster like she'd had a breakthrough. "We should start there. It would be helpful if you made a list of anyone who would benefit from seeing you off the team."

Carly watched Trevor's expression change from dejected to hopeful, and she regretted the ray of hope she'd given him since she figured it was pointless because this case was no longer about whether or not Trevor had harassed his ex-girlfriend. A woman had been murdered, and the prosecutor was out for blood.

The rest of lunch consisted of Jane filling in details about what Trevor could expect procedurally for the foreseeable future, and answering questions for Shelby about the process. When Trevor rose to leave, Carly realized they hadn't discussed anything about the Houston police reports she'd dug up in preparation for this meeting.

"Trevor, before you go, I was hoping we could ask a few questions about—"

"We'll have more questions later," Jane interrupted. "But for right now, go on about your business. The only thing we ask you to do is to keep a very low profile. Avoid social media, no comments to the press, and run any press engagements by us before you agree to appear on TV or give any interviews."

"Trevor has several appearances tied to his endorsements," Shelby said. "What about those?"

"Run everything by me. We'll call those on a case-by-case basis. I know you have obligations, but right now, we have only one, and that's to make sure Trevor stays a free man. Understood?"

Shelby nodded, but she didn't look happy about it. She stood to leave and Landon rose beside her. "I'll walk you out," Landon said. Carly rolled her eyes, but when she saw Shelby sigh with relief, she wished she'd thought of the tactic. Landon had the whole "rescue the damsel in distress thing" down.

After they left the room, Carly confronted Jane. "When are we going to get to talk to Trevor about the information I found in Houston?"

"Not now."

"Obviously, but you agree it's important that we know more, right?"

"Of course, but he's not going to tell you anything incriminating in front of his agent, and if he merely denies any wrongdoing right now, then he'll get entrenched in that position and never change his mind. First, we'll find out what Donna knows, and then find a time to talk to Trevor, just you and Landon. He'll be more likely to talk to you when he doesn't feel like he's going to lose face in front of the woman who sells his brand to the world."

Jane's words made sense, but surely Trevor would think his freedom was a little more valuable than saving face in front of his agent. Besides, his agent seemed to be pretty distracted by Landon's attention, a fact that annoyed Carly more than she wanted to admit. "Okay. I'll do some more digging. I know Donna, though, and she's not going to share much about her case before she presents it."

"Maybe we can leave that to Landon," Jane said. "She seemed to be working magic with Shelby."

"No," Carly replied too quickly. The very last thing she wanted to do was suck up to Donna Wilhelm, but no way was she going to let Landon hog this entire case and steal the partnership out from under her. She'd earned this partnership, and if she had to step out of her comfort zone to seal the deal, then she was going to make it happen. "I've got this."

"Got what?"

Landon walked back to the table and slid into the seat next to hers. Again with that little self-satisfied smirk. Carly imagined her flirting with Shelby all the way to the door, and the idea of that bothered her way more than it should. Suddenly feeling very warm, she shifted in her seat. "Just talking over a little case strategy. Thanks for hand-holding the clients."

"Hand-holding is half the battle, right, Jane?"

"True," Jane said. "Carly, once you've gotten Donna to talk to you, fill Landon in and both of you meet with Trevor to discuss that business in Houston."

"You don't want to be there?" Carly asked, ignoring the curious look on Landon's face.

"I think he'll feel less intimidated about discussing things with just you two." She stood. "Besides, one of you is going to be a partner after this case, so it's time to start doing partner level work. Just let me know what you find out. I'm headed downtown for a hearing in the Gosling case. See you back at the office."

A moment later, she was gone and Carly stared at her half-eaten salad.

"You should've ordered the lobster mac 'n cheese," Landon said, pointing at her own empty plate. "It was off the hook."

"My salad was great."

"Said no one ever."

"You eat your food and I'll eat mine. If I'm not trying to shove it down your throat, then I don't see why it matters to you what I choose to have." Her anger was irrational, but she couldn't seem to stop herself. She stood. "I've got to go. I have work to do."

"Is this your first murder case?"

"No." Not entirely a lie, but not entirely the truth either. Carly shot back, "Is it yours?"

"Not hardly. I don't know what kind of cases you've worked before, but just a word of advice. You have to gain the client's trust before you can get him to open up to you, and part of that is gaining the trust of the people around him. It's pretty clear Trevor takes his lead from Shelby, so you might want to spend some time getting her to warm up to you."

"Thanks for the tip." Carly edged away from the table. "And here's a tip for you. You could be a damn sight more subtle when you're flirting. It makes it seem less like you're trying to give legal advice and more like you're trying to get a date." She didn't wait for a reply before she turned around and walked out, leaving the infuriating Landon Holt to stew in that.

CHAPTER FIVE

The next morning, Landon pushed through the front doors of the Frank Crowley Courts building but stopped short when she saw the long line waiting to go through security. One of the beleaguered women in line looked up at her and pointed back toward the door. Damn, the line snaked outside, about twenty feet from the door. Landon started back out of the building to find the end of the line, when she heard a voice call her name.

"Landon Holt, what are you doing here?"

She turned and came face-to-face with one of her old law school classmates, Nick Glass. "Hey, Nick, what's up?"

He pulled her into a hug. "Lots of stuff considering it's been five years since I've seen or heard from you."

"Yeah, I guess it's been a while." Landon wasn't sure what else to say about it. When she'd split for Austin, she'd hadn't looked back.

"You doing okay?"

"I am." He pointed at the building. "Working my way up the ladder."

"You're with the DA's office?"

"Started right after the bar exam. I'm number two in Parker's court."

"And here I had you pegged for some white shoe firm." Landon supposed she shouldn't be surprised. "Of course, you were the star of our Crim Pro class. Glad to see you're putting it to good use."

"And what are you doing here?" Nick asked. "I thought you'd be working in the family business." His face took on a surprised expression. "Wait, there's no trouble in the land of all things Holt, is there?"

"I wouldn't know. This Holt makes her own way in the world." She pointed to the line. "Speaking of which, I have a meeting inside, so I better get in line."

He shook his head. "Lines are for people who don't know people. Come with me."

She followed Nick back through the doors, past the waiting crowd. When they reached the security guard who was ushering everyone through the metal detectors, Nick flashed his ADA badge and said, "She's with me," and a second later she was standing in the lobby. "See?" he said. "Now where are you headed?"

"Donna Wilhelm. Not sure what floor. Hate to admit it but this is my first time here. I've been working in Austin since the bar. With Sturges and Lloyd."

"She's up on nine." He narrowed his eyes. "Wait a minute. Are you working on Trevor Kincade's case? Holy shit, can you believe he's about to be indicted just when the regular season's about to start?"

Landon heard the fanboy in his voice. "You want to tell me what you know?"

"Not much, but you know how it is when someone like that gets arrested, everyone's talking. Donna's a straight shooter, but don't act like an out-of-towner or you'll ruffle her feathers. She hates when defendants hire some fancy-pants out-of-town attorneys to handle cases."

"Do I look fancy-pants to you?"

"Maybe just a little, but that's because I haven't seen you in forever." He rubbed his chin. "Feel free to drop my name. We hang sometimes."

"Is hang a euphemism?"

"Don't even." He held up his hand and pointed at a ring. "I'm happily married. Something you would know if you kept in touch." He smiled to soften the jab.

"I'm sorry, Nick. It's not just you, though, if that makes you feel any better."

"It doesn't, but you can make it up to me with a beer or three."

They exchanged numbers and agreed to meet. Landon wasn't sure she'd keep her end of the bargain, but it was nice to see a friendly, familiar face. Maybe a bit more of the same would help her acclimate to being back in Dallas.

She followed Nick's suggestion and took the escalator to the fourth floor and the stairs the rest of the way to avoid the overcrowded elevators. By the time she reached her floor, she was winded and resolved to start working out since this was probably the first of many trips to see Donna Wilhelm. She located the desk for the family violence unit and waited for the receptionist to finish texting on her cell phone before she announced her presence.

"I'm here to see Donna," Landon said. "She's expecting me."

The woman gave her a funny look, but picked up the phone and dialed. "There's a Landon Holt here to see you. Would you like me to tell her you're busy?"

Landon was about to butt in and say she had an appointment, but the woman held up a hand and spoke into the phone. "Okay, I'll send her back." She hung up and shoved a clipboard and a visitor's badge across the counter. Landon scrawled her name and clipped the badge on her lapel. The receptionist buzzed her in and called out "third door on the left" before she went back to punching on the screen of her cell.

Landon counted down to the third door and found it partially ajar. She knocked once and waited until she heard a voice call for her to come in before pushing it open. As the door swung into the room, Landon blinked when she spotted a second familiar face. "Carly?"

"Oh, hi, Landon," Carly said, cool as a cucumber. She made a show of looking at her watch. "I wasn't sure you were coming, so we decided to get started."

Landon stifled a growl. Carly must have gone through her calendar at the office because she sure hadn't mentioned she was coming down to the courthouse this morning. Of course, she really had no right to be angry since it had been her plan to cut Carly out of the loop, but her anger had more to do with Carly beating her at her own game. But showing her anger would only give Carly a win, so she offered a big smile and made up a little lie. "No problem. I'm sorry I'm late, but I had to go over some important information with our client." She stuck out her hand at the woman behind the desk. "You must be Donna. I'm Landon Holt. Nice to meet you."

Donna's smile was a tad forced, but Landon didn't blame her. The notoriety of this case cut both ways. On one hand, a conviction could make Donna's career, but on the other, most of Dallas was probably sending her hate mail for tying up their favorite player in court proceedings. If she botched the case in any way, she'd be blamed from all corners.

"Holt?" Donna asked, her forehead scrunched in a thinking frown. "Are you one of the—"

Landon knew where she was headed and cut her off fast. "Yes, I'm with the Austin branch of Sturges and Lloyd, but I'm here in Dallas for a while to work on this case. All hands on deck." She winced inwardly at the cliché.

"You're going to need them. Your guy is a killer, and I've got a solid case."

Okay, so that was how it was going to be. Landon looked over at Carly. She was staring daggers at Donna, who was leafing through papers on her desk. Carly opened her mouth to speak, but Landon jumped in first. "Care to share? I mean if you have him cold, let us know what you've got and maybe we can shortcut this entire process."

"You're kidding, right?"

Donna steepled her fingers and maintained a neutral expression, but Landon could tell by the gleam in her eyes she was salivating at the prospect of working out a plea before she had to take the case to grand jury. "Depends on the evidence. From what I've seen you don't even have enough to indict, but if there's something I'm not seeing, feel free to let me know." She heard Carly clearing her throat and turned to look at her.

"Us."

"Excuse me?" Landon asked.

"Us. If Donna has some evidence to share, she should share it with us," Carly declared. "So, Donna, as I was saying before we were interrupted, I would like to get a copy of the full police report. Can you make that happen?"

Donna looked at them with a curious expression. "Sure, but some sections are going to be redacted for now. And it's the usual pre–grand jury procedure—you can look at it here, but you can't take it with you or make copies."

Landon watched as Donna handed Carly a stapled stack of papers. She wanted to act like it was nothing, but she couldn't resist the urge to get a glimpse, so she walked over and stood behind Carly, reading over her shoulder. Carly read fast, faster than she did, and flipped the first page before she could scan a third of it. She was barely into the second page before Carly flipped again. Either she was a demonic speed reader or she was jacking with her. Landon started to say something, but a knock on the door interrupted them, and a guy in a suit, probably another ADA, stuck his head in the room. "Donna, I need you to settle something. It's urgent."

"I'll come out there. No room in here." She stood. "Be right back."

Landon waited until she heard the click of the door behind them and pulled out her phone.

"Whatever it is, it can wait," Carly said, flipping to the next page. "She's not going to let us sit here all day."

"You're right about that, which is why we're going to get what we need and be on our way." Landon held up her phone like a camera and held out her hand. "Give me that."

Carly eyes widened and she clutched the papers tightly with both hands. "No way. You heard the rules."

"I heard what she said, but it included absolutely nothing about taking a picture of what we're reading. Clearly, I don't read as fast as you do, so I'm at a disadvantage." She reached over and grabbed the report from Carly's hand. "I'm merely taking steps to level the playing field." Without waiting for a response, she snapped pictures of the document, ignoring Carly's glare. She was on the last page when the handle to the door turned. She shoved the document back into Carly's hands and slipped her phone into her bag.

"You get what you needed?" Donna asked as she walked back into her office.

"Almost," Landon said. "I can see why the police charged Mr. Kincade, you know because of the relationship, but I'm still not convinced you have enough for an indictment." She pointed at the police report in Carly's hand. "Do you have anything besides what's in that report?"

She was bluffing, especially since she hadn't had time to read the report in between snapping photos of the pages, but Donna didn't know that. She glanced over at Carly who, to her credit, maintained a neutral expression.

"We're always working to develop evidence in our pending cases and we'll comply with the rules of discovery."

Donna delivered the words with an expression of smug satisfaction. There was something else and it wasn't in the report. Landon guessed whatever Donna knew, she wasn't going to share unless they wound up in trial. Time to get out of here, read what they did have, and make a plan to find out the rest.

❖

"What the hell was that?" Carly spat out the words as they walked down the hall and away from the DA workroom.

Landon shrugged. "It's called using your resources. She left us alone in the room with the documents. It's not like I stuffed them in my shirt."

In spite of herself, Carly shot a look at Landon's chest. She wore a form-fitting dove gray shirt under her navy suit jacket, and there wasn't a lot of room for a stack of paper along with her C-cups. Damn. She needed to find a way to keep from being distracted by the good looks and charm of Landon Holt. "It's called breaking the rules, and talented attorneys don't need to cross the line to get things done."

"So now you think I'm not talented. But you hardly even know me." Landon smiled broadly, which was only more infuriating. "Tell you what, let's have lunch again and get to know each other. This time you pick the place."

Carly started to snap that she wasn't remotely interested in sharing another meal with Landon, especially not after the stunt she'd just pulled, but Jane's words about working together echoed in her head. Plus she hadn't had time to finish reviewing the police report, and now Landon had the only copy they could access. If she didn't make nice with Landon now, she'd be at a distinct disadvantage.

"Fine. But I'm driving." Carly didn't wait for an answer before taking off at a brisk pace to the stairwell, down all nine flights, and out of the building. She smiled as she heard Landon puffing behind her as she strode into the parking garage, but her pleasure quickly dispersed when she realized what she'd done. She didn't drive a fancy convertible, and she could just hear Landon making fun of her decade-old Honda Civic. She probably should've suggested they meet at the restaurant, but chances were good she would've changed her mind about the whole thing if Landon weren't in the car. She took a deep breath and pointed the key fob at her vehicle to unlock the doors. "Ready?"

Landon nodded and slipped into the passenger's seat. "Where are we headed?"

"Not far." Carly maneuvered out of the garage and took side streets to Maple Avenue. Landon pointed at a popular Mexican restaurant up ahead on the left.

"I haven't been to O'Jeda's in forever. I'm swooning at the prospect of their fajitas."

"Keep swooning because that's not where we're going."

"Okay. Mind filling me in?"

"The way you filled me in before you started taking pictures of evidence?" Carly turned into a tiny parking lot across the street from O'Jeda's and parked in front of a small brick building. She took the key out of the ignition and reached for her purse, but Landon's hand on hers stopped her in mid-grasp. She looked up at Landon. "What?"

"I could tell you that police reports aren't evidence, but I'm thinking you're a better-than-average lawyer since you're in the running for partner, so you probably already know that. So I'm pretty sure there's something else going on here that extends beyond friendly competition to account for why you don't like me, especially since you barely know me." Landon grinned. "People generally like me. It's my thing."

For the first few seconds of her speech, Carly had been fixated on Landon's hand on hers. It was warm and soft, but her touch was firm and electrifying and she hadn't wanted her to move. Ever. But as she kept talking, it became clear Landon Holt was used to getting her way, and would do anything to make that happen, including touchy-feely hand-holding just for show. Carly moved her hand out of reach. "I hope your 'thing' works out for you since you'll need it when you don't make partner." She opened her door. "Come on. I'm hungry."

Octavio Avila, owner of Avila's Mexican Restaurant, greeted them at the door and immediately pulled Carly into a big hug. "Carly, it's been weeks. Where have you been? And who is this lovely lady?"

She tunneled her way out of his arms in time to catch Landon's wide grin. Lovely lady, indeed. Octavio's assessment was on point if you judged by looks alone. Landon pulled both of Octavio's hands into her own while sporting her trademark smile.

"I'm Landon. I work with Carly. Nice to meet you." Landon looked around. "This is a beautiful place. I can't believe I've never been here before."

Carly watched Landon work her big bunch of charm. Others might fall for the package, but Carly wasn't one of them. Nope, not even. Octavio showed them to her usual booth and handed Landon a menu before walking away.

"Hmm," Landon said. "You don't need a menu, which means not only do you know the owner, but you have a 'usual.' Let me guess—the house salad?"

"You're hilarious."

"Some people think so."

Octavio reappeared and asked if Landon was ready to order. She handed her menu back and said, "I'll have whatever she's having." Carly waited until he was out of sight before picking up where they'd left off. "Speaking of being hilarious, I want to be perfectly clear that what happened back at the courthouse wasn't funny. You're new here, but I've been handling cases with these prosecutors for years, and I've been careful to earn their trust. If Donna had walked in while you were taking pictures she'd never trust me or anyone else from our firm again. Maybe those stunts have worked well for you in Austin, but not on my watch."

"Not on your watch? What are you, a cop? Because you're acting like you're on the other side. We represent Trevor and we're supposed to do everything in our power to help him, not suck up to the people who are trying to put him in prison for a crime he didn't commit. If I take a few pictures of a police report so I can read it in my own time instead of huddled around a prosecutor's desk, then I consider that perfectly acceptable advocacy."

Carly wanted to argue the point but she couldn't fault Landon's rational explanation. She kept to the rules because that's what people did, and when they didn't bad things happened. Besides, she'd always gotten good results for her clients by keeping a clear separation between right and wrong, something Landon clearly didn't get. "Let's agree to disagree. Now show me what you got."

Landon handed over her phone and had the good sense not to make any snide remarks about the fruit of the poisonous tree. "I glanced in the car. There's not a whole lot there, but skip to page five and let me know what you think."

Carly swiped the screen to the page Landon referenced and used her fingers to enlarge the image. This particular page of the report listed the witnesses the police had talked to in the course of their investigation. She skimmed the list of familiar names, neighbors of the victim and her family and friends, but one name stood out as unfamiliar, Kyle Dandridge. She pointed at the screen. "Who's that?"

Landon's jaw dropped. "Seriously?"

Carly shifted in her seat and looked at the name again. Okay, maybe it did sound a bit familiar, but she couldn't place it. Wishing she'd kept her mouth shut until she could Google it, she went all in. "Seriously."

"He's only the best running back in this division, maybe even the entire league. He was Trevor's roommate in college and probably knows him better than anyone else on the team. How is it possible that you live in Dallas and don't know this?"

"Uh, maybe football isn't really my thing."

Carly felt the burn of a blush as she spoke and waited for a sharp rebuke, but Landon merely shook her head. "Unbelievable. Well, you have a lot to learn."

"I don't need to learn the game of football to defend Trevor unless he's alleged to have committed the offense during a game."

"'Alleged to have committed'? Really?"

"Oh, so now you want to make fun of the way I talk?" Carly was about done with Landon having fun at her expense. "I was able to get Trevor's suspension lifted without knowing a damn thing about the sport. So what if I speak legal jargon? I'm a lawyer and a damn good one. You'd do well to take notice."

Landon's eyes widened during her diatribe, and Carly braced for whatever additional crap she wanted to dish out. To her surprise, Landon merely said, "You're right. Good job on the suspension, by the way."

Carly waited a beat, but apparently the compliment wasn't accompanied by any sarcasm. "Thanks." She sighed. "Maybe I should know a little bit more about the game."

"I could teach you."

Warning bells sounded in Carly's brain as she pictured the two of them perched in front of a giant screen TV, because that's what she imagined all sports fans had in their living room. Landon would be standing over her shoulder, leaning in close to point out some finer point of the game, and she'd graze her—

"So, what do you think?"

"About what?" Carly scrambled to clear her head.

Landon cocked her head. "You and me and ESPN."

"Uh, sure," Carly replied, wishing she had a firm grasp on what she'd just agreed to. Before she could backtrack, Octavio appeared with two steaming platters of food.

"These plates are very hot," he said as he sat the platters down in front of them. "Would you like some tortillas?" He directed the question at Landon, who looked to Carly.

"Do I?"

"No, you do not." Carly suppressed a grin as she watched Landon gape at her enormous plate of food.

"This," Landon said, pointing with her fork, "is not a salad."

"Are you making fun of me again?"

"Not even. I might be a little in awe. What have we got here?"

"Chile rellenos. The best in Dallas. Probably the best in the state, but I haven't made it to every place that serves them. Yet."

"Ah, so it's salads and Mexican food for you. Any other surprises?"

"Nope," Carly said, tucking into a large bite of relleno. She adored this place and this food, but the portions were insane, and she'd be eating the leftovers for the rest of the week. Landon was well into her plate of food, and at the rate she was going, wasn't likely to have anything to take home. "You like?"

"I love. And I too am a Mexican food aficionado, so there's that."

Carly smiled, but a small voice in the back of her head told her it was time to steer the conversation back to more professional and less social topics. "So what do you think Kyle Dandridge is doing on the list of witnesses?"

"That's a good question. It could be just for general background information, but that question needs to top the list of things we ask Trevor. Speaking of which, I asked Rhonda to set up a meeting with him for tonight. He wants to meet at his place. Do you want to ride together?"

Instinct told Carly to say no. She should drive her own car, maintain her independence.

So she was as surprised as anyone when she opened her mouth to politely decline and said, "That would be perfect."

CHAPTER SIX

Trevor's house rated on the moderate scale for football greats. Landon pulled into the drive and spotted a shiny red Corvette, pretty much the kind of ride she'd expect for a pro player. She was pleasantly surprised when Shelby stepped out of the driver's side.

"Oh great," Carly groaned. "I was hoping we might get to talk to him alone."

"Really?" Landon returned Shelby's wave and parked behind her car. "I mean, it seemed like he opens up more when she's around. What's their history?"

"She's been his agent his entire career. She's a few years older than Trevor, but they met when he played with her brother in high school. Apparently, Trevor was like another son to her folks. His own parents were doctors, and not into sports at all, so Trevor hung out with Shelby's family more than his own."

"Is Trevor an only child?"

Carly nodded. "Although I'm pretty sure he considers Shelby and her brother Randy honorary siblings. Randy plays for the Falcons."

"Look at you, spouting off football facts like a pro."

"As if." Carly jerked her chin toward the door. "Are we going in or not?"

Landon followed her gaze. Shelby waved at them from the front door. What Landon really wanted was to stay here and keep her conversation with Carly going, especially now that they'd established a rhythm, but they had a lot of work to do. "Guess we better go in."

Trevor's house was a giant man cave, and Landon loved every inch of it. The slate entryway led into a den that featured a wall of large screen TVs worthy of a high-end sports bar. On the opposite wall was a full bar, complete with beer pulls, barstools, and a spotless mirrored back wall. She idly wondered how often the maid came to visit, and whether Trevor hired a bartender to work when he was watching games at home. Too bad they weren't here for fun.

Shelby ushered them into the room, and a chubby black French bulldog lumbered toward them. To Landon's surprise, Carly hunkered down and rubbed his wrinkled jowls. "Hey, cuteness, who are you?" Carly said to the Frenchie, who snorted and licked her hand in response.

"That's Dijon," Shelby said. She frowned and stepped back as the dog turned her way at the sound of his name. "Trevor's sidekick."

"He's adorable," Landon said, but the really adorable one was Carly, who was still at dog height, giving Dijon a world-class petting.

"Trevor's finishing up a call," Shelby said, clearly moving on. "Would either of you like a drink?"

"Sure," Landon said before she caught sight of Carly's frown as she gave Dijon a final stroke and stood. Taking advantage of the fact Shelby was headed across the room, Landon whispered, "What?"

"You really think it's a good idea to belly up to the bar?"

"It's one drink." Landon pointed at Dijon. "If he asked, I bet you'd say yes."

Carly scowled, but before she could speak, Shelby called out, "What's your poison?"

Landon ignored Carly's pointed look and walked toward the bar. Shelby cocked her head and said, "You strike me as a tequila girl, am I right?" Without waiting for an answer, Shelby pulled a bottle from underneath the bar and held it up. "I socked this bottle away so I have something besides the usual whiskey and beer that the guys drink when they hang out here. Don't be fooled by the pretty bottle. There's actually a really old, sophisticated extra añejo inside. Join me?"

Landon flashed back to the night of her birthday party. Hard to believe it had only been a few days ago. She never imagined then that she'd be sipping expensive tequila with the agent of a pro football player while sitting in his fancy house. Carly could be as uptight as she wanted, but Landon could tell that getting Shelby on their side was the key to Trevor opening up, and if that meant she had to enjoy a fancy glass of tequila, well, she was up to the sacrifice. "Absolutely."

"Carly, how about you?" Shelby called out. "Wait, you're not a big drinker, are you?" She made a show of looking around and pulled out a bottle of Perrier. "Sparkling water okay?"

"Actually, I'd love a glass of tequila, especially if it's as good as you say."

Landon looked back and forth between them, trying to gauge whether the undercurrent of animus she'd just heard was all in her head. There was some history here, and if it meant Shelby wasn't real fond of Carly, then maybe she could use it to her advantage. The realization was a mixed bag of opportunity and regret. She'd been fully prepared to do battle with Carly, but she kept getting little glimpses that she was human after all and an interesting one at that. She was definitely gorgeous, even if her beauty was all buttoned-up. She just needed to let her hair down. Literally. Landon imagined reaching up to unfasten the barrette that kept Carly's hair tucked in place, and she sucked in a breath at the mental visual of Carly's auburn waves cascading to her shoulders.

Landon shook away the thought. It wasn't productive, and it wasn't going to happen no matter how much tequila they drank. She and Carly had to work together, plus they were competitors, and she'd do well to remember that. She felt a touch on her hand and accepted a short heavy glass full of amber liquid from Shelby. Shelby maintained eye contact with her for a few seconds, and then whirled around and poured another glass for Carly. Carly raised her glass in a mock salute and took a healthy sip.

"Nice," she said.

Landon stopped with her glass halfway to her mouth, riveted at the sight of sexy Carly sipping tequila. This needed to stop and right now. She took a taste and glanced over at Shelby, who was throwing side-eye in Carly's direction. Landon made a note to find out what the issue was between them, but for now, she decided to break the ice. "This is the best tequila I've ever had. And I've had quite a bit."

"I can always spot a tequila girl." Shelby took a drink from her glass. "I'm going to go see what's keeping Trevor. He had a call with one of his sponsors, but I expected it to be over by now." She squeezed Landon's hand. "Be right back."

She sashayed out of the room and disappeared into the cavernous house. Landon raised her glass again and looked at Carly. "Do you really like this or were you being polite?"

"Do I strike you as the type to mask how I really feel?"

"Maybe. Like I can tell there's some bad blood between you and Shelby, but you seem to be handling it like a pro even though she keeps goading you."

Carly waved a hand. "She didn't always agree with our strategy when we were fighting the suspension. Rather than blaming Jane and Mark, she focused her disapproval on me. Comes with the territory. If you expect clients to like you all the time, you'll be sorely disappointed."

Landon knew she wasn't the "you" Carly had been referring to, but she couldn't help but feel like the message was meant for her. Fact was, she did like it better when clients liked her. It sure made it easier for them to confide in her. If Shelby wanted to play favorites, she wasn't going to protest.

Trevor's voice sounded from the entry. "Sorry to keep you waiting." He pointed at the phone in his hand. "But I'm not really in a position to turn down calls from my sponsors right now." At the sound of his voice, Dijon sprang from the bed he'd collapsed into after his attention from Carly and ran toward his owner. Trevor smiled, but his eyes were red and he looked haggard as he petted the lovable Frenchie.

"Everything okay?" Landon asked.

"I don't know. Brands are dropping me like crazy, but Shelby's convinced a few to keep me on at least until the grand jury determines if they're going to indict me. It's kind of unbelievable that in the court system you're innocent until proven guilty, but in the court of public opinion one allegation and you're history."

Sounded suspiciously like a sound bite and something Shelby had prepared. Landon spoke carefully. "I get that it's tempting to tell your side of the story and shout that you had nothing to do with Vanessa's death, but I promise the public will twist anything you say into a bigger pretzel than the prosecution. You have absolutely nothing to gain from talking to the press." She pointed at Shelby. "Besides, that's what you have Shelby for. I'm sure she has access to some great PR folks who can speak on your behalf. Trust me, we'll get you through this."

"Shelby tells me she has good instincts about you." Trevor strode over to the bar and pulled a beer. "So, what's on the agenda for tonight? Jane said you might have some background questions." He took a deep drink from the beer glass. "Whatever you want to know, ask me."

He motioned for them to have a seat on the huge leather sectional that took up most of the room. When they were settled, Landon decided not to waste any more time. "Tell us everything you know about Kyle Dandridge."

Trevor's eyes narrowed. "I don't get it. What's Kyle have to do with this?"

"Good question. He's listed as a witness in the police report, and since he wasn't arrested, I'm thinking he's a prosecution witness. When's the last time you talked to him?"

"I called him yesterday."

"How did he act?"

"He didn't. I didn't reach him. I left a message."

"What did you say?"

He looked surprised at the question. "I don't know. Probably something about needing to talk to him because all this stuff is weighing on my mind. Why?"

"Because you can bet that if Kyle really is a prosecution witness," Carly said, "he's handing over every message you leave to the prosecutor, and the words 'stuff is weighing on my mind' sounds suspiciously like someone who has something to confess."

"Well, that's crazy." Trevor tossed back the rest of his beer and stared at Carly with a hangdog expression. "Is that what you really think?"

Shelby stared daggers at Carly, and Landon almost felt sorry for her. "Let's take it back a notch," Landon said. "Trevor, tell us everything you know about Kyle. Start from where you met him to what kind of relationship you have now. I mean, realistically you probably don't spend a lot of time together, right?"

"Actually we've spent a lot of time together this off-season. We took a trip to Aruba and I spent a couple of weeks at his place in Cabo."

Landon cut a glance at Carly, who nodded. She took out a piece of paper and wrote at the top *Attorney Client Work Product/Confidential* and handed it to Trevor. "You don't have to do this right now, but after we leave, I need you to write down everything you can remember about those trips. Who you talked to, what you said, what other people said to you. You get the idea, right?"

"I do."

Shelby's phone buzzed. "Sorry, I need to take this. I'll be back in a minute."

Trevor leaned back in his chair and sighed. "I just can't imagine what Kyle would have to say about Vanessa. I mean, he knew we had kind of a tumultuous relationship, but he was my go-to when I needed to get away from all the drama."

"Well, let's talk about that. I know you probably discussed your relationship with Vanessa with Carly while you were fighting the suspension. Do you mind going over everything again with both of us?"

"Carly has been great. I'm pretty sure we never would've gotten the suspension lifted without her."

Out of the corner of her eye, Landon saw Carly puff up at the compliment. Obviously, Trevor didn't share Shelby's animus for Carly. Landon made a mental note to figure out more about the hostility between the two women. Maybe there was something there she could use to her advantage. The moment she had the thought, she felt a tinge of regret. This whole race for partnership thing put her in a weird spot. She was used to being a tough competitor, but that was when she was fighting with someone on the opposite side. She and Carly were working toward the same goal, and it didn't feel right to be looking for ways to undermine Carly's success to make herself look good. Besides, despite Carly's uptight ways, Landon actually enjoyed their banter. She needed to adjust her approach. Maybe the key to getting the partnership wasn't to undermine her competitor but to strike a balance between making them both look good while delivering winning blows against their real opponent, the prosecution. She liked this plan. Especially since it meant she could get a little closer to Carly than sparring would allow.

Carly waved off Landon's attempt to open the car door for her. "We're not on a date, Holt."

Landon winced. "Don't call me that, please."

Filing the nugget of intel away to be explored later, Carly slid into the passenger seat and yawned. They'd spent the last two hours grilling Trevor under Shelby's watchful eye. Whenever they tried to play devil's advocate, Shelby intervened, and Carly was exhausted from the effort. They hadn't learned much more than what Carly already knew. Vanessa had confronted Trevor several times about threats she'd received and whether he was seeing other women. On at least two occasions, the police had been called. Trevor denied ever sending the emails, and he insisted Vanessa was just paranoid. That much hadn't changed since she'd last grilled him on the subject, but when Landon asked him if he'd ever cheated, he squirmed, finally admitting that one time, he and Kyle had picked up some fangirls in a bar after an away game and taken them back to the team hotel. Infidelity wasn't illegal, but at least now they had a more definite reason for why Kyle might be on the prosecution witness list. Tarnishing Trevor as a cheating boyfriend could bolster the prosecution's case.

A hand passed near her face, and she looked over at Landon.

"Earth to Carly. Are you more tired or hungry?"

Carly laughed at the surprising question. "I think it's a dead heat."

"Why are jocks such bad hosts?" Landon asked. "I mean, the guy could afford to have a chef on hand around the clock, but the only food in the house was pretzels. Lawyers cannot live on party mix alone. At least not this lawyer."

"Me either. My relleno faded long ago."

"I could use a burger, if you're up for it."

Carly surreptitiously glanced at the dashboard clock. It was late. She was no stranger to working late, but a big dinner after nine would keep her up half the night. Her plan had been to go home, have a cup of the soup she'd saved from the day before, and do a little research before turning in. A greasy burger and the fries she was certain Landon would order were definitely not part of her plan. She diverted. "How is it that you know so many places to eat in Dallas if you haven't lived here in years? Do you come up often?"

"Not even. I guess I just remember the good places."

It was too dark to see Landon's expression, but her tone had morphed from fun loving to somber, and Carly wanted the fun version back. "Ah, that explains the progression of comfort foods." At that moment her stomach rumbled, and they both laughed. "I guess that settles it. Take me to your favorite burger spot."

Keller's was hopping for a weeknight. Carly had driven past the old drive-in burger joint plenty of times and, like tonight, it was usually crowded with fancy cars parked next to Harleys owned by the many bikers who frequented the place. Landon pulled the car to a stop. "This okay?"

"Sure." Carly decided to embrace trying something new. Landon turned on her flashers, and a few minutes later, a woman sporting a beehive with a paper pad in her hand wandered out to the car to take their order. The food came fast, and when it did, Carly bit into her cheeseburger and tried not to mind that it dribbled down her chin. "There are not enough napkins in the world for this experience," Carly said.

"True. But if you're focused on the napkins, you're doing it wrong." Landon took another bite of her burger and moaned. "Better even than I remember."

"No good burgers in Austin?"

"There's plenty, but Dallas wins, hands down."

"This is amazing."

"It's no salad, that's for sure."

Carly smiled, and a second later, Landon touched a napkin to her face, dabbing at the corner of her mouth. Carly reached for the napkin, and her fingers closed over Landon's and held for a moment, enjoying the warmth of the simple touch. Warning bells clanged in her head and she reluctantly let go. "Salads aren't so messy."

"They are when I eat them. Of course I load them up with tons of dressing and toppings. Lettuce is merely a palette."

"How in the world do you look the way you do when you eat stuff like this all the time?" The words were out before Carly could censor them and she was instantly mortified.

"You like the way I look," Landon said with a grin.

"That's not what I said, and you know it. It's a question of science. If I ate like you do, I'd never fit through my front door."

"Maybe I have a very large front door." Landon chomped down on a French fry. "Seriously, I've always been this way—overactive metabolism. I do work out, but that's mostly to burn off energy."

"Was that comment supposed to take away the sting, because it just made me hate you more."

"You don't hate me."

Carly paused before answering. It was true, she didn't hate Landon. Not at all. In fact, the more time they spent together, the clearer it became that she actually kind of liked her. Which made it more difficult to wrap her head around kicking Landon's ass while working on this case. "Okay, *hate* is a strong word."

"See?" Landon scrunched her hamburger wrapper into a ball and started the car. As they drove away from Keller's, she said, "I know we're rivals here, but if we set some ground rules, we might actually both have a better shot at winning."

Intrigued, Carly said, "Name them."

Landon ticked the rules off on her fingers. "Number one, we share all information we learn. If we're working for the good of Trevor, then it's our duty to do the best we can."

"Got it. Next?"

"We present a united front. Trevor, Shelby, and especially Donna Wilhelm don't need to know we're competing against each other. If Donna finds out, she could try to take advantage."

"Agreed. I've got the next one. We do all witness interviews together whenever possible. That way we each get a fair glance at the veracity of the witness."

Landon nodded. "I have only one more. You let me teach you about the game of football. I can't have you going around using the wrong vocabulary and not knowing anything about the players and organization. You'll make us both look bad. And don't say you can learn all about it on the internet, because you can't. There's no substitute for the real thing."

Carly stammered for a response, but Landon was right. Right or not, she proceeded with caution. "And how do you propose to teach me?"

"We'll start slow. Have you ever been to a game?"

"That's a pretty broad question, counselor."

"Okay, have you ever been to a pro game?"

"Fairly certain you know the answer to this one. And that would be no."

"Excellent. Then I'll have the pleasure of escorting you to your first game. Prepare to be amazed."

Landon's words were silky smooth and probably weren't intended to convey strong flirtation, but Carly's senses were all on high alert at the promise in her voice. "What should one do to prepare?"

"One should not talk about oneself in the third person, for starters."

And just like that, Carly's eagerness for the new adventure was buried in embarrassment. Thank God Landon had just turned into the office parking lot. "Yeah, it's okay. I think I can figure out what I need to know on my own. My car's right up there. You can let me out here."

Landon ignored her and pulled into the spot next to her car. "Hey, I'm sorry. I was just teasing."

Carly shrugged. "I get it. I'm just tired."

"You don't like to be teased."

"Does anyone?"

"I guess I'm used to it. I have two brothers. It came with the territory."

Carly's ears perked up at the first mention of some detail of Landon's family, but she decided not to press. She wasn't at all sure why she cared about Landon's personal life, but she wrote it off to knowing her opponent. Sure, right, that was it. For now she was just glad for the focus not to be on her and her own insecurity. "I should go."

"Okay."

Neither one of them moved. Carly had no desire to leave because it would mean Landon's hand would no longer be touching her. Completely irrational. Landon was everything she wasn't. Gregarious, easygoing, good-looking—the list went on and on. They had absolutely nothing in common but this case, and the fact they both wanted to make partner—both excellent reasons for why she shouldn't be attracted to Landon and why she definitely shouldn't act on her feelings. It might be a little too late for that first thing.

CHAPTER SEVEN

"Why are we taking an Uber again?" Carly asked.

Landon looked up from her desk. Carly was framed in her doorway, and Sunday-at-the-office version of Carly was wildly different from regular workday, office-ready Carly. She was dressed in jeans, Chucks, and a light cotton hoodie, and her hair, normally pinned up tight, cascaded around her shoulders like a gorgeous auburn halo. "Your hair is almost red when the light hits it."

Crap, she could tell by the strange look on Carly's face that she'd said that out loud. "I mean that's interesting. Like a strange effect. You know. Of the light. On your hair." *Shut up, shut up, shut up.* Now Carly was smiling at her in a goofy way, so Landon stood and grabbed her cell. "As for why we're taking an Uber, you'll see. Ready to go?"

Perfect timing—the car showed up just as they stepped out of the building. It was a gorgeous fall Sunday, and the air was crisp with the promise of cooler temperatures. Like Carly, Landon was dressed for play in jeans and her favorite sweatshirt purchased on a recent trip to Provincetown. When Carly asked her about the P-town logo, she was surprised that she hadn't heard of the popular gay vacation destination. "It's at the tip of the cape about two hours from Boston. Super popular in the summer, and they have a full week of events just for women every October." She watched for a sign of recognition but got nothing. Maybe the gay vibe she thought she'd been getting was something else. But then Carly had made that comment about not being on a date when she'd held open her car door, but that wasn't definitive. She shook her head—they were here on business, and Carly's sexual orientation was a non-issue, or at least it should be.

"I don't vacation much."

"Don't like to travel?"

Carly seemed surprised by the question. "I don't mind the destination, it's the preparing for and getting there part I'm not particularly fond of. Besides I've been pretty busy with work the last few years, you know, trying to make partner."

"Oh yeah, that." Landon smiled. "Well, if you hate the getting there part, you'll appreciate not having to park at the stadium." She pointed out her window at the long lines of vehicles waiting to get into the parking lot. "We're about to be dropped off at the entrance." She leaned over the seat and gave the driver specific instructions about where to locate Will Call. She was excited about seeing the game in person, even though the star player would be absent. It would be the second time this season they'd played without Trevor. They'd crashed miserably the first time, but they'd had little notice since he'd just been arrested. Now that the team had had more than a week to regroup, hopefully they'd be up to the challenge.

"Is Trevor here for the game?" Carly asked.

"No. He discussed it with the coach and they decided that even though he isn't technically suspended right now, his presence would be a distraction. They want the press to focus on the game and not spend their time shouting questions about the case. Although after the way they played last week, they might welcome a distraction." She looked for a sign of agreement on Carly's face, but all she got was a blank stare. "You really don't follow football, do you?"

"It's not just football," Carly replied. "I like to think I'm equal opportunity when it comes to not giving a rat's ass about professional sports."

"Do you hate the Olympics too? Because if you do, I may not be able to hang out with you."

Carly smiled. "No, I'm not a heathen. The Olympics are way more commercial than they used to be, but they still have that 'root for the home team vibe' about them." She pointed at the stadium. "We're going to watch the Dallas Cowboys, but we had to drive from Dallas to a completely different county, not to mention city, to get to the stadium. Not a lot of home team feel about it."

Landon grinned. "That's because they're America's team, baby."

She looked up in time to see the driver nodding at her words, and she pointed. "See!"

"You're hopeless," Carly said.

"I may be, but it's time to roll." Landon tipped the driver and held the door for Carly. As they walked up to the gate, Landon suppressed an instinct to grab Carly's hand, but her earlier thoughts echoed. They were here on business, and this wasn't a date. But that was no reason they couldn't have fun. "Last one to the gate is a rotten lawyer." She didn't wait for a reply, instead dodging around the family walking in front of them and charging toward the entrance. When she reached her destination and turned around, Carly was standing a few feet away, but she slowed in her tracks and a wall of seriousness fell over her expression. "What?"

Carly didn't speak, but Landon followed her eyes and zeroed in on Shelby Cross standing just inside the ticket gate staring at them with a sour face. "Oh."

It wasn't that Landon didn't like Shelby. She seemed nice and capable and like she had Trevor's best interests at heart, but she'd wanted this day to be her and Carly, discussing strategy without the client or the client's stand-in watching over their shoulders.

"Did you know she was going to be here?" Carly asked with an accusing tone.

Landon raised her hands. "Not even, but I guess it makes sense since Trevor was the one who arranged for our tickets that he'd send Shelby to be our host when he decided not to come. Maybe she won't stay after she gets us settled."

"Have you seen the way she looks at you?" Carly shook her head. "She'll stay."

Landon's reply was cut off when Shelby strode up. "Hey, you two. I've got your tickets. Trevor asked me to meet you and make sure you got the VIP treatment. Are you ready?"

Landon faked a smile. Trevor was the client, and Shelby was his agent; both facts were a solid reminder that she was here to work, not make eyes at her competitor. Maybe Shelby joining them was a good thing. Who knew what information they might be able to get from her under the guise of casual conversation? With a quick reassuring look at Carly, she said, "We're ready. Lead the way."

When they reached the elevator to the suite level, Landon hesitated. "Where are we headed?"

"The Zion suite," Shelby answered. "They always save seats for Trevor's guests."

Landon started to say she thought they'd just get some random seats in the stadium, not the cush digs of the executive suites, but the words sounded silly when she played them in her mind. Of course Trevor would have access to luxury seating. He'd been the brand spokesman for Zion Athletics for a while, and Zion probably had a luxury suite in every stadium in the country where Trevor's guests could enjoy catered food and an open bar during the game. Not exactly the experience she'd planned to show Carly when she'd had this brainchild. "Hey, do you mind if we make a quick stop before we head upstairs?"

Before Shelby could answer, she motioned for Carly to follow her and walked toward the concourse. She hadn't been to a game here in years, but she'd scoped the layout online and had a mental map of exactly where she wanted to go.

"Where's the fire?" Carly said as she caught up and matched her long strides.

"Are you hungry? I'm starving."

"Sure, but is there a reason you're leaving the client in the dust?"

"Shelby's not the client." Landon looked back and tossed Shelby a fake smile and a friendly wave. "The food in the suites will be good, I'm sure, but it's going to be faux football food. In order to have the true experience, you need food that isn't sitting in fancy silver chafing dishes, warmed-over and soggy. Trust me on this."

"I do."

Carly delivered the simple statement with exaggerated seriousness, and they both burst out laughing. They were still laughing when Landon located her destination. "May I order for you?"

"Sure, why not?"

Landon looked back at Shelby and motioned to ask if she wanted anything, but Shelby shook her head, the puzzled look on her face signaling she thought Landon had lost her mind. Maybe she had. Before she could give it any further thought, she stepped up to the counter and asked for a large order of pulled pork nachos and two large draft beers. She forked over way too much money for the overpriced food and handed one of the beers to Carly.

"I guess I should've mentioned I'm not much of a beer drinker," Carly said.

"Let me guess. You tried it in college and hated it. I bet it was at some frat party where the brothers were tapping the keg themselves."

"Maybe."

"Maybe, my ass. I'm right and I know it. I also know the beer you have in your hand is nothing like the beer of your college days."

"Care to bet a partnership on it?"

"You're hilarious." Landon grabbed the nachos and her own beer, and they walked back to Shelby. "Thanks for indulging me. I've been craving these nachos ever since we decided to come to the game, and I've found that if I don't indulge my cravings, bad things happen."

"I see."

The lilt in Shelby's voice was subtle, but Landon instantly regretted her careless words. A quick look at Carly yielded no hint of what was going through her mind in response to the exchange, but she figured it was best to change the subject. "Shall we head upstairs?"

They followed Shelby to the Zion suite, where an attendant offered to fetch them a drink. Landon held up her beer by way of answering. Carly took a sip of her own beer and smiled. "Hey, this is pretty good." She looked at the attendant. "I'll stick with this, thanks."

"Try not to sound so surprised," Landon whispered as the attendant indicated where they should sit. "Prepare to be blown away by these nachos."

Carly's expression was dubious. "I hate to tell you this, counselor, but your nachos are looking a little wimpy."

Landon took a look at the basket in her hand and had to agree. The chips, weighted down with extra cheese and pork, had started to sag and the result was a gooey mess. She grasped a chip and pulled, but it tore under the weight of all the ingredients. Not at all the hearty meal she remembered from her last visit. "I guess it's been a while since I've had these. The memory isn't holding up to reality today."

Carly smiled and pointed to the back wall of the suite. "Guess we'll wind up exploring those chafing dishes after all."

Shelby pointed to the buffet. "You girls help yourselves. I have to make a call, but I'll be back soon."

Landon and Carly filled their plates with appetizers and settled in. The suite was large enough to hold at least twenty people, but they were the only two guests so far.

"When are you going to start schooling me on the game?" Carly asked.

"I was going to let you get fortified first, but if you're ready, so am I."

Carly sipped her beer and pointed to the large screen TV that hung over the twenty-yard line. "I thought the whole point was to watch the game live. What's with the TV?"

"It's in the top five largest hi-def televisions for a sports stadium in the world." Landon pointed at the upper rows of seating across the way. "It's so the folks in the cheap seats, and I mean that in the most relative sense, can see what's happening on the field." She took a long pull from her beer and studied Carly's face, which was scrunched in a frown. "Right now, you're thinking what's the point of paying big money for a ticket, fighting traffic to drive to the stadium, and standing in line for nachos if you're going to watch the game on TV?"

Carly grinned. "Hey, mind reader, with skills like that, you're going to be stiff competition for sure."

Landon returned the grin and pointed to the field. "Game's about to start. They're doing the coin toss now." She motioned to Carly to join her at the rail and spent the next few minutes pointing out various aspects of the game.

"I guess there is something to being here live. On TV you only see what they want you to see," Carly said.

"Exactly. And while they're at commercial, we get to see even more." Landon leaned in close and pointed downfield. "Look—it's the full contingent of Dallas Cowboy cheerleaders." Carly turned to look in the direction she was pointing, and the move placed her snug in Landon's arms. Landon breathed deep, enjoying the light scent of lavender and the warm edge of Carly's closeness, but mostly she enjoyed that Carly didn't push away or act weird about their proximity.

Seconds later, the spell broke when the door to the suite opened, and Landon heard Shelby's voice call out, "We have some more guests."

Damn. Irrational as it was, Landon had hoped she'd have the afternoon alone with Carly. She told herself her hope had to do with discussing the case, but as she stood with Carly in her grasp, she didn't give a damn about anything to do with football or the court case. Not good. Not good at all. Summoning reserves of willpower, she turned to greet Shelby and whoever else was going to share the suite for the rest of the afternoon.

One of the men with Shelby handed his coat to the attendant and turned to face them. And that's when the day went completely to hell.

"Landon?" the man said, his voice laced with more displeasure than surprise.

Her first instinct was to head for the exit, but that was a childish response. One she'd employed many times before, but today was different. Today she was working. Today Carly was with her. Today, if she ran, she would look foolish to someone other than the man standing in front of her.

"Hello, Dad." She managed an overtly friendly tone with only an undercurrent of annoyance. He hated being called Dad. Too casual. Too familiar. Which was silly since there had never been any danger of them becoming too familiar.

Shelby introduced the other man, Robert Zion, founder of Zion Athletics. Robert looked off-kilter at the exchange between Landon and her father. He cleared his throat as if that would cut the tension hanging in the air. "I was going to introduce you all to my business associate George Holt, but it looks like you know one another already."

Landon piped up before anyone else could respond. She stuck her hand out to Robert, after all, he hadn't done anything to her yet. "Pleased to meet you. I'm Landon Holt, George's daughter, and this is my associate, Carly Pachett." She refrained from any specifics about the fact they represented Trevor because it wasn't clear yet what her father was doing here. "Thanks for letting us use the suite today. Are you here for the game or for business?"

Robert looked uncomfortable. "Some of both." He glanced at the attendant who was talking to Shelby and lowered his voice. "Since you're a lawyer, I'm sure you appreciate my desire not to speak too openly in public, but we are in talks with your father about the future of the company, and Trevor's future as our spokesperson is a big factor in our negotiations. When I spoke with Shelby about our concerns, she thought you might have some insights to share."

It was a lot to digest, so Landon picked it apart word by word, suddenly clear about why dear old Dad was here. "You're buying

Zion," she hissed in his direction. "And you're worried about whether Trevor Kincade is going to besmirch the brand, aren't you?" She didn't expect an answer. She wanted to tell Robert Zion to run, run as fast as he could because once George Holt owned his company, he would change it from a family-owned business dedicated to good products into a sweatshop concerned only with the bottom line, but she owed it to Trevor to hold her tongue. Besides, she wasn't about to give her father the satisfaction of seeing her lose her cool. "Well, this should be interesting."

Unsure of what she might say or do next, Landon walked back to the railing at the front of the suite and caught Carly staring at her with an inquisitive expression. She wanted to say something about what a jerk her father was, that his only interest in Zion was as an acquisition, not a brand to build on, but she didn't say anything and the irony wasn't lost on her. The desire to share her feelings with Carly was exactly the kind of thing her father would've warned her about. She could hear the echo of his voice telling her it wasn't wise to share personal information with a competitor, that they would only use it against you. She hated to admit it, but her father was right. Against her gut instinct, she ignored Carly's stare and focused on keeping her feelings hidden.

Carly felt the mood in the suite shift after the arrival of the other guests and tried to piece together what was going on. Only two things were perfectly clear: Landon's father was here, and Landon and her dad did not get along. She'd seen Landon stiffen the minute George Holt came close to them and Carly felt the ice form between them.

"May I get either of you another drink?" the attendant asked. Carly looked at George, Robert, and Shelby who were talking on the far side of the suite. Before she could respond, Landon pushed her beer to the side. "Bourbon, neat." She looked around like she dared anyone to find fault with her choice.

If straight bourbon was the bar, Carly wasn't going to try to hurdle it. Considering Trevor's biggest sponsor was here, one of them should attempt to stay sober. Not wanting to offend their host, she ordered a vodka and club soda, figuring she could switch to just soda for her next drink and no one would know the difference. While the bartender fixed their drinks, she attempted to get Landon to open up. "I'm guessing you and your dad aren't on great terms."

Landon choked out a laugh. "Understatement. Big one." She accepted the glass from the attendant and took a healthy swallow. "He's big business, and I'm his greatest disappointment."

"Hmm," Carly replied and fished around for something genuine to say. She understood the concept of disappointment because she'd worked hard her entire life to avoid being the cause of it, while being driven by the fear of it. "Seems a little hard to believe that you, a lawyer up for a partnership in one of the top firms in the state, would be disappointing."

"It does, doesn't it?" Landon tossed back the rest of her drink. "Yet somehow I manage." She pointed at the group huddled on the other side of the suite. "Let's go mingle. This is a work thing, after all."

Carly heard the bitter edge in Landon's voice. Was it possible Landon was as disappointed as she was to have their casual outing interrupted by not only work, but also by family drama of the highest order? Carly had no business being disappointed. No matter how Landon made her feel when she was standing close, this wasn't a date, not even if it had started to feel like one. Landon's family dynamic wasn't her concern, nor should it be. "You're absolutely right."

Ignoring Landon's outstretched hand, Carly stood and walked over to Shelby, Robert, and George, whose voices all trailed off as she approached. Summoning reserves of assertiveness she didn't actually feel, she said, "I'm guessing none of you are here to watch the game. Shall we talk?"

George was the first to speak. "If the firm is taking this case seriously, then why isn't Jane or Mark here to represent Trevor?"

Ass. Carly offered him an exaggerated smile. "Here? At the football game? There's not a lot of 'representing' to be done during a Sunday afternoon game, but what there is Landon and I are perfectly capable of handling. I assume you have questions about Trevor's future."

"I have many."

"Let's hear them." Carly crossed her arms and enjoyed the twinge of discomfort George Holt exhibited at being called out. She spotted Landon watching the exchange but couldn't get a read on her reaction.

"Trevor Kincade has become the face of Zion Athletics, and the company has taken a big hit with the news of his arrest. Is he going to fight the charges? If he plans to take a plea, I need to know before we invest any more energy in this deal."

"Mr. Holt only invests in sure things," Landon called from across the room. She pointed her glass in his direction. "Ask him. He'll tell you."

George stiffened but didn't respond. Carly willed Landon to shut up, but apparently she was just getting started.

"Mr. Zion, you're a smart man," Landon said. "You've built a trusted brand from the ground up. Why in the world would you want to sell to Holt Industries?"

Robert gave Shelby a save-me-from-this-conversation face, and Shelby was quick to intervene. "Robert, you know Trevor would never let you down. He has been with your brand since the beginning when other names were courting him, but he wanted to be part of something new, different. I promise he is going to fight these unfounded charges and we will make sure that whoever represents him is willing to go to whatever lengths necessary to make that happen."

She made sure to emphasize the words "whoever represents him" as she stared down Carly and Landon. Alarm bells went off in Carly's head. Landon's family feud was about to get them both, not to mention their firm, tossed from the case.

"Mr. Zion," Carly said. "Shelby is right. We will do whatever it takes to exonerate Trevor. He's in good hands, but if a lawyer or anyone else makes you a promise about outcomes, then they are lying because there's absolutely no way to predict what will happen." She looked at Landon's father. "It was nice to meet you, Mr. Holt, but we're going to leave now. We have work to do and you have business to discuss. The two don't necessarily mix." She looked across the room. "Landon, let's go."

Carly didn't say another word as they left the suite and took the elevator down to the main concourse with Landon following a few feet behind. The earlier mood that had her imagining a fun day spent in the company of an attractive woman had passed, but she decided it was for the best. Landon was her opponent, not her friend, and she'd do well to remember that until she was promoted to partner.

CHAPTER EIGHT

On the way back to the office, Carly wished she'd stayed there instead of making this ill-advised trek to the Cowboys game. The day had started with such promise, but the spark between her and Landon had fizzled when the reality of their work stepped in. She couldn't deny she was curious about Landon's relationship with her father, but Landon, who had performed the role of rebel back in the Zion suite, now appeared cowed by the encounter and sat staring out the car window, sullen and withdrawn. After thirty minutes in traffic, Carly had had enough of the brewing silence between them and reached over and tapped Landon on the shoulder.

"What?"

"Are we going to talk about what happened back there, or are you going to stew all by yourself?"

Landon kept her face down and hunched her shoulders. "I don't have anything to say."

"Well, I have questions. How about we start there?" Carly glanced up at the Uber driver who didn't appear to be remotely interested in what might be going on in his back seat. "So, you're the spawn of one of the richest men in Dallas. What's that like?"

Landon's head jerked up and she squinted at Carly like she was trying to figure out if she was for real before a slight grin slipped past the frown she'd been wearing. "Spawn, huh? You know, you're pretty funny for someone who acts like they read legal memoranda for entertainment."

"Now look who's being funny," Carly replied with a grin of her own. "FYI, just because someone takes her job seriously doesn't mean she can't have a sense of humor."

"And look, she talks about herself in the third person—bonus dork points."

Carly studied Landon's face. She was probably kidding, but the words still stung. Landon must've detected something was wrong because she immediately said, "I was only kidding."

"Sometimes kidding around is only funny to the person doing it."

"Touché." Landon made a mock bow. "Please accept my apology. My nerves are a little raw, but I shouldn't take it out on you."

"True. Now you can make it up to me by telling me what the hell happened back there."

"I will under one condition."

"Name it."

"Watch the game with me. We can still catch it on TV even if we don't have the fancy digs."

Carly hesitated. It wasn't like she had anything else planned, and she wouldn't have been home for hours if they'd stayed at the stadium. Knowing her enemy would be a good idea, but she ignored the voice that argued spending the afternoon with Landon wasn't exactly gearing up for battle, still she quickly agreed. "There better be nachos and not soggy ones."

"I know just the place."

Landon gave an address to the driver, and Carly started to ask where they were going, but Landon was punching numbers into her phone and held up a hand to hold her off. Resigned to waiting, Carly looked out the window, pretending not to eavesdrop on Landon's conversation.

"Hey, Ian, it's Landon." Brief pause. "I know, I know." Longer pause with Landon inserting uh-huhs here and there. "Now that you've got that out of your system, do you mind if I join you for the rest of the game?"

Carly perked up at Landon's question. She'd envisioned a sports bar, but she couldn't quite picture one that Landon would have to call first and engage in a long, mostly one-sided conversation to gain entry. Where was Landon taking her? She poked her on the shoulder, but Landon merely waved her off.

"Okay, great. We'll be there in about five minutes. Save us some beer." She clicked off the phone. "That's settled."

Carly stared. "What's settled? Where are we going? Who was that?"

"You ask a lot of questions."

"In my experience that's how you find out information."

"Don't you like surprises?"

Carly considered the question for all of two seconds. "No."

"Then it must be hell for you to be a litigator."

"I'm—" Carly stopped the words before they left her mouth. Landon didn't need to know that her experience with litigation was mostly behind the scenes or dealing with the fallout on appeal. Besides, she dealt with plenty of surprises even if she wasn't out front in the cases the firm tried. She didn't mind the unexpected when it came to cases, but surprises in her personal life were another thing entirely.

The thought brought her up short. When had this day turned into something personal rather than a business outing? *The minute you agreed to go with Landon anywhere.* Carly wanted to regret her decision to go wherever the hell they were going, but the truth was she didn't. On some level, she was enjoying the adventure, and it wasn't like they were going far since Landon had told the person on the other end of the call they were five minutes away. If the adventure became too, uh, adventurous, she'd be able to escape with a simple click on the Uber app.

The car stopped in front of a modest-looking stone house in the M Streets. She wasn't fooled by the smallish size—properties in this area ran upward of half a mil for two to three bedrooms. While Landon tipped the driver, Carly got out and looked around. Not a lot of activity on the street, but it was clearly all residential. Whose house was this and why was this the place Landon had chosen to bring her?

"You ready?"

She started to ask for what, but decided instead to embrace this newfound sense of adventure. "Yes. Yes, I am." But when the front door to the house swung open and the male version of Landon ran down the steps, she wasn't at all sure what she'd gotten herself into.

"Landon!" the man called out as he swept her up in a hug. "The prodigal daughter returns."

Landon shook her head. "Takes one to know one."

"Yes, it does. Besides, I know you're only here for my famous spread."

"I made promises. I hope you're ready to deliver." Landon reached back for Carly's hand. "Meet Carly. She's another lawyer at the firm. We're on an important mission to research football and nachos. Tell her we've come to the right place for both."

The man looked at their joined hands, and Carly let go of Landon like she was a hot potato to avoid giving him the wrong idea. Still unsure who this guy was or why Landon had chosen to bring her here, she navigated the situation cautiously. She stuck out her newly released hand. "Nice to meet you…"

"Ian," he offered easily, grasping her hand in his and cocking his head. "I'm Landon's brother. Older."

"By like a minute," Landon protested.

A light bulb went off and Carly said, "You're twins."

"She's a smart one," Ian said to Landon. "I knew one day you'd bring a smart one home."

Carly started to protest Ian's assumption about her role in Landon's life, but Landon beat her to the punch.

"Don't be a jackass. Ian. We're doing research for a case, and the research involves football, which Carly knows little about. Care to invite us in and share your wisdom?"

Ian bowed with a flourish and ushered them into his house. As they walked through the entry, he and Landon locked arms and chattered like long lost souls while Carly walked a few steps behind. Normally, she wouldn't mind being left alone, but Landon's quick denial that there was anything more than a professional relationship between them left a lingering sting. *And you were so quick to drop her hand when Ian was looking.* Carly caught the irony, but she couldn't seem to shake the dueling feelings. The real question was what was she going to do about it?

❖

Landon watched Carly sitting off to the side of the small crowd of guys in her brother's den. She was staring raptly at the television, but Landon wasn't convinced she was actually interested in what was happening on the football field. Coming here might have been a mistake, for many reasons. First clue was when Ian started in on her the second she walked in the door and hadn't let up yet.

"Are you home for good? Have you talked to Mom and Dad?"

"Do you have any beer in this place?" Landon asked by way of putting him off.

He led the way outside to the patio and pointed to a cooler full of iced-down bottles. "There's whiskey in the cabinet over there if you want something stronger."

She did, but it wasn't a good idea. She grabbed a local brew and popped the top using the bottle opener under the deck railing. "Are you ever going to give up living in a frat house?"

"You say that, but you know you secretly wish you had a place like this." He tilted his bottle back toward the house. "My buddy Eric is a Realtor. You want to talk to him about finding a place now that you're back?"

"Who said I'm back?"

Ian cocked his head. "Well, it sure seems like you're back. I mean you're standing here in my house, and you brought a 'coworker.'"

She punched him in the arm. "Just don't with the finger quotes. Carly is a lawyer at the firm. She and I are assigned to work on a case, and the case is here in Dallas. That's it. There's nothing more going on. Got it?"

He raised both hands. "Got it. I'm just glad you're home. I miss you."

Landon heard the sincere emotion in his voice, but she needed to set the record straight. "I miss you too, but this isn't home. Austin is home. I'm here on a case. That's all." Not true. If she won the partnership slot, Jane would expect her to move back to Dallas, but Landon refrained from amending her answer. Ian would start in on her to find a permanent place before she could get the words out of her mouth, and she didn't need to add house hunting to her list of work right now.

"Sure. Whatever," he said. "Wait a minute. You're both working on a case and it involves football?" His eyes got really big. "You're representing Trevor Kincade, aren't you?"

She grabbed his arm and shushed him. "Yes, but I don't want to get stuck answering a bunch of questions about a pending case by your buddies. Okay?"

"Okay, but that goes for my buddies, not for me, right? I mean what's the point of having an attorney in the family if I don't get the inside scoop?"

Landon took a pull from her beer and handed him the bottle. "I'm out of here."

"No, you aren't." He shoved the bottle back at her. "Drink your beer and have a good time." He drew a line across his lips. "I won't say a word, and you and your lawyer friend can watch the game on the biggest big screen you've ever seen."

"Not hardly. We were actually at the game. Pretty sure Jerry Jones has you topped when it comes to televisions."

"Wait a minute. You were at the game and left to come here to watch it on TV? What gives?"

Landon wished she'd kept her mouth shut, but it was too late now. "Let's just say Dad showed up."

"Oh, got it." Ian looked like he wanted to say more, but he just said, "I'm sorry."

"No need for you to be sorry. Just took me by surprise. But here's a tip. If you have any interests in Zion Athletics, get out now." She shouldn't have said that, but her father's condescension had her worked up. Before Ian could respond, she started walking back toward the house. "Are you coming or not?"

When they reentered the living room, Landon was surprised to see Carly deep in conversation with a tall blond guy sporting a Trevor Kincaid jersey. The guy was standing really close to Carly and gesticulating wildly. It almost looked like he was pretending to call a play, and when he pulled his right arm back in an imaginary pass, Carly started laughing. The sound was magical, and Landon was momentarily irritated that someone else had elicited the departure from Carly's usual reticent manner. If she didn't know better, she'd think Carly was actually flirting with this guy.

But she didn't know better. She didn't know much about Carly at all. Maybe the signals she'd been getting were way off, and Carly was totally into guys. Maybe she was bi. Determined to rectify her lack of knowledge, Landon strode right up next to them. "Getting your lesson elsewhere, I see."

Carly turned quickly, and Landon took a step back. Carly's eyes were shining and her smile was bright. She was having a good time and Landon felt stupid for interrupting.

"This is Luke. He was attempting to explain some of the finer points of the game."

"That's great. I'm glad." Landon shifted in place. "Uh, I'm going to grab some food. Have fun." Determined to save face, she walked away but Carly followed and maneuvered her to the side.

"Where are you going?"

Landon jerked her chin at Luke. "You seem to be in good hands."

"Key word *hands*. Luke's not exactly shy, and this little lesson has run its course." Carly dropped her voice even lower. "Save me. I'm begging you."

Landon leaned in close. "Follow my lead." Without waiting for a response, she laced her fingers through Carly's. In a louder and somewhat suggestive voice, she said, "Sorry, babe, I know I promised you nachos. You ready for me to deliver?" She tugged Carly toward the kitchen, trying not to focus on how good it felt to hold her hand.

Ian's kitchen was bigger than she remembered, and she enjoyed watching Carly take it all in. "In direct contrast to the man cave you just saw," Landon said, "Ian keeps an immaculate, fastidious kitchen. He's a chef. When I promised you nachos, I meant business." Ian appeared in the doorway. "Speak of the devil."

"Watch your mouth, sis. I can tell when you're hungry. What's the matter? Didn't find anything out there that you liked?"

Landon pointed back toward the den. "It was a little hard to get to the food through the cloud of testosterone. Besides, I told Carly I was taking her to the world's best nachos. Please do not disappoint her."

"Nachos, huh? Sorry about that. I was trying out some new dishes for the restaurant and nachos aren't on the menu, but I bet I could whip some up."

"Seriously," Carly said, "don't do that on my account. You have a ton of food already."

"Nonsense. There can never be enough food." Ian was already pulling chips out of the pantry, followed by a block of white cheese and what looked like pulled pork out of the fridge. "I will put you to work, though. Landon, grab the cheese grater and get busy. Carly, you can chop this cilantro. You're not a cilantro hater, are you?"

"I love it."

Ian pointed a knife at Landon. "I knew I liked her. Do you want me to turn on the game in here?"

Landon looked at Carly, who shrugged. "I think I've got the gist of it," Carly said. "Fight for the ball, run it down the field, cross the goal line. Repeat."

"That's about it." Landon drew the block of cheese along the grater. "That's not what I wanted you to get out of today, though."

"I know."

"You do?"

"Sure. You wanted me to get the feel of being in that ginormous stadium with thousands of people cheering on their team. To experience the feeling that you're cheering for something more than a contest, but for a sense of community and loyalty to where you live."

"Wow." Landon was genuinely surprised at Carly's summary of the game. "When did you have time to get all of that?"

"While you were arguing with your father." Carly deftly chopped the cilantro and showed it to Ian for inspection. "Do you not get along with your father either?"

"Nice job," Ian said, pointing a knife at the cilantro. "As for Dad, he wasn't too keen on the whole chef thing and he's constantly telling me how I could sell my concept to a bigger company and then do something else, but I'm better at ignoring him, so overall, we get along okay."

"What's the difference? I mean, Landon's a successful lawyer. Doesn't that rate his approval?"

"Uh, excuse me, but I'm right here," Landon said. She watched Carly and Ian turn to look at her like they were surprised she was listening to their private conversation. "First of all, my relationship with Dad is private, and second, I know exactly why he doesn't approve."

"Care to share with your friend?" Ian asked. "I mean, if you're going to have a fight with Dad and then bring her to your brother's house and force her to make her own food, it seems like you should at least share."

He had a point. He usually did. Between them Ian had always had the level head, putting practicality before emotion. He'd accepted the strings that came with the family money to start his own business, figuring he could break free later, and he had, mostly. But she'd chosen to walk away from any monetary connection to the Holt fortune to make her own choices.

"I'm guessing your dad didn't want you to become a lawyer."

"You'd be wrong. Dad didn't have a problem with me going into the legal profession. Matter of fact, the minute I announced my plans, he was on the phone with the deans of admission at the stuffiest schools in the country to find out what size donation he needed to make to get his wayward daughter accepted in their incoming class."

"I'll guess again. UT Law School wasn't his first choice."

"Hardly. Only Ivy League for dear old Dad."

"Which is exactly why she decided to go to UT instead," Ian said. "They barely spoke all three years she was there."

"True," Landon said. "He did show up for graduation, though. He said, 'Now that you've had your fun, I've secured you a spot in the legal division of Holt Industries. It's entry level, but Holts aren't afraid of hard work, and it's time you stopped acting like a child.' I tossed him out of my apartment and we hadn't spoken again until today." She crossed her arms. "In the scheme of things, I know there are worse problems, but you would never guess how many people assume that because my last name is Holt, I had a leg up."

"I didn't," Carly said.

Landon considered. She'd had her doubts, especially since Carly had pressed her to talk about family on more than one occasion. Was it possible that Carly's questions had been more in the realm of getting to know her and less about social gossip? The sincere look on Carly's face was all the answer she needed. She could trust Carly to tell her the truth. "I know. Thank you." She cleared her throat. "Now enough about unpleasant family. We have nachos to make."

Later, when they were slouched on the patio drinking beer and eating the best nachos ever, Landon wondered if she should've told the rest of the story about her father, and how his attempt to manipulate her personal life, not just her professional one, was the real reason she'd shut the door on their relationship. Ian was the only one she'd ever told. Sharing her story with Carly was a whole new level of personal, and while she might be ready to hold hands, baring her soul wasn't on the agenda. Not now anyway.

❖

"I had fun today," Carly said as the Uber driver pulled up to the offices of Sturges and Lloyd. The ride from Ian's had been shorter than she'd anticipated, definitely not long enough to explore the newfound feelings of respect and camaraderie she'd developed for Landon. Probably best anyway to unpack all this emotion later, out of Landon's bigger-than-life presence.

"Me too, although I'm not sure I delivered as promised."

"You did." Carly wanted to say more. Like how she couldn't remember the last time she'd had this much fun. How she enjoyed feeling part of something and hanging out with a bunch of people who had no preconceived notions about her lack of social skills or intense focus on her work. But when she looked at Landon, shadows danced across her face and her full lips parted, and Carly's words faded into the night air.

They stepped out of the car. "I should go."

"Okay."

Had she heard a trace of regret in Landon's voice? It was only one word, so not likely. "Okay."

"Can I walk you to your car?" Landon asked.

"Yes, please."

Landon tipped the driver and sent him on his way. The parking lot was empty, which made sense since they were the only two attorneys at the firm likely to be working late on a Sunday. Landon didn't take her hand, but their arms brushed as they walked across the lot. With each step, Carly cast about for a way to prolong the contact. She opened her car door and hesitated before getting in. "I could give you a ride to your hotel."

"It's just across the street."

"I know." Carly held Landon's gaze and waited. She was taking a big risk because she didn't know what came next. She held her breath as the moments ticked by, the expression on Landon's face unreadable.

Without saying anything, Landon leaned close to Carly's ear, her breath light and caressing. "I had fun today too, but I should go." She didn't wait for an answer, but placed her hand on the car door and drew it open wider, inviting Carly to step in. Carly slid behind the wheel and watched Landon in her rearview mirror, walking farther and farther away. When Landon was no longer in sight, Carly drove off, unsure if she was disappointed or relieved to be driving home alone.

CHAPTER NINE

Thursday afternoon, Landon stretched her legs across her desk and reread the file private investigator Skye Keaton had prepared on Vanessa Meyers. She'd already read it five times, but she kept hoping she'd come across something, anything that would cast some light on who else might have had a motive to kill her. She'd turned up nothing except a list of character witnesses Donna Wilhelm would likely call to demonstrate exactly how big a loss it was when Vanessa died because everyone loved her. Everyone except Trevor.

But that was the thing. Except for the two calls to the police, all evidence pointed to Trevor loving her too. Friends reported he'd even been looking at rings and started making plans to pop the question. Landon was well acquainted with domestic abuse cases and how outward appearances often didn't have anything to do with what was going on inside a house, but Trevor's emphatic denials that he'd ever threatened Vanessa or harmed her in any way were pretty believable. And there was no actual evidence to support past violence. There was more to this mystery, but one thing was clear—all the evidence was circumstantial, which was likely the reason Carly's brief in support of getting Trevor's suspension tossed had been granted even if the victory was short-lived.

Landon pushed the file aside. She'd spent a lot of time over the last week avoiding thoughts of Carly, but proximity in the office made it impossible to ignore her existence. Not that she wanted to ignore her. All she really wanted was for all her thoughts—make that feelings— about Carly to fade into the background so she could concentrate on her work, but she was failing miserably. She should've kissed Carly the other night in the parking lot and gotten it out of her system.

Except she was a little scared acting on her impulses would only have her coming back for more, and more would be a distraction that could derail her chance at the partnership. Memories of a warning her father had once issued rang in her head: *It's not true that business isn't personal. Good business is always personal, which means you have to guard against letting anyone or anything rank higher than your professional desires or your business will fail.*

She'd spent her life rebelling against and suffering the consequences of his callous approach, but she had to admit he'd been spot-on before, even if she'd been too stubborn to admit it. If she was serious about winning this partnership, focus was key. Kissing Carly was the very opposite of focus, which was probably why she couldn't stop thinking about it.

Her desk phone buzzed and Russell's voice interrupted her obsessive thoughts. "Landon, you have a visitor."

She glanced at her cell phone calendar, hoping she hadn't forgotten an important appointment. Nope. "Who is it?" she asked.

"It's your brother, you know, the good-looking one." She looked up at the sound of the voice coming from her doorway, where Ian stood wearing a big grin. "It's lunchtime, and I want to try this new place downtown. Come with?"

"You know, most people wait until the person they come to see agrees to see them. Proper channels and all."

"Since when are you proper?" Ian didn't wait for an answer. He walked into the room and sat in one of the chairs across from her desk. "Before you tell me you're busy, let me extol the virtues of food on the brain. Hungry people make bad decisions."

Landon glanced from the pile of paperwork on her desk to her bulging email inbox. Greg had been sending messages on the regular with questions about her pending cases in Austin, and she was beginning to feel like she was holding down two jobs. Maybe a bit of a break was in order. "Okay, but not some long, lingering, order one of everything on the menu lunches. I have work to do."

"Fine. We'll shove one entree each into our mouths as fast as we can so you can get back to it. Come on, let's go."

Landon shook her head and grabbed her suit jacket. "Where are we going?"

"Nowhere long and lingering." Ian followed her out of her office. "Hey, where's Carly? Should we invite her?"

Before Landon could respond, she heard Carly's voice.

"Hi, Ian, invite her to what?"

Shit. Carly was standing in the hallway outside of her office. Two more minutes and they would've escaped without seeing her. Landon wanted to grab Ian's arm and run out of the building, but the sight of Carly in tall boots, a wool skirt, and a figure-hugging sweater had her rooted in place. Carly was gorgeous, and the sight of her had Landon questioning the whole kissing not kissing decision again. Exactly the reason she should be running.

"Lunch," Ian said without missing a beat. "Some people understand how important it is to fuel the mind, but my sis here? Not so much. Where do you fall on the feed a starving lawyer spectrum?"

"I'm sure Carly's too busy for lunch," Landon said before Carly could respond. "We're working on a deadline. Besides, it would be boring since we're just going to discuss that family thing." She pointed to the door. "We should get going or we're going to be late." She didn't wait for an answer and pulled Ian with her to the lobby and out the front door.

"Hey," Ian protested. "That was rude."

Landon punched the elevator button several times in quick succession. "You know what's rude? Not asking a person if they want another person to join them for lunch. That's what."

The door dinged and they stepped inside. When the door closed, Ian took up a position with his back to the door. "You're not leaving this car until you tell me why we just ditched Carly."

"I thought we were going to lunch, just you and me."

"Uh-huh."

"What?"

Ian cocked his head and flashed a knowing smile. She hated that expression and wanted to wipe it off his face. "Stop acting smug. You've got this all wrong."

"Care to tell me what I'm missing?"

Landon fished around for something to tell him and settled on the truth. Partly. "Carly is not my office friend or lunch buddy. She's my fierce, competitive rival. Got it?"

Ian took a minute to consider her words. "Okay." He nodded slowly. "Do we hate her?"

Landon silently cursed. Things would be a lot easier if she hated Carly, but right now she'd have to settle for acting like she did to keep from acting on how she really felt. "*Hate*'s an awfully strong word. How about we just agree that she's someone to be cautious about? I'll keep you updated."

"See that you do."

Landon moved quickly to steer the conversation in a different direction. "What's for lunch?"

"I'm thinking sushi. You up for that? We can even walk if you're game."

"Lead the way." The office was close to one of the urban dwellings that had popped up all over the city. Condos surrounded by shops and restaurants so the busy, single professionals who lived in the condos didn't have to wander far to spend their salaries. As they walked past the rental office, Landon grabbed a brochure.

Ian waited until they'd ordered at the restaurant before pointing to the paper in her hand. "You looking for a place to live?"

"Maybe."

"In Dallas?"

"Maybe." She looked up into his grinning face and smacked him with the menu. "Quit acting like it's a done deal."

"I can't help it. You're my favorite sibling."

"Jerry," she said, referring to their other brother, "isn't a sibling. He's an android programmed to do Dad's will without question. You and I are obviously the product of some kind of gene experiment."

"I can't argue with you there." Landon often lamented the lack of closeness with her older brother while simultaneously praising the gods for Ian. She couldn't imagine having to grow up as the only wild child in the family. "The whole moving to Dallas thing is contingent on whether I make partner."

Ian brushed his hand through the air. "As if you wouldn't. Jane loves you. She talks about you to Dad all the time."

"That probably makes him crazy." Landon hated that Jane ran in some of the same circles as her father.

"Maybe a little. But seriously, I'm certain she'll promote you."

She wanted to just nod in agreement and not get into the whole plan Jane had hatched, but she'd always shared the truth with Ian, and frankly she could use a confidant right about now. "There's a catch. They do plan to promote an associate this year, but only one, and they've narrowed it down to two people."

Ian sucked in a breath. "Oh no. Gorgeous Girl is your rival?"

"Don't be an ass—that's not her name."

"You don't be an ass. I know her name. So, how is Jane going to decide which one of you to promote?"

The waiter appeared with their order, and they were momentarily distracted by the beautiful omakase platter, listening intently as he described each piece. "This looks amazing," Landon said, grabbing a piece of tuna with her chopsticks and swooning at the buttery taste of the fish melting in her mouth. "I haven't had sushi in forever."

"We'll get back to that travesty, but in the meantime, tell me more about this race for the partnership. How's it going to work?"

"Simple really. We're supposed to work together on Trevor Kincade's case, and when it's over, Jane promotes whichever one of us did the best work."

"Which she measures how?"

"Hell, I don't know. She may wind up flipping a coin for all I know."

"You don't sound like you really want the gig."

Landon rolled his comment over in her head. She did want it. She wanted it bad. The promotion would be a symbol of her hard work, but mostly it would be a big fuck you to her father. She wondered what motivation Carly had for wanting the job, and that was a problem. What Carly wanted shouldn't factor into her plan. Not one ounce. Not at all.

"I do want it, but more importantly, I'm going to get it." Landon inserted all the conviction she could muster into the words. Eventually, she would believe them, and as for how her win would affect Carly, well, she'd deal with that when the time came.

❖

Carly reached into her bag and fished out the half of the sandwich she hadn't eaten at lunch. She hadn't been hungry then, and she wasn't particularly hungry now, but munching might keep her mind from wandering to thoughts of Landon and what she was doing right now.

Silly really. Landon's office was two doors down, and she should just get up and wander over there and check in. Except there were two problems with that approach. First, she kind of hated it when coworkers showed up in her doorway unannounced. Second, Landon obviously didn't want to hang with her based on the not so subtle way she'd ditched her at lunchtime. She shouldn't care, but after feeling so included when Landon took her to Ian's house, Landon's abrupt snub had stung.

It was for the best. She was busy formulating her strategy for the grand jury packet and didn't need the distraction of Landon's effortless good looks and bigger than life charm. If she wasn't careful, she'd get sucked into letting Landon show her up on this case. It wouldn't be hard. Carly was used to being the behind the scenes hero, letting her mad research skills prop everyone else up onstage. If she was going to win this partnership, she needed to step up her game and take center stage. No more second chair, no more managing the fallout. She needed to make things happen.

Loaded with resolution, she grabbed her iPad and took the long way around the floor to Jane's office. She'd timed the trip perfectly because Rhonda would be in the office kitchen brewing her afternoon tea right now. Jane's door was slightly ajar, but she gave it a solid knock, determined to make her case.

"Come in. I'm almost finished with it."

Carly stood in front of Jane's desk, waiting for her to look up. Jane's office was the epitome of power femme. Glass and steel combined with orchids and pops of color. Nothing about her space resembled Carly's office, where the walls were bare except for bookshelves lined with reference materials.

When Jane finally looked up, her expression was one of surprise. "Oh, hi, Carly. I thought you were Rhonda. Have you seen her?"

"I haven't, but if you have a minute, I'd like to run something by you."

Jane pushed aside the files on her desk and motioned for Carly to take a seat. "Sure. Let's hear it."

Carly hesitated for a second but pressed on, mentally chanting *go big or go home.* "It's about the grand jury hearing. I've reviewed all the evidence we have so far and, if left unrefuted, I think there's a better than even chance Trevor will be indicted."

"I think you're right."

Carly masked her surprise. She wasn't used to hearing Jane say anything negative when it came to case outcomes. She'd cheer her team on even when everyone in the office knew all hope was lost. Carly had always figured it was Jane's way of trying to get them to go the extra mile, not to mention the solid optimism helped convince the client to keep funding the retainer. "Then why do you have us working so hard on a grand jury packet?"

"It's a good exercise, and we'll be even more prepared for trial. Trevor's going to want a quick trial, and like Landon suggested, a speedy trial request is likely to leave the prosecutor scrambling. Donna Wilhelm is swamped right now with several other complex cases, and I'm willing to bet she's pulling together a bare-bones case with just enough evidence to get Trevor indicted. If she has to get ready for trial quickly, she's going to be in over her head."

"What if he didn't get indicted? Would he be back on the field this season?"

"Shelby has the team's word that if the case gets kicked for any reason, Trevor will be back in uniform, catching passes faster than you can say touchdown." Jane shook her head. "But let's be real. That's a pipe dream."

"What if it wasn't? What if he gets a no bill?"

Jane smiled indulgently. "Tell me what's on your mind."

Carly pointed at her iPad. "Donna's going to have the arresting officer testify, and he'll regurgitate what he included in his report. The grand jurors will be bored out of their minds, but they'll indict Trevor because they'll only hear one side of the story. The flat, dry story." She paused before making one last decision to commit to her idea. "What if the story wasn't flat at all? What if it was personal and vibrant and compelling, but not in favor of the prosecution, but for Trevor?"

"You want him to testify, don't you? Are you crazy?"

Carly started at the sound of Landon's voice behind her, but she resisted the urge to turn around and face her. What the hell was she doing barging in here while she was having a private conversation with Jane?

"Carly, is that where you're headed?" Jane asked. "You want Trevor to testify at the grand jury?"

She was already committed to this path, so she stuck with it. "Yes. Trevor's a smart guy and if we prepare him, which I believe I can, he'll be ready," she said, placing extra emphasis on the *I*. "We'll be right outside and he can ask for a break to consult with counsel if he hits a rough patch. I think he'll charm the socks off the grand jurors." She ticked off several points on her fingers. "He's a superstar. He's charming. He's known as a stand-up guy. It'll be much harder for them to true bill his case to his face."

"That's ridiculous," Landon said, her voice rising. "Once he's in that room, he can't walk out to consult with counsel unless he wants to look like he's got something to hide. And he might be a master on the playing field, but put him in the hot seat and he'll crumble just like everyone else who winds up on the other side of a criminal investigation. What's going to happen if he gets in there and they start asking him about the past allegations of abuse with this victim?"

Carly looked at Jane, who was nodding. She had to talk fast to sway her to her side. "We'll prepare him for all of that. It's no different than putting a witness on the stand. You can't be sure what will happen, but sometimes the gamble is worth the risk. I wasn't aware you were one to play it safe." Right after the words spilled from her lips, she regretted them. Well, mostly she regretted making things personal in front of Jane who'd warned them about playing nice. But playing nice didn't mean getting railroaded.

Landon pointed at Jane. "You can't really think this is a good idea, can you?"

"I'm not convinced yet that it's a completely awful plan. Tell you what. Why don't you two put together a pros and cons list. Make sure you cover every possible contingency, and we'll meet first thing in the morning. Trevor is coming by at ten, and we'll make a decision by then."

"Sounds great," Carly said before Landon could respond. She stood. "I'll be in my office. You can meet me there." She waved to Jane and stalked past Landon on her way out the door. When she reached her office, she slumped in the chair, her energy spent. She wasn't entirely convinced Trevor testifying before the grand jury was a great idea, but she needed some strategy to offer, and she believed there was some merit to this one. Maybe Landon would be able to talk her out of it. The key would be whether she would hear a word Landon said through the haze of attraction that was clouding her judgment.

CHAPTER TEN

L andon returned to her own office and gathered her notes, but she was in no hurry to meet with Carly, at least not until she got her anger under control. They were supposed to be working on this case together. Where did Carly get off thinking she could march into Jane's office and propose a crazy stunt like having Trevor testify before the grand jury? And why hadn't Jane dismissed the idea out of hand? It wouldn't matter if Trevor were Prince Charming; letting a target of an investigation go into an adversarial proceeding on his own was professional suicide.

Landon looked at her phone to check the time and spotted a text from Ian. *Come to the restaurant for dinner. My treat.* It was almost six. Sushi at lunch had been really tasty, but she'd need something more substantial soon to keep from going all hangry on Carly, and she'd be much more persuasive if she kept her cool. Carly didn't have as much litigation experience. She simply needed to take Carly through the reasons why her idea, though creative, wasn't appropriate when the stakes were this high. The damage to Trevor's reputation had already been done with the arrest, and the only way to truly clear his name now was a not guilty from twelve of his peers. Landon took a deep breath, confident now she would be able to convince Carly her idea was ill-advised, and bonus—she was going to do it over food. Good food.

When she arrived at Carly's doorway, she had her head down, reading through a file. Landon started to knock, but instead spent a moment observing her at work. Carly's face was bunched up in a pensive frown as she skimmed whatever she was reading on her iPad.

Her hair, normally pinned back, was showing signs of the wear of the day, and wispy strands fell around her shoulder, careless and out of place, completely at odds with the buttoned-up image Carly generally projected. Landon wanted to brush those strands with the back of her hand and feel Carly's skin against her palm.

"Are you going to stand there all night or get in here and start working?" Carly didn't glance up as she asked the question.

"Are those my only two options?"

Carly tilted her head and locked her in a steady gaze. "You have something else in mind?"

"I'm starving. Let's have a working dinner. I know a good restaurant that isn't far from here, and there are plenty of quiet spots in the back where we can work and eat." Landon grinned. "I promise I'm much easier to convince when I've been fed."

"I don't know that I've ever met a woman who loves food as much as you do."

Landon wasn't sure how to take the remark. Carly's tone wasn't sarcastic or otherwise hurtful. It was more like she was curious, and Landon wanted to satisfy her curiosity. "I've never been one for hiding my likes and dislikes."

"And you like food."

"Immensely, but to my credit, I have wonderful taste."

"We're still talking about food?"

Landon paused before answering, unable to read the expression on Carly's face. Was Carly flirting? Should she take the bait? Remembering her resolution to keep things businesslike, Landon simply replied, "Sure." She looked down the hall. "Everyone else is gone. It's not like you're going to get extra credit for working late. Come on, I'll drive."

Carly hung back. "Give me the address, and I'll meet you there."

"Are you planning to bail on me? I'm going to show up at the restaurant and wind up sitting on my ass waiting for you to show up while you're home in your pajamas, sipping a glass of red and getting a head start on Jane's assignment." Landon saw Carly's eyes twitch and she pointed. "I'm right, aren't I?"

"Maybe." Carly sighed. "Or maybe I just want to have my own wheels."

"So you don't get trapped."

"More like so I have options."

Landon nodded. She could respect the need to have options. "Fair enough. How about this? We set a time now and check in at the halfway point. If you decide you want to leave earlier, I'll call you an Uber, and I'll even pay for it." She wasn't sure why it was so important to her that Carly ride with her to the restaurant. Maybe it was because she really did believe that left to her own devices, Carly would make some excuse and ditch their date. Date. Wrong word. Completely wrong. And if it wasn't a date, then pressuring Carly to ride with her was just weird. *Let her take her own car. Quit being a stalker.*

"Okay," Carly said.

"What?"

"I'll ride with you."

"Great. Okay then." Landon jingled her keys like a super nerd. "Let's go."

Ian's restaurant was downtown in the area near the Klyde Warren Park. A few years ago, a few rich people in the city had raised a bunch of money and convinced the city it would vastly improve tourism and overall quality of life to have more parks in downtown Dallas. With limited options for suitable venues, city engineers had come up with the idea of changing an overpass to an underpass and turning the over part into the biggest park in the area, and since most of the money came from private funds, the city leapt on board with the idea. Now cars roared, unseen, through the underground tunnel while food trucks and yoga classes occupied the space above. Ian's restaurant was one of several that had existed in Dallas before the change, but he'd moved to a funky new space along the edge of the park when it opened to take advantage of the boon. Landon had been to the site when the building was in the early stages, but hadn't been back since he'd opened his doors.

When they pulled up in front of the Salt Block, Carly shifted in her seat. "What's wrong?" Landon asked.

"This place is kind of fancy-pants."

"True, but one can't live solely on sandwiches one brings from home."

"Oh, so now you're spying on me at the office."

Landon considered carefully before responding. *Spying* wasn't the word she would've used, but it was probably appropriate. She had wandered by Carly's office a few times during the day, more out of a desire to chitchat about the case than as a voyeur, but every time she'd wandered by, a voice inside said she had an ulterior motive and she kept walking. "Spying isn't exactly what I was up to, but I did figure if we're going to work on this case together, we might need to talk at some point."

Carly nodded. "Got it. I'm used to working on my own."

"I gather that. Look, how about we take tonight to see if we can find some common ground?"

"Yeah, okay."

Not the enthusiasm she'd been looking for, but Landon figured Carly's agreement was a step in the right direction. She handed the keys to the valet and led Carly into the restaurant. Ian, decked out in a chef coat emblazoned with the restaurant's logo, was waiting at the bar. With a quick nod to Landon, he held out his arms and embraced Carly.

"Thanks for coming! I was hoping you could make it."

Carly returned the hug, but when she turned back around, she was frowning at Landon. "I have a feeling I've been led astray."

"Only slightly," Landon confessed. "Ian's been wanting me to come by and try out his new menu, and he asked me to bring someone who doesn't have to say they like his food just because they're related to him. And he has a nice, quiet table in the back where we can work." She lifted her shoulders. "What can I say? I like to multitask. Are you mad?" she asked, hoping she wasn't.

Carly looked at Ian who wore a hopeful expression. "No, I'm not mad. In fact, now that I smell food, I'm starving."

"Perfect," Ian said. He pointed at a waiter coming toward them. "This is Beckett. He'll take you back to the private dining room and hook you up with whatever you want to drink. Settle in, and we'll have the first course ready for you shortly." He gave Carly's arm a squeeze. "Any food allergies or things you absolutely hate?"

To Landon's surprise, Carly shook her head. She wasn't sure why, but she expected that someone who brought her own sandwiches to lunch every day probably had some very specific preferences.

Beckett led them to an intimate private dining room designed to seat about a dozen guests. "We've got a legit Sazerac on special tonight."

"We'll take two," Landon said before Carly could respond. A

couple of drinks would go a long way toward breaking the ice between them. When Beckett left, she noticed Carly glancing around. "Looking for an escape route?"

"Do you do that with everyone or just me?"

"Do what?" Landon was genuinely confused.

"Observe my every move."

"Ah." Did she? Landon had become a careful observer at a young age, gauging her father's moods in relation to what she wanted and needed at the time, but her close observation of Carly was about something else altogether. "Maybe I'm just trying to figure you out."

"You make me sound like a puzzle. What you see is what you get." Carly offered a guarded smile as she delivered the cliché.

"Would you like me to tell you what I see?" Landon asked.

"Wouldn't you rather get started on work before the food arrives? Besides, I promise that I'm not nearly as mysterious as you seem to think."

"Who said anything about mysterious? Intriguing maybe."

"And what exactly do you find so intriguing?"

Beckett burst through the door with a tray in one hand. He made a production of describing how the Sazeracs were made, and that the special ingredient consisted of bitters made personally by Ian. By the time he was finished, he sounded like he'd spent the day studying bartender.com, and it took all of Landon's patience not to shoo him out the door. When he finally left, Carly took a sip of her drink and placed a hand over her heart.

"I think I might be in love with your brother."

Carly took another sip of her drink and tilted the glass toward Landon. "Aren't you going to try it?"

"Ian's single. If you're interested, I could put in a good word for you."

Carly set her glass down and eyed Landon, trying to figure out if she was kidding. "Did you bring me here with some ulterior motive?"

Landon squirmed under her gaze. "What are you talking about?"

"Your brother seems like a really nice guy, and based on the food

I sampled at his place, I'm sure he'll make someone an excellent date, but I'm not in the market."

"Is it because he's…"

"A chef?" Carly filled in the words, certain they weren't even close to what Landon was about to say, and then she laughed with Landon, enjoying the release that came with their hearty laughter. "If I was interested in dating anyone, which I'm not, your brother is not my type, you know, because he's a guy."

Landon nodded. "Cool. You're into girls."

"When I'm into anyone, which I'm not right now, I am into girls, correct."

"Duly noted."

"That was super nerdy."

"I'm aware." Landon lifted her drink and motioned for Carly to do the same. "Let's toast to nerdy lesbians everywhere." She tilted her glass and clinked it with Carly's. "Now that we've identified we have something in common, shall we get to work?"

Carly heard a trace of reluctance behind Landon's words, and she wanted to recapture the playful banter. "We should probably wait until we've eaten at least one course. I can't be responsible for my mood when I'm starving."

"Fair enough. Care to share any other personal insights that might help me get to know you better?"

Loaded question and one Carly didn't want to answer. She'd done well so far, getting Landon to do the bulk of the sharing, but Landon didn't strike her as the kind of person who would let that go on for long, which was why she probably shouldn't have agreed to this dinner in the first place. Walls were easier to keep in place when they were at the office, where their roles were clear.

Ian brought the first course in himself, crispy polenta squares with braised pork belly, and they looked delicious. Carly suppressed a smile about their conversation, while Ian talked about incorporating new versions of comfort food into his fall menu, and how he'd braised the pork belly in a bourbon reduction to enhance the flavor. When he left the room, it was like the air had been sucked away, and she and Landon were left in awkward silence. Landon reached for a square and chewed slowly, offering no comment. The silence made Carly realize how much she really enjoyed Landon's running commentary and constant questions. "I'll tell you something if you tell me something."

Landon grinned. "You first."

"I loved law school."

"Do we get to ask follow-up questions, because I'm going to need to ask follow-up questions."

Carly sighed. "I should've known. Yes, you can ask one question."

"Hmm, let me see. I assume you didn't love other schooling because you mentioned law school specifically instead of saying 'I love school.'"

"Is there a question in there, counselor?"

"I'm getting there." Landon picked up another square and munched. "Okay, here it is. Why law school as opposed to undergraduate school?"

"Because it was the only school I attended where being the smartest person in the room was a good thing. A thing that was rewarded." Carly prayed Landon didn't ask more, but knew she would.

Landon nodded. "I get that. I mean, I wasn't that person, but the smartest people in law school were rock stars. In undergrad, we mostly just made fun of those folks."

"Oh, so you were one of those." Carly bit her lip, but it was too late.

"'One of those'?"

"You know what I mean. The popular kids who trade on social currency instead of smarts and make fun of the rest of us."

"Wow. Assume much. You don't know a thing about me and my experience."

Carly thought she did, but Landon was right. Everything she thought she knew was an assumption. "You're right. I'm sorry. Maybe we should just get to work and dispense with the small talk because clearly I suck at it."

"Well, this wasn't exactly small talk, but I am enjoying getting to know you better."

"Is that so?"

Landon crossed her heart. "Absolutely. You're kind of a mystery around the office. You keep to yourself a lot. Everyone says so."

Carly's first reaction was to demand who'd been talking about her, but she wasn't entirely sure she wanted to know. "I work hard, which doesn't leave a lot of time for socializing."

"I work hard too."

Landon's tone was defensive, and Carly's first instinct was to tell her to suck it up, but then she remembered Landon's encounter with her father at the Cowboys game. Landon had probably spent her whole life defending her choices to her well-respected, dominating father. Carly decided to give her the benefit of the doubt. "I guess you're used to people thinking you have it made because of your family name."

"I don't know that I ever get used to it. It was better in Austin. Totally different scene there, and big business isn't revered the same as it is here. I could actually go to a party and have no one there assume I was an heiress to an empire."

"Is that why you moved to Austin?"

Landon reached for another square, a move Carly now recognized as a stall tactic. People had worse food habits, she supposed. She reached for one too, figuring she could wait Landon out because she really wanted to know the rest of the story.

"I moved to Austin partly for anonymity, but mostly for a girl. She was going to UT Law School, so I chucked the offer from Harvard that my father had worked so hard to obtain and headed down south."

"Really?"

"You sound surprised. Haven't you ever done anything impulsive because you thought you were in love?"

Carly was surprised, though she wasn't sure why. And as for Landon's question, she couldn't recall an instance where she would have sacrificed a significant opportunity for a personal relationship, a fact about which she'd once been proud, but now felt some shame in admitting to Landon. She replayed Landon's words *because you thought you were in love* and found a way to dodge the question. "So, this love wasn't the real thing?"

Landon placed her hand under her chin and appeared to consider her answer carefully. "I thought so at the time, but looking back, it was more about an escape route than a path toward something lasting. Apparently, she thought so too, since she wound up moving to Chicago after our first year. Turns out my father pressured the admissions committee at Northwestern to recruit her for their new human rights clinic, which he paid for with a generous endowment. His way of proving everything has a price."

"Did she know he was behind the move?"

"Yep. She said she couldn't pass up the opportunity, even if it was his way of trying to tear us apart. She even promised we could make it work, but once she left, I never heard from her again."

"That's rough," Carly said because it seemed like the kind of thing people said in these situations, but what she was really thinking was that Landon probably did better in school without the distraction of a girlfriend, especially one that didn't have a sense of loyalty. Thankfully, Ian entered the room again before Landon could turn the conversation back around to her.

He set down two loaded plates and described the food in glowing terms. "What's the verdict on the first course? Too much on the bourbon or just right?"

"Just right," Carly said. "I don't think I've ever had food this good."

"She doesn't get out much," Landon said with a grin.

Carly started to protest that Landon couldn't possibly know that, but as she watched Ian play slap Landon, she realized Landon's playful banter was vastly different than being made fun of—a pleasant distinction. "Food like this definitely inspires me to get out more. Maybe if I can get Landon to do her fair share of the work, I could find the time."

Landon leaned back and narrowed her eyes. "Touché."

Ian raised his hands in the air. "Not to worry. I'm out of your hair. Beckett will be back in to check on you. By the way, is Beckett the most hipster name you've ever heard? I mean it can't be his real name because how would his parents have known that one day he and his skinny jeans and love of all things artisanal would merit such a moniker? Like oracles of the hipster generation." He shook his head and started to back away. "I'm gone. Enjoy!"

When he cleared the door, Carly stabbed her fork into the pan-fried Gulf snapper and tasted it. "Every time I think I've tasted the most amazing food ever, he tops it. What is it with your brother?"

"I know, right?" Landon cocked her head. "You sure you don't want to date him?"

"I don't want to date anyone." She saw the question in Landon's eyes and plowed on. "Not right now anyway. Not with this case and the partnership at stake." She stopped abruptly, feeling like she'd over-shared, but Landon's own openness left her feeling she had to qualify her definite no dating remark.

Landon merely nodded and pointed at the rémoulade. "Did you try this? It's amazing."

Carly dipped her fork in the sauce and brought it to her lips. "Delicious," she murmured. Everything about being with Landon heightened her senses, which made her feel excited and fearful at the same time. She turned to her usual solution when the personal became uncomfortable. "At some point don't you think we should talk about the case?"

"I suppose. I mean, I've resisted the urge to tell you again how crackpot I think your idea of having Trevor testify in front of the grand jury is, but if you really want to ruin this fabulous meal by having me say it again, I'm happy to oblige."

"How do you do that?"

"What?"

"Back at the office you were pissed off, but now you're smiling and sharing a wonderful meal with me like we're old friends, and when I bring up the case again, you actually sound like you're teasing me."

"It's not personal. The case, I mean. We can disagree about something at the office, but that doesn't mean we can't be friends, right?"

Intellectually speaking, Landon was right, but Carly wasn't accustomed to marking the difference between personal and professional in such bold terms. Still, she could sense that saying so would make Landon give her that funny look again, so she merely nodded and dove back into where she felt most comfortable. "I've spent a lot of time with Trevor. I'll be the first to admit I don't know much about football, but I do know that a large measure of his success isn't his pure skill. It's his ability to influence the people around him to be better than they think they can be. He's not just charming, he's influential. Think about it. People in Dallas love football. Trevor's a hero. When the NFL issued the statement about the suspension, people went crazy defending him. No one wants to believe he's guilty of killing someone, let alone a woman he was in a relationship with, especially when a judge determined the suspension was unjustified. The grand jurors will be predisposed to believe in him. All he has to do is go in there and answer honestly that he doesn't know a thing about what happened. He can admit to disagreements with her, like any couple has, but maintain that he's not capable of the kind of violence it would take to do her physical harm."

"And what if he is?" Landon asked. "What if the Trevor you've seen isn't the real deal, and he has some low simmering anger that Donna Wilhelm is able to coax out of him right there in front of all the grand jurors?"

Carly started to respond, but Landon held up a hand to stop her. "And there's more. All you need is one woman on the grand jury who has hashtag #MeToo on her social media profile, and Trevor is toast. The headline will be Trevor Kincade told his side of the story, and they indicted him anyway. Everyone will think he's guilty, and most won't bother parsing out how a grand jury proceeding is different from a jury trial. His entire career will be over."

"The same thing could happen at trial, but at least this way we'll get two shots at winning."

"We could put together a grand jury packet without him having to testify, and include letters from people that know him, respect him, know the nature of his relationship with Meyers."

"Dull, lifeless. I would've expected you to be more of a gambler," Carly said.

"Why?"

"I don't know." Carly considered. That wasn't entirely true. Landon's entire personality evoked a sense of living on the edge, taking risks. Why was she playing things so close to the vest in this case? "Maybe I'm off base here, but someone who shirks Harvard to chase after love seems like the kind of person who doesn't play things safe."

"Ah, but that was personal and this is professional. Even someone like me can tell the difference between the two."

Carly wondered why it seemed so easy for everyone else but not for her.

CHAPTER ELEVEN

The next day, Jane sat at the head of the conference room table and explained the pros and cons of testifying before the grand jury to Trevor. Shelby was seated on Trevor's right and Carly on his left, and Landon sat across the table, feeling like her presence was superfluous.

"I hate to come off like a dumb jock," Trevor said, "But I could really use an explanation about what exactly a grand jury does." He turned toward Carly. "How is it different from a trial? Do I get both?"

Jane nodded at Carly, who appeared eager to jump into the conversation. "Before the police arrested you," Carly said, "they presented evidence to a judge to convince him that there was probable cause to believe you committed the crime. In Texas, whenever someone is arrested on a felony, the prosecutor is required to present evidence to a grand jury—a panel of twelve people—to let the grand jurors determine if the arrest should stand and if there is indeed probable cause to keep the charges in place. The prosecutor can present the same evidence as what the police gave the judge to support the warrant, or they might have new evidence. Sometimes, we present evidence to the grand jury to get them to no bill, or decline to indict. If you were to testify, your testimony would be the bulk of our evidence. We would also prepare a packet for the grand jurors with letters in support of your innocence."

"Do you get to pick who is on the grand jury?" Trevor asked.

"No," Carly replied, her tone gentle and even. "Unlike a trial jury, the grand jurors are selected by the chief judge of the county courts. These jurors don't just hear your case. They hear lots of cases over the course of several months, so they will be fairly savvy when it comes to reviewing the evidence, but they will also likely have a good rapport with the prosecutors because they've been spending lots of time with them."

"If the grand jury…" Shelby paused. "What's it called when they decide to throw out the case?"

"No bill," Jane said. "And that doesn't mean the case is thrown out. It just means they've decided there is not probable cause to support the charges at this time."

"Meaning they could charge me later?" Trevor asked.

Landon heard the trepidation in his voice. She couldn't blame him for being a bit on edge since Jane had decided to let him make the call about whether or not to testify. If the decision had been left up to her, she would've been a bit more heavy-handed when it came to managing the client, basically telling him this was the way it was going down.

"The prosecutor could try to indict you again, but without some new evidence, she'd be facing an uphill battle."

Landon coughed into her hand to cover her grunt of disagreement, but Shelby perked up and focused on her. "What? You don't agree? What do you think will happen?"

Landon ignored Jane's pointed stare and scrambled for an answer that would be authentic but would also keep her out of trouble with the boss. "It's a gamble all around. The only thing that wouldn't be a gamble would be if Trevor wanted to take a plea to a fixed prison term, and I think we can all agree that's not up for debate?" She held Shelby's gaze until Shelby nodded that she understood. "Okay, then we should explore all of Trevor's options. This is just one of them."

"Right," Shelby said. "That makes sense. What would you do if it were you?"

Ah, the classic question every criminal defense lawyer had to tackle multiple times in their career. Landon looked around the table to see if anyone else wanted to weigh in, but it was clear Shelby had meant the question for her. Her stock answer, the one she gave at cocktail parties—it depends—would only beg the question, and Trevor deserved better than a theoretical discussion since his life was on the line. Maybe Carly was right. Maybe this was the time to take some risks. She folded her hands and focused first on Shelby, but then turned to Trevor and spoke directly to him.

"If I were accused of something I didn't do, something this unthinkable, I'd take every opportunity I could find to proclaim my innocence. I'd have a press conference telling everyone who wanted to know that I didn't do it. I'd show up for the grand jury and demand to tell them in my own words that I am innocent. If they indicted me, I'd demand a speedy trial so I could put this travesty behind me, and when the judge at trial asked me to stand up and enter my plea, I'd be out of my chair in a flash to say that I'm innocent of the charge."

Trevor nodded, his eyes bright and flooded with confidence, and Shelby smiled broadly. Out of the corner of her eye, Landon caught sight of Jane, who stared at her like she'd grown another head, but Carly's astonished expression was the one Landon lingered on, taking time to flash a grin her way before returning her attention to Trevor.

"Now, that said—" she started to say, but Shelby cut her off.

"Yes!"

"Excuse me?"

"That's the spirit we've been waiting to hear," Shelby gushed. "I'm so glad you're on the team. Trevor, don't you agree?"

"Absolutely," he replied. "Sounds like we've got a plan. I'm going to testify. What do we do next?"

Shit. Apparently, she'd been a little too heavy-handed, but in the opposite direction. Landon bit her bottom lip, considering whether she should counterbalance her impassioned speech, but then decided screw it. She and Carly could prep Trevor well enough, and if he crumbled in front of the grand jury, they'd deal with the fallout.

"We prepare," Jane answered for Landon. "Carly and Landon will work out a schedule with you. The key is to be ready for any question they might throw at you, but still appear natural."

A few minutes later, they all filed out of the conference room. Before Landon could reach the door, she felt a light tug on her arm and looked back expecting to see Carly ready to give her an earful about the sudden change of heart. But Shelby was standing behind her, crooking her finger to motion Landon back into the room. Landon cast a look over at Carly who shook her head and kept going. When she and Shelby were the only ones left in the room, Landon asked, "What's up?"

"I like your style."

A simple phrase, and it could have been innocent, but Landon wasn't getting innocent vibes. Sensing that asking Shelby what she meant would only invite extra, unwanted attention, Landon simply said, "Thanks."

"Who do I need to talk to to make sure you're the lead on Trevor's case?"

Shelby moved closer as she spoke, and Landon tried really hard not to run for the door. Normally, she welcomed being the focus of a good-looking woman, but Shelby's aggressive approach turned her off. It shouldn't. She should welcome a chance to have the client, or at least the client's representative ask Jane to have her take the lead. Carly wouldn't be able to fight the client's choice, and it would give Landon an advantage in their race for partnership.

But it felt off, like Shelby was going to want something from her in exchange for the favor. Again, not normally something she'd mind from a gorgeous woman, but a voice in her head told her Carly would think less of her for it. To her surprise, she cared more about what Carly thought of her character than taking advantage of this opportunity. She backed toward the door. "No lead here. Trevor has a team of good attorneys, and we'll all work hard to make sure justice is served."

Before Shelby could respond, Landon ducked out of the room and walked swiftly down the hall, not caring about rudely ditching a client. When she walked through the door of her office, Carly was leaning against her desk. Landon broke out into a smile. "Hey, you—"

"When did you change your mind about the grand jury?"

Carly's question was more like an accusation than a casual request for information, and it took Landon off guard. "What's up?"

"What was with the rousing speech about proclaiming innocence? You sounded like Tom Cruise in *A Few Good Men*. You know if we really are going to work as a team, it makes more sense that we get our act together ahead of time."

"Wait. You're mad at me for agreeing with you?"

"No, I'm annoyed that suddenly my idea became your idea served in a brighter package. It's like you swooped in and took all the credit in hopes you'd win the client into thinking you're taking the lead on his case."

Landon started to protest but couldn't deny that was exactly what had happened. But hey, that was what was supposed to happen, right? They were in a contest. If she just so happened to come around to Carly's way of thinking about the case, and it bought her brownie points with the client, then bonus for her. "Maybe I actually just realized that you were right all along."

"And this flirting thing you have going on with Shelby had nothing to do with your sudden change of heart?"

"It didn't." Too late Landon realized she hadn't denied the flirting. "It's a good idea."

"I know it is. Maybe I just wished you'd given me some credit when you decided to jump on board." Carly stalked toward the door. "I'm going back to my office to work on another good idea. I'll let you know when it's ready for you to reject and then embrace."

She was out the door before Landon could respond. Carly was right. The whole thing had been Carly's idea, and Landon had as much as called her crazy for it. If she was going to change her mind and jump on board, it was only right to give Carly credit for coming up with it in the first place. The best thing she could hope for right now was that Trevor's case got kicked by the grand jury to put an end to this stupid contest. It couldn't happen fast enough.

CHAPTER TWELVE

The elevator doors opened and Carly, thankful the press had been restricted to the lower floors of the building, led their group to the lobby of the eleventh floor of the Frank Crowley Courts Building. Shelby hung back, walking beside Landon, but Trevor stayed close, whispering last-minute questions in her ear. She wanted to tell him to shut up because his nervous tone on top of her persistent internal voice whispering that this was a big mistake was threatening to make her head explode. But it was her job to handhold, to guide, to reassure, and she wasn't going to fall down on the job today. Big risk, big reward. She silently chanted the words as she pulled Trevor off to the side, out of the earshot of any of the people wandering the halls of the courthouse.

"Listen to me. You've got this. All you have to do is go in there and be yourself. You know, the self that walks out onto the football field in that insanely large stadium and keeps his cool while tens of thousands of people, not to mention millions more watching from home, cheer you to victory. They don't just do that because they love the game, they do it because they love you. You're personable, authentic, and likable. Everyone either wants to be you or be with you. Remember all this when you go in there, and use all those superpowers to get them to hear the honesty in your account."

He nodded and stood a bit straighter. "Got it. You know, you should be a coach."

She smiled, pleased her lack of football knowledge hadn't gotten in the way of the pep talk she'd rehearsed that morning. "I'll take that as a compliment. Now, let's review the main points."

"Listen to the questions, and make sure I understand them before answering," he said, ticking off the point on his fingers. "No offense, no defense—just the facts. The only emotion I should show is the sorrow I feel at the loss of someone I cared about. If I'm in a jam, I can call a time-out, but I only get one, so try not to use it."

"Good," Carly said. And it was pretty good for a layperson, despite all the sports analogies. Truth was, he could call all the time-outs he needed, but once he used one to talk to his lawyers, the chances he was getting indicted went up sharply, so she'd cautioned him not to ask for a recess unless things were going way south.

"Maybe when all this is over, we can have dinner and, you know, talk about something besides indictments."

Carly stared at Trevor's hopeful expression, hesitant to dash his expectations so close in time to his looming testimony. Thankfully, Landon chose that moment to walk up with Shelby tagging close behind.

"Are you ready?" Landon asked.

"I am," Trevor said with a lot more confidence than he'd displayed moments earlier. Carly took in the trademark smile he usually saved for the cameras and decided maybe she'd read too much into his dinner offer. "He's good," she said. "I'll check with the clerk to see where we are on the docket."

Carly walked up to the counter and got in line. The lawyer in front of her was asking to see a copy of a police report for a case that was set the following week that hadn't been assigned to a prosecutor yet. The clerk sighed and yelled back to one of her coworkers, asking for the file. Figuring she was going to be waiting for a bit, Carly looked back over at where Trevor, Shelby, and Landon were waiting. Shelby was standing between them, but much closer to Landon than Trevor. Like super close. Oh, and then she laughed and reached out and picked a piece of lint off Landon's suit. Like an orangutan. And then Shelby straightened Landon's collar. Was it her imagination or did Shelby's fingers linger on Landon's lapel? Was she looking into Landon's eyes? Like a girlfriend?

Stop it. Shelby was just one of those women who thought she had to suck up to everyone in the room to get what she wanted. *Except she's never sucked up to you. Not even close.* Before she could dig further into what might or might not be going on between Landon and Shelby, and why she cared so much, Carly saw Skye Keaton run up to Landon and press a file into her hand. Skye gestured in Carly's direction, and then leaned in close to whisper something in Landon's ear. Damn, were all the good-looking women at the courthouse going to flirt with Landon right in front of her?

"Can I help you?"

Carly pulled her gaze away from Landon and turned to the clerk beckoning her to approach the counter. She started to walk toward her, but then she heard someone calling her name. She looked back and practically ran into Landon, who'd apparently snuck up behind her. Landon held up a hand to the clerk. "Sorry," she said. "We'll be back in a minute."

"What are you doing?" Carly asked as Landon tugged her out of line and back across the foyer.

"Trust me, you're going to want to hear this. Come on."

Landon led her over to Skye, who was waiting near the windows that overlooked downtown Dallas. They were about ten feet from Trevor and Shelby, who were both staring at them with puzzled expressions. Carly looked at her watch. "I was checking in. Donna's going to be ready for us any minute now."

"Damn right, she's ready," Landon said. She punched Skye in the arm. "Tell her. Better yet, show her."

Skye handed her a folder. "I'm sorry I didn't find this before today, but it required a helluva lot of digging. My guess is that Donna wanted to keep this under wraps, but I have a friend in the Houston DA's office who helped me get my hands on this report."

Carly opened the folder and skimmed the contents. Body found. Evidence of strangulation. Identified as Jocelyn Aubrey. Carly racked her brain. The name. It sounded so familiar.

Holy shit. She jabbed her finger on the page. "This is one of Trevor's old girlfriends. From when he lived in Houston." She took her whisper down a few notches. "What's going on?"

"Apparently, Jocelyn went missing last week. She lives by herself, and because she's a flight attendant who travels all the time, no one noticed right away until Houston PD showed up yesterday to serve her with a grand jury subpoena for Trevor's case."

"Why are we just now hearing about her death?" Carly asked, still trying to process what it all meant.

"My guess is Donna was planning to question Trevor about it when he was in there all by himself," Skye replied.

Carly nearly dropped the folder. This was her fault. She'd been mere minutes away from sending Trevor into an ambush. Her strategy had almost doomed his case. She glanced over at where Trevor and Shelby were waiting. How was she ever going to face him, and how was he supposed to trust her counsel from here on out?

"Carly, are you okay?"

She looked at Skye, but then she felt someone take her arm, gently this time.

"She's fine," Landon said, her voice injected with a confidence Carly didn't think she'd ever feel again. "We just need a minute to talk. Do you mind going over there and keeping them calm while we regroup?"

"On it." Skye walked off. Landon said, "Let's start with breathing. We caught this in time. No harm done."

Carly stared at her dumbstruck. "No harm done?" She heard the edge in her own voice and took a breath to stay calm. "He was about go in there. With my blessing. He would've been sacked or whatever you call it, and there is nothing we could have done about it."

"We'll figure this out. Right now, we just need to get out of here with as little fuss as possible."

Carly shuddered. The press would still be waiting downstairs. A few local stations had followed them into the building, and more were set up outside on the front steps, ESPN and all the major networks among them. Summoning her reserves, she motioned to Skye, and when she rejoined them, Carly asked, "You know a lot of the sheriff's deputies. Any chance some of them are football fans and would be willing to help us smuggle Trevor out of here?"

"I think I can make that happen," Skye said. "But you need to get off this floor before Donna comes out. If she sees you here with Trevor, she's going to make a big deal of it with the press, saying that he showed up but didn't have the guts to testify."

Carly started to protest at the characterization, but she knew the truth didn't matter, only how the facts were spun. Landon appeared at her side.

"You go with Skye and Trevor," Landon said. "I'll stay here and be the bad guy."

"What are you going to do?"

"I'll think of something. Now go."

Carly hesitated. This was her mess, but she couldn't be in two places at once. She looked over at her client, who'd placed his trust in her plan, and realized she had to stick with him and trust that Landon would take care of handling the fallout. Funny, trusting Landon didn't seem like such a big leap, and she wondered when that had happened.

❖

Landon watched Skye escort Carly and Trevor down a back hallway, wishing she could go with them and avoid the confrontation that was about to occur.

"Are you sure you know what you're doing?" Shelby asked.

"Yes," Landon lied. Shelby's tone wasn't harsh; she sounded like she was genuinely curious, and Landon figured it was better to fake confidence than spread the uncertainty coursing through her. She had gambled by having Shelby stick around, but since she wouldn't have Trevor to parade in front of the cameras, his agent would be the next best thing. "I'm going to need you to do exactly what I say. First rule, I do all the talking. You don't say anything to the press, to the prosecutor, to anyone. Understood?"

Shelby nodded slowly, and Landon could tell by her frown she was reluctant to agree. She'd have to trust that Shelby would keep her word. She looked over at the counter where Carly had been standing earlier. No one was waiting, and she hoped she could do what she planned and get out of here before Donna came looking for them. "Come with me."

When the clerk appeared at the counter, she stuck out her hand. "Hi, I'm Landon Holt. I have a client with a case set on the docket today, and I just wanted to make sure you received the materials we sent over earlier this week." She knew they'd received the packets filled with letters from Dallas bigwigs in support of Trevor's innocence since she had a receipt from the courier, but since this was all for show, she played it up as best she could, complete with what she hoped was a friendly, "I just want to help" expression.

Before the clerk could respond, Landon heard a voice behind her say, "Oh, we got your packet."

She stifled a grimace and turned to face Donna Wilhelm. "Hi,

Donna. I don't know if you remember me. I work with Carly Pachett. Sturges and Lloyd?"

"Oh, I remember. Is your client ready to testify?" Donna made a show of looking around. "Where is he?"

"I'm not sure where he is, but he's not here. Mr. Kincade is confident the grand jurors are smart enough to know you don't have a case. Are you?"

"I know exactly what I've got." Donna narrowed her eyes. "And I have a feeling you do too or we'd be having a completely different conversation right now." She looked at Shelby. "Who's this?"

"Shelby Cross, meet Donna Wilhelm, the prosecutor handling Mr. Kincade's case. Ms. Cross is Mr. Kincade's agent."

"Hope she has some other high-profile clients to get her through the lean times ahead because Trevor Kincade is going to prison."

Landon felt Shelby shuffle beside her, and she shot her a hard look, rushing to speak first. "We can trust you to share the contents of the packet with the grand jurors, right?"

"Sure," Donna said. "For all the good it will do. I have plenty of other information to share with them."

"Have a great day." Landon grabbed Shelby's arm and led her toward the stairs. Once they were in the stairwell, Shelby let loose.

"What is up with that bitch?"

"Whoa there," Landon said, taken aback by the vitriol. "Look, we're both on Trevor's side here, but if you think that was bad, you need to brace yourself for what's coming. When the grand jury reports out with an indictment, every sportscaster across the country will go all Apostle Peter on Trevor, and if you're not in a position to prop him up when the going gets rough, then he's not going to make it through this."

"I don't get why you can't go in there and tell those people how the evidence is circumstantial, that he didn't do it."

"It doesn't work that way." Landon looked back over her shoulder. The stairwell at the courthouse wasn't the ideal place to be having this conversation, but she needed Shelby to get her head together before they walked outside. Chances were decent no one from the press would recognize her, but they all knew Shelby, and reporters were used to her reputation for always having something to say. "Trevor's lawyers only get to go into the grand jury room if they're invited, and we weren't." She didn't bother pointing out that circumstantial evidence was the norm for most criminal cases since it was rare for defendants to be caught with a smoking gun. "Let's see if we can get out of here with as little fuss as possible. Remember what I said about talking to reporters?"

"I have no comment and don't even say no comment. Got it."

They walked down the eleven flights in silence, only running into a couple of other people on the way. When they reached the doors that led out into the lobby, Landon paused. "Walk at a normal pace. If they accost us when we get out the door, I'll make a short statement and then we go. Don't say anything. Understood?"

Shelby nodded, but when Landon started toward the door, Shelby grabbed her by the arm. "Promise me something."

"What?"

"I want Carly Pachett off this case. This whole grand jury thing was her idea, right?"

"Why do you think that?" Landon said, mostly to stall and partly because she was genuinely curious. Jane had presented the idea like it was groupthink, not the brainchild of any one in particular.

"Trevor told me. He said she told him so."

Landon struggled to process the information. Had Carly told Trevor it was her idea to ingratiate herself with the client? If so, that idea had backfired horribly. Now Shelby was handing her a way to clear her path toward partnership by getting Carly kicked off the case. So why did it make her feel nauseous to think about throwing Carly under the bus? "Let's get through the next few minutes. If you and Trevor have a problem with how the case is being managed, tell Jane. She makes the calls." She placed a hand on the door. "Let's do this."

They made it two steps into the lobby without drawing any attention, but within seconds, reporters crowded around them. Jane would've loved this, Landon thought, remembering her penchant for talking to the press. Rumors at the firm reported that sometimes she even tipped them off herself when she was going to have the opportunity to share some breaking news. But not today. Today was all about saying as little as possible and escaping the spotlight.

"Shelby, where's Trevor? Is he upstairs testifying?"

"Do you think the NFL is going to impose another suspension?"

"Did he kill Vanessa Meyers?"

Landon stepped in front of Shelby and held up a hand. "Good

afternoon, my name is Landon Holt and I'm one of Mr. Kincade's attorneys. Ms. Cross and I just spoke with the grand jury clerk to confirm they have received a packet we submitted in support of Mr. Kincade's innocence. Now it's up to the good citizens of Dallas County to say what we already know. There is no credible evidence to support the prosecution of Trevor Kincade, and he should be allowed to resume his normal life so everyone can put this tragedy behind them. Thank you."

She smiled and waved, and then began to edge away, ignoring the shouted questions that continued behind her as they took the escalator down to the underground tunnel to the parking garage. She walked Shelby to her car. "What I said about talking to the press still holds."

"Got it. And I meant what I said about Carly Pachett. You can talk to Jane or I can, but either way, she's off this case."

Landon didn't answer, but Shelby wasn't the kind of person who cared about other people's responses as long as she got to say her piece. Once Shelby drove away, Landon walked to her car and drove back to the office, conflicted about what to do next. It could have just as easily been her who came up with some risky strategy. After all, Jane had encouraged them to think outside the box and do whatever it took to defend the firm's high profile client. Risks were the name of the game. So why was she so relieved that the idea for Trevor to testify before the grand jury hadn't been hers in the first place? Either way, she dreaded the fallout even if she wasn't the one who was about to get axed from the case. At the next stoplight, she reached for her phone and thumbed through her favorites, unsure who to call—Jane to give her a heads-up about Shelby being on the warpath, or Carly to warn her about the fallout of today's misadventure? Conflicted, she tossed the phone on the passenger seat and drove to the office. Whatever bad news she had to report was better delivered in person, but she couldn't help hoping that Carly wouldn't hate the messenger.

CHAPTER THIRTEEN

Carly heard Mr. Jasper calling out to her, but she pointed to her ear in the universal "I'm on the phone" motion, unlocked her apartment door, and pushed her way inside. She wasn't on the phone, but she had no desire to talk to anyone. Ever again.

The adventure of getting out of the courthouse had been an ordeal, with Trevor asking a million questions, and Skye trying to get them both to shut up and follow her. After they'd delivered Trevor safely home, Skye dropped Carly at her apartment and she sent Jane a text saying she'd report in later, later being very loosely defined. Right now, later felt like never.

Once inside, Carly kicked off her shoes, tossed her briefcase on the floor, and walked into the kitchen. She poured a tall glass of water from the filtered pitcher in the fridge, wishing it were something stronger. Further inspection of the fridge told her what she already knew. Unless she wanted to drown her sorrows in Greek yogurt, salad mix, or grapes, she was out of luck. Healthy living was going to be the death of her. The thought rousted memories of sharing a big, juicy burger or steaming chile rellenos with Landon. If Landon were here, there would probably already be a pizza on the way, and there wouldn't be any vegetables marring the surface.

But Landon wasn't here, and that was a good thing. She had no desire for anyone to witness the aftermath of her humiliation, especially not Landon. Was it because she liked Landon or because they were rivals? She wasn't sure, but she did know that she had some things to figure out, and until she did, she wasn't going back to the office or to work on this case—partnership be damned.

Carly made a pot of coffee, and while it was brewing, she dragged her briefcase open and pulled out the file Skye had brought to the courthouse. Jane would probably have a fit if she knew she'd taken it home, but she didn't care. She was probably going to be booted off the case, but in the meantime, she'd figure out where she'd gone wrong.

Jocelyn Aubrey, Trevor's girlfriend during the time he played for the Houston Texans, was one of his least high-profile girlfriends. A flight attendant, she was often traveling, which meant their schedules didn't always sync, and she rarely made personal appearances with Trevor and almost never showed up for his games. The entertainment press had speculated that her desire to remain out of the spotlight was the main factor in their breakup. When she'd asked Trevor about her, he said Jocelyn had told him she loved football when they met, but she seemed to have lost interest the longer they dated. He brushed it off, saying that a lot of women romanticized dating a pro player, but the reality was far from ideal since he spent the entire season consumed by practice, travel, and games, and in the off-season, he was doing photo shoots for sponsors and other marketing to enhance his income. According to Trevor, he had very little time for a girlfriend, and most women didn't appreciate the lack of attention.

She flipped the page. The police had found Jocelyn's body yesterday and managed to keep the news under wraps so Donna could use it as her secret weapon at the grand jury hearing. She didn't blame Donna for employing the tactic, but she did hate her a little for making her look bad. Would she have cared as much about being bested if Landon hadn't been there to witness her downfall? She didn't like the answer that surfaced, but she'd have to live with it.

Carly fired up her laptop and signed onto the firm's network. Something was bugging her, and she knew the only way to work it out was to review everything one more time. Jane might be about to kick her off the case, but Carly would have answers.

Trevor had a habit of serial monogamy, selecting one lucky girl to be his arm candy in every major city where he'd played ball. None of those women had followed him when he was traded, and he'd usually taken a little while to get acclimated in the new place before finding his next girl. Were there any other surprises in Trevor's past that Donna Wilhelm either had or was about to unearth?

Her own notes were sketchy on the subject. While they'd talked to

Trevor about his past relationships, their questions had been focused on whether there had been any reports of domestic violence. It had never occurred to her to ask if he was an experienced killer, and apparently, it hadn't occurred to anyone else either. Or had it? Landon had pressed her about going easy on Trevor, but she'd brushed her off, insisting that she knew the guy after working with him for months on the NFL suspension and there was no way he'd killed Vanessa Meyers. She buried her head in her hands. Maybe she should just give up.

A knock on the door roused her from her self-doubt. Mr. Jasper had probably found some of her mail mixed up with his again. She knew from experience it was better to answer since he wouldn't give up if he'd seen her go inside. She tilted her laptop cover shut and walked to the door, swinging it wide, but it wasn't Mr. Jasper on the other side.

❖

"What do you mean she's not here?" Landon said. "Skye's text said they left the courthouse almost an hour ago."

Rhonda shrugged, seemingly unaffected by the urgency in Landon's tone. "I don't know where she is. I only know she's not here, and Jane wants to see you both."

"Tell her I'll be right there." Landon didn't wait for an answer before stalking off toward Carly's office. It wasn't that she didn't trust Rhonda's word, but she wanted to see for herself that Carly had bailed when it was time to report to Jane about the shit storm that had just happened.

Carly wasn't in her office, and it looked exactly the way it had when they'd left together for the courthouse that morning, brimming with optimism about the direction of Trevor's case. Damn, that had been misplaced. Landon sank into the chair opposite Carly's desk and contemplated where they'd gone wrong.

"Were you going to come see me anytime soon?" Jane stood in the doorway with her arms crossed.

Landon stood. "Sorry." She motioned toward Carly's desk. "I was checking on something first."

"Where is she?"

She fished around for a good response, but came up lacking. "I don't know, but she might be with Trevor. She left the courthouse with him."

"I know. I just got off the phone with Shelby. She gave me an earful about how I have the most incompetent lawyer working for me, and if I didn't yank her off the case, she'd take Trevor's business elsewhere. I don't need to tell you how much we billed this year dealing with the suspension and this case. We have an opportunity to take on his transactional work as well, but all that is going to disappear because I signed off on this stupid grand jury idea."

Landon didn't know what to say. She could say she'd been the first one to say it was a bad idea, but that verged on "I told you so," and that wasn't her style. Now was the perfect time to stick it to Carly, who was already teetering on the edge. All Landon had to do was push ever so slightly, and Carly would tumble right out of this partnership competition. But something was holding her back. She knew what it was, but if she acknowledged the thought it would make it too real. *Don't mix business and pleasure.* She could adhere to that admonition without killing Carly's career. Right?

"You don't have anything to say?" Jane asked.

Landon had plenty to say, but not until she talked to Carly. She wasn't going to win by ambush. They would talk it out, and then Carly could explain to Jane what had happened and make her case. Landon wasn't sure it would do much good, but at least then she could win fair and square, not by backstabbing. "I know we have a lot of work to do, but I need to check on something. Give me the afternoon and we'll start fresh in the morning."

Jane stood still for a moment before nodding curtly, but Landon was already on her way out the door. Her haste was more about keeping herself from changing her mind than about whether Jane would be angry that she was taking off. In the elevator she pulled up a file and plugged an address into her phone. Fifteen minutes later, she was standing in front of Carly's door, now suddenly unsure of whether she'd made a hasty decision.

"She's home."

She looked over at an elderly man opening his door across the way. He smiled and pointed at Carly's door. "She got home a little while ago. Not in a great mood. Could probably use some company."

Landon wondered if that was true, and even if it was, whether she was the kind of company Carly wanted right now. She nodded her thanks to the neighbor, and before she could think it through, she knocked firmly on the door. Seconds later, it swung open.

Carly was standing in the doorframe wearing the same clothes she'd had on at the courthouse, but she was barefoot and her hair was down. The sight of her robbed Landon's breath, and she stood silent, staring into Carly's apartment.

"What are you doing here?" Carly asked, frowning.

"Can I come in?" Landon glanced back over her shoulder, certain the old man was staring out his peephole. "Please?"

Carly's answer was to turn and walk away, leaving the door standing ajar. Landon followed her in, shutting the door gently behind them. "I know I'm probably the last person you want to see right now." She waited a few beats, but Carly didn't respond, didn't even look at her. She sat back down at the kitchen table and stared at her laptop while Landon fished around for something to say. "You weren't at the office, so I thought I'd come by and see—"

"Either sit down or go, but quit towering over me," Carly snapped.

Landon wasn't going anywhere until they had a conversation, so she walked over to the table and, on the way, took the opportunity to glance around the apartment. Small, tidy, absolutely nothing out of place. It resembled Carly's office, reflected her personality, which made it all the more surprising that Carly had ever even brought up the idea of Trevor testifying. The risk wasn't calculated or logical, but a crapshoot. Carly didn't strike her as the type to ever engage in crapshoots.

"Why did you do it?" she asked, more to herself than Carly, but too late she realized she'd spoken the words out loud. She decided to go all in. "Defendants almost never win at the grand jury. It would have been so much easier to just let them true bill the case and deal with the outcome. Save your strategy maneuvers for trial."

Carly looked up from her laptop. "Easier? I guess you don't realize I want this partnership as much as you do, and playing it safe isn't going to get me there. I don't have your...your..." She pointed her finger in Landon's direction and sputtered out the words. "Your charisma, your big personality, whatever it is that makes everyone think you have all the answers before you even open your mouth. I have to work harder and be smarter if I want to even the score, and if I want to win, I have to come up with something big."

Carly finished the diatribe with her hands waving in the air, and Landon wasn't sure what to say. She could tell that Carly was frustrated, but she couldn't quite tell if the angst was directed inward or at her. What she did know was that Carly was wrong. "I have to work hard too. Everyone I meet thinks because I'm a Holt, I have it made. This name opens doors, but the opportunities come with expectations that a connection to me is an automatic link to the Holt fortune and access to my father. I've never had anyone judge me on my merits alone. This case, this partnership, is my chance to shine, to show everyone that I can do something big all on my own." She took a breath and noted her misstep. "And I don't mean all on my own, but you know what I mean."

"I'm sure Jane knows who was behind today's disaster."

"I just left the office. She wants to talk to both of us. I bought us some time, but you know Jane."

"You mean Jane 'If I asked for it today, you should've known I was wanting it yesterday' Sturges?"

Carly laughed at her own assessment of their boss, and Landon joined her, thankful for the levity. She should warn Carly that Shelby was insisting on her removal from the case, but bringing it up now would dampen the mood even more. There would be time to talk when they got back to the office. "You ready to go see Jane?"

"No."

"No?"

"No," Carly said, more firmly this time. "If I go back to the office, Jane is going to tell me I made a stupid decision, ignore the fact she signed off on it, and the entire exercise will be a colossal waste of time."

Landon nodded slowly. "Okay, so you're just going to hide out here until her anger fades?"

"I'm not hiding. I'm working on Trevor's case."

Landon looked at the contents of Trevor's file spread around the table. From the looks of it, Carly wasn't sitting around licking her wounds, she was working, which was exactly what she should be doing instead of checking on the personal well-being of her rival. Landon reached over and tapped a finger on the papers in front of Carly. "Found anything new?"

Carly stared at her for a moment like she was trying to figure out if she should share or keep whatever she'd been doing to herself. Finally, she shoved a page of handwritten notes across the table. "We haven't been looking deep enough. We've asked about and researched other domestic violence issues both in the prep for the suspension hearing and for the grand jury, but what we should be looking for is what no longer exists."

"I'm not following."

"Trevor has played for three different pro teams and then there's his time in college. He's the kind of guy who likes to have a steady girlfriend, someone on his arm at all of his public appearances. We know, because Skye checked, that the only ones who ever called the police were Vanessa and Jocelyn, but we assumed because there were no police reports with any of the others that nothing was ever wrong. Where are these other women, and what do they have to say about their relationship with Trevor? Two of them have turned up dead. Are the others alive? Have they given statements to the police? For all we know Donna plans to parade them or pictures of dead bodies at trial to show Trevor's a serial offender."

Landon picked up Carly's notes and skimmed the page. "And these are the women?"

"Yes."

"We should call Skye and get her to start looking for them."

"I already emailed her when you were casing my apartment a few minutes ago."

"I wasn't casing your apartment."

"Yes, you were."

"Maybe I was just trying to get to know you better by being aware of your surroundings." Landon grimaced as she spoke. "Okay, that sounded dumb, but you know this place looks just like your office."

"What is that supposed to mean?"

"Nothing in particular. You apparently like to keep things very, uh, clean and organized."

"There's something wrong with cleanliness and efficiency?"

Landon stood and paced the room. "No, of course not, but if I were trying to get to know you, I'd get nothing from either here or your office." She gestured at the walls. "No pictures, no knickknacks." She pointed at the plain white mugs hanging in the glass-doored cabinet.

"I can tell you like coffee, but none of those mugs have logos. It's like this whole place jumped off the Pottery Barn catalog page into your apartment."

Carly's face blushed red. "Maybe it did."

"Oh." It was Landon's turn to be embarrassed. "It's nice. It just doesn't have any personality."

"You're saying I don't have any personality."

Landon walked over and placed a hand on Carly's arm. "That's not what I'm saying at all. I mean the room doesn't reflect the personality of the occupant." She bored her gaze into Carly's until she couldn't stand the heat sparking between them. "Besides, it's just one room."

"Yeah, about that," Carly said. "You probably shouldn't go into any of the other rooms." She ducked her head. "Pottery Barn might've been having a sale."

They both broke into laughter. "Well, I'm all about a sale," Landon said, sitting back down at the table while her mind drifted to thoughts about what the rest of Carly's place looked like.

"You make fun, but seriously, I just wanted my place to look nice, but I don't have the first clue about picking out furnishings and interior decorating."

"Your mom must not be like mine. She was constantly redecorating our house when I was growing up. I think it was her secret way of putting one over on my father. He'd come home from the office, always late, to trip over the new furniture arrangement."

"My parents weren't really big on anything to do with home. They're both workaholics who barely noticed they had a child at home, let alone things like drapes and furniture. I was raised by a string of academic interns who babysat for the chance to get a fellowship from the dynamic duo of professors who spawned me."

Landon heard the bitter tone in Carly's voice. "Sounds like we both have plenty of parental baggage. Do you still keep in touch with your parents?"

"It's more a question of whether they keep in touch with me. I try to follow their travels, but it's hard when they jet off around the world, often forgetting they have a child. I expect one day I'll get a call from their lawyer, asking me what I want done with the bodies, but in the meantime, we talk a few times a year—major holidays mostly. But enough about them, it's time to refocus on this case."

Now, Landon thought. Now was the time to warn Carly that Shelby wanted her off the case. But doing so would ruin this already tenuous connection, and she didn't want to let go. Let Jane deliver the bad news. It was her job. Landon's job was to work this case, and for as long as possible, she was going to do it with Carly.

CHAPTER FOURTEEN

Carly looked up from her desk at Keith Worthington leaning against her doorframe. "I'm busy," she said, dropping her gaze back to her computer, hoping he would get the hint and go away. "That's not what I hear. Word is you're about to be taken off the Kincade case. I just stopped by to see if you want to go ahead and give me your files since I'm the natural choice to take your place. What can you tell me about Landon Holt? Is she single?"

Carly's stomach dropped at the mention of the case and Landon, but she faked nonchalance. "Don't believe everything you hear."

Keith started to say something else, but Jane's clipped voice sounded through the intercom on her phone. "Carly, please come see me. Thanks." Jane was off the line before she could respond. She looked back at Keith and wished she could reach him to claw the grin off his face, but he waved and walked off down the hall.

Carly took a moment to breathe. She'd known this was coming and she'd spent the night preparing her response. If there was one thing she'd learned from Landon, it was that bravado opened doors. After all, she'd opened the door to Landon the day before when she'd planned to spend the entire day licking her wounds. She might not feel totally natural emulating Landon's brash style, but she was attracted to it, just like she was drawn to her wit, easygoing manner, and the sexy confidence she exuded in everything she did. *Landon's confidence isn't the only sexy thing about her.* Carly shook away the thought for the distraction it was. No good could come of thinking about Landon that way.

Carly took a few more minutes to review the notes she'd made last night, and satisfied she was as ready as she ever would be, walked down the hall to Jane's office. When Rhonda looked up, Carly gave her a smile and Rhonda's eyes grew wide like she thought she was crazy. Carly pointed at the door. "Jane wants to see me. I'll let myself in." She strode past Rhonda's desk and pushed open the partially closed door without knocking first. Jane was staring at her computer and didn't immediately look up, a power play Carly recognized from many other similar occasions but had never challenged. Today was different.

"You wanted to see me?"

"Have a seat, Carly. I'll be just a minute."

"I'll come back. I'm sure you'd rather have me working on cases than sitting here waiting while you finish up."

Jane tugged off her glasses and turned to face her with a look of surprise. Carly didn't look away, daring Jane to call her out for being insubordinate. The way she figured it, she had nothing to lose after what had happened yesterday, but if she left the firm, Jane would lose a lot. Carly might not be Landon Holt, full of charm and personality, but she was smart and thorough and a billing machine.

She owed most of her newfound confidence to Landon's visit. They'd both ignored Jane's repeated calls and texts, and spent the afternoon reviewing everything in their files about Trevor's case and conferencing with Skye about what they needed from her. When the grand jury reported out, they'd be ready for whatever Donna Wilhelm had to throw their way.

Jane pushed her monitor to the side. "You're right. Let's talk about what happened yesterday."

Carly took a deep breath. She'd practiced this, and she was ready. "We were ambushed, rather I was ambushed. I took a risk and it didn't work. You're not used to me taking risks because I always give you the sure thing—the solid research, the absolute answer. But you've asked me to step up and show you that I'm partner material, and that's what I'm doing. Every move I make isn't going to be a winning one. I bet not every move you made when you were building this firm was a winner, but you learned from every decision you made—good or bad. Am I right?"

To her surprise, Jane merely nodded and motioned for her to go on, but this was as much as she'd practiced. If she was going to show she was just as capable at litigating as Landon, then she needed to dig deep. "You can yank me out of the running for partner, but you can't yank me off this case. I've worked with Trevor for a while now, and he trusts me. Ask him if you don't believe me."

"I already have. And you're right. He won't work with us unless you stay on the case." Jane folded her arms and leaned back in her chair. "I have to say, I've always admired your smarts, but this more aggressive side of you is really something."

Carly's first instinct was to say thank you, but she decided instead to channel Landon. "I prefer to call it assertive, and I hope by 'really something' you mean you appreciate my candor. I've worked really hard for you over the years, and I've rarely made a bad call."

Jane shook her head. "Ultimately the call was mine, and it was worth a shot. We make decisions based on the best information we have at the time. It's not our fault if our client doesn't give us all the facts."

Jane's words prickled Carly's conscious. "You think he did it?"

"I have no idea, and I don't care either way, but I find it pretty odd that two women he's been serious about in the past two years have turned up dead, don't you?"

"I guess."

"But we have a more pressing matter. The NFL commissioner is putting pressure on the team to fire Trevor."

"Will they? If they do, Donna might ask for a new bail hearing and assert that if he doesn't have a steady job he doesn't meet the qualifications of his bond. On top of that, the Houston DA could file charges any minute, and he could be arrested and dragged into court down there."

"Exactly. I need you to get a copy of his contract from Shelby and see if there are any loopholes to the morality clause. Also, either you or Landon should talk to Donna and take her temperature about the bond. Trevor's paying us out of his own pocket, and neither one of us can afford for those pockets to go empty. Understood?"

Carly nodded, deciding not to fight back on Jane's characterization. She often talked about clients in terms of their ability to pay, and Carly hated it, but she recognized Jane had a duty to keep them all employed. She stood to leave the room, but Jane stopped her.

"How are you and Landon getting along?"

It was a loaded question, and Carly took her time sifting through potential responses before she settled on one. "Good. We both have the same goal. That's what's important, right?"

"Yes, yes, it is. Please close the door on your way out. Thanks."

Carly walked out of the office, past Rhonda, who humphed as she went by. What she should do was go directly to her office and start researching whether the team ownership could break their contract with Trevor before he was actually found guilty of any wrongdoing. But her legs betrayed her by walking directly to Landon's office. When she reached the open door, she spotted Landon on the phone and started to turn away, but Landon waved her in.

Landon placed a hand over the receiver. "It's Skye. She found a former roommate of Jocelyn who's willing to talk. She lived with Jocelyn when she was dating Trevor. She lives in Austin now, and Houston PD has been trying to get in touch with her, but she just got their messages. Thankfully, she called Skye back first and she's willing to talk today if we can find the time. It's a bit of a haul, but if we leave now, we could be back late tonight."

"Set it up." Carly mentally ran through her to-do list. She could get a lot of it done in the car on the drive down, assuming Landon would drive. She had a vision of her papers flying out of the convertible onto the highway as they raced down I-35. "I have some research to do today, but I can do it in the car if…"

"If I keep the top up and don't drive like a speed demon. Got it." Landon told Skye they'd be there in a few hours and hung up the phone. "This'll be great. I need to check on my place anyway—just a quick drive-by to collect mail and pick up some more clothes." She started scooping her notes and her laptop into her bag. "How soon can you be ready to go?"

"An hour?" Carly saw Landon's frown and revised her answer. "Thirty minutes?" Still with the frown. "Fifteen? Give me a break. You should know by now that spontaneity is not my strong suit."

Landon laughed. "I do know, and I'm making it my life's mission to change that fact." She stood and hefted her bag over her shoulder. "Meet you at the elevator in five minutes."

Carly shook her head as she watched Landon take off. She ran through a mental checklist of what she needed to take to avoid having the time on the road become a work vacuum, and then she walked swiftly back to her office to gather her things. She was more excited than she was willing to admit about the prospect of a road trip, and her excitement had nothing to do with talking to a potential witness.

❖

Landon sped down I-35, glad Skye's call had come after rush hour. Once they were out of Dallas, they should make good time, although at any given time, stretches of this road were under construction. She set the cruise control to make Carly happy and settled in to enjoy the ride. "Did you talk to Jane this morning?"

"Why do I think you already know the answer to that question?" Carly asked.

"You know what they say. Never ask a question unless you already know the answer."

"That goes for trial witnesses, not, you know…"

"Friends?"

"I was going to say coworkers."

"Fine. How about coworkers who became friends? If I win the partnership, then we'll be working in the same office. Wouldn't it be nice to have a friend?"

"There are a bunch of things wrong with that assumption. First of all, you winning is a big 'if.' And you're assuming I don't have other friends."

Landon was assuming, but her assumption was based on observation. Carly arrived and left alone. She ate alone, she lived alone, and Landon never saw her glued to her phone on calls or texts. She bypassed Carly's comment. "I guess I thought it would be nice to be friends with you, but if you have a wait list, that's cool. Put me on it, and I'll wait my turn."

"What if things happen the other way?"

"Other way?"

"What if I make partner, not you?" Carly asked. "In the unlikely event everyone forgets I messed up with the grand jury. Will you stick around Dallas or go back to Austin?"

"I don't know." Landon wasn't being cagey. She actually hadn't let her mind drift to thoughts of what would happen if Carly got the partnership instead of her. The question was bigger than where would she live and work. Would she and Carly ever speak again? "I really don't know," she repeated. "I love Austin and Dallas for very different reasons, but life is simpler in Austin. For me anyway."

"Because of your dad?"

"Mostly, but also because the name Holt doesn't automatically conjure up unrealistic expectations for everyone I meet."

"So having a chick-magnet name like Holt isn't a good thing?"

Landon looked over at Carly, relieved to see her smiling. She needed to lighten up. "It's not necessarily a bad thing, but too often the second date comes with not so subtle questions about how involved I am in the family business."

"How do you handle it?"

"I don't go on second dates." The second she said the words, she regretted them, but she wasn't entirely sure why. She glanced over at Carly, but she was looking out the window. For the next few minutes a weighted silence hung between them. Landon focused her attention on the road, trying to ignore her growing affection for Carly. She hadn't forged any close friendships at the Austin office, partly because she'd never been certain she would stick around and partly for the same reason she didn't go on second dates. But Carly didn't care about her family name, and she liked that when Carly chose to be around her it was because she liked her company, despite their supposed rivalry. If she did wind up losing the partnership to Carly, she wouldn't be surprised. Carly was not only a hard worker, she was a genius. With a little work on her people skills, she'd outpace most lawyers Landon knew.

The rest of the drive was spent discussing various aspects of the case, and Carly used portions of the road with a decent cell signal to do some internet research on contract terminations. By the time they pulled up at the Austin office of Sturges and Lloyd to pick up Skye, they'd exhausted all non-personal topics of conversation, and Landon was relieved to have a third person in the car.

Jocelyn's old roommate, Mandy Hauser, lived in an area of north Austin not far from Landon's condo. The neighborhood was lined with small bungalow houses, but Landon wasn't fooled. "Pricey neighborhood. I thought you said she was a flight attendant." She directed her comment to Skye.

"Key word 'was.' She got married about six months ago to some bigwig at Dell and quit her job with United. No more roommates for her. Not that it matters, but she's pregnant and a tiny bit emotional, so be gentle, okay?"

"Gotcha."

"How's your little girl, Skye?" Carly asked.

Skye's face broke out in a big grin. "Amazing. She just turned five, going on thirty. She definitely knows how to give us a run for our money."

"You have pictures?"

Skye swiped through her phone and handed it over. Carly oohed and aahed as she viewed the photos. Landon watched the exchange, curious about this side of Carly. "You like kids?" She'd blurted out the question without thinking and instantly regretted her incredulous undertone.

"Sure. You know, before they get to the mean stage." Carly looked back at Skye. "Not that Olivia ever will. She's such a cutie."

"Thanks," Skye said with a broad grin. She pointed ahead. "That's the house, up there on the right." Landon turned into the drive. "She knows you're coming, but let me go in first to give her a heads-up. Remember, go easy. She and Jocelyn were really close, and she's pretty broken up."

While Skye walked up to the door, Landon said, "How about I take the lead?"

"Let me guess. Because you're the kinder, gentler lawyer?" Carly asked.

"Maybe."

Landon braced for blowback, but Carly surprised her by saying, "It's true, you are. Use some of that magic Holt charm and get her to tell us everything she knows. I'll linger in the background and feed you questions." Carly pointed to Skye who was waving from the front door. "Looks like they're ready for us."

Carly was out the door before Landon could reply, although she wasn't sure what she would have said anyway. Magic Holt charm. What was that about? Was Carly being sarcastic or did she really think she was charming, and why did the idea make Landon flush with excitement? *She's only talking about your ability to talk to witnesses, so get over yourself.* Still, she couldn't help but feel a flutter of anticipation at the prospect of showing off her skills, and charming Carly in the process.

❖

The house was small, but perfectly furnished. Unlike her own sterile apartment, Carly noted the furnishings here were eclectic, but not in a thrown together mishmash way, but in the "carefully selected by an interior designer" kind of way. This chick hadn't ordered the already put together room from the Pottery Barn catalogue.

"Have a seat," Mandy said. "Would you like something to drink or eat? Skye said you drove down from Dallas?"

"We did," Landon said. "We have an office here in Austin, and I had to get some things from there anyway, so we thought it would be nice to talk to you while we were here."

Mandy visibly relaxed, and Carly noted how Landon's explanation for their trip put Mandy at ease. "I'd love a glass of water," Carly said, in her own attempt to act like this was a friendly visit instead of an interrogation. "If it's not too much trouble."

"No trouble at all." Mandy looked at Landon and Skye, who both shook their heads, and then she wandered off to the kitchen. Carly took advantage of Mandy's absence to look around. The mantel was lined with a grouping of photos. Mandy, wrapped in a hug with a man who was probably her husband. A family portrait, that based on the resemblance, must be Mandy's parents and siblings, and finally a shot of Mandy with Jocelyn.

"I miss her every day. She was my best friend."

Carly turned and almost bumped into Mandy, who was holding out a glass of water. Carly took the glass and thanked her. "I'm sorry for your loss."

"Do you think he killed her?" Mandy asked. "The police think he may have killed her."

Damn. Way to jump right in. Carly resisted the urge to look over at Landon. Mandy seemed fixated on her, and she wanted to show she could be just as gentle with the witness as Landon could. "No, but it doesn't really matter what we think, only what the state can prove. We need to know the truth, which is why we're here." Not entirely true, but not a lie either. "Anything you can tell us will be helpful."

"I don't know much. We were both flying a lot during their relationship, but she did talk to me about things."

Carly motioned to the dining room table in the room adjacent. "How about we have a seat and talk?"

"Of course. Sorry."

When they were all four settled around the table, Skye started the conversation. "I think it would be helpful if you tell Carly and Landon what you told me."

Mandy drummed her fingers on the table. "I have this tremendous guilt that I never mentioned this to anyone, but Jocelyn always brushed it off and I suppose I just took her lead."

Carly resisted grabbing her by the collar, shaking her, and demanding to know what "it" was. She injected her voice with as much calm as she could muster. "What was going on with her?"

"About three months into dating Trevor, she started getting hate mail. Well, I called it that. She referred to it as what comes with the territory when you're dating a big star. She was completely smitten with Trevor at that point, so she'd do anything to keep the status quo. When she mentioned the messages to him, he brushed her off."

"Were they messages or actual mail?"

Mandy abruptly stood and left the room. Carly looked at Landon, who merely shrugged. A moment later, Mandy returned holding a laptop and an envelope. She set the envelope on the end table, settled in next to Carly, and pointed at the screen. "Jocelyn's laptop was always on the fritz, so she used mine quite a bit. She shut down her social media accounts when she and Trevor broke up, but her password is saved on here, and you can sign in and see the kind of messages she was getting." She booted up the laptop and used the saved password to sign onto Facebook Messenger. A smiling profile pic of Jocelyn greeted them along with a list of messages. Mandy started typing, "Some of these are from friends, but there's one in particular from someone named Only One that I thought was a little disturbing." She clicked a few more keys and then turned the laptop so they could all see. "Here you go."

Landon stood up and read over Carly's shoulder, and she struggled to ignore the disconcerting proximity and focus on the words on the screen.

He doesn't love you. He only loves one person, and he only ever will. You're just one of the many pretty girls he parades around for the cameras.

Carly skimmed the rest, but it was more of the same. On the surface, the message wasn't threatening—more like the ramblings of a jealous fan, but there were a total of six similar messages, and it was hard to ignore the repetition.

"What do you think?" Landon asked, placing her hand on Carly's shoulder.

Carly's first instinct was to reach up and touch Landon to complete the connection, but she was all too conscious they were not alone. "Hard to tell." She directed her attention back to Mandy. "Did Jocelyn have any idea who was sending her these messages?"

"Not a clue. We looked up the profile, but it's like any one of those trolls who signs up and doesn't post any personal information."

"Do you know if she told anyone else about the messages?" Landon asked.

"No, I don't, but I'm sure she didn't. She was pretty embarrassed when Trevor broke up with her. She did get wasted a few times and acted out."

"The 911 call?" Carly asked, as gently as she could manage.

Mandy nodded. "Yep. She was mortified the morning after."

Carly looked at her notes. "Were you living with her when the incident with the burning clothes happened?"

"No. I'd moved out the week before. I was a little worried about leaving her on her own, but she seemed to be getting back to pre-Trevor normal."

"Do you think there's any chance she might've set the fire herself as kind of a way to get Trevor's attention?"

"I guess anything's possible," Mandy said. "But I don't want to give you the wrong impression. Jocelyn wasn't crazy, just crazy about him."

Carly patted Mandy's hand, sensing she was about to start crying and hoping she could head it off. What she really wanted was a copy of the messages on Mandy's computer.

As if she could read her mind, Mandy said, "A detective from Houston PD is coming by later today to download copies of the messages, but Skye asked if I could make you a copy." She handed over the envelope. "Here it is."

Donna Wilhelm was going to come unglued, but there was no way

Carly wasn't going to take her up on her offer. She took the envelope from Mandy and thanked her. "We should get out of your hair."

Landon followed her lead and stood, adding, "Skye might have a few follow-up questions for you."

Mandy hesitated for a second. "Sure, no problem." She turned to Carly and pulled her into an awkward hug. "Thanks for listening." Carly stayed in the embrace several seconds past uncomfortable before extracting herself and joining Skye and Landon on their way out. They huddled near Landon's car.

"I think we should get an affidavit," Landon said. "Skye, do you mind sticking around and getting her to sign a sworn statement? Tell her Carly asked for it—she seemed pretty taken with her."

"I can do that," Skye said. "I'll catch an Uber back to your office, but then I need to get back to Dallas pretty quickly for a family thing."

"No worries," Landon said. "We'll be heading back soon too. Let's hook up at the Dallas office tomorrow. Have her detail exactly what she found on her computer and everything she knows about when Jocelyn received the message and her reaction to them. And if you can, get her to put in writing that she never witnessed any violence or threats between Jocelyn and Trevor, and that Jocelyn never mentioned any incidents between them. See if she'll let you grab screenshots of the Facebook messages since they might make for better graphics than the printouts." Apparently satisfied Skye knew what she wanted, Landon turned to Carly. "You handled Mandy like a champ. Ready to go?"

Carly fumed inwardly at having been so casually dismissed, so she merely nodded. Once they were in the car and pulling away, Landon seemed to notice her mood had changed.

"What's the matter?"

"Until such time as you become partner, we're still equals. Would it kill you to treat me like one?"

Landon gave her a blank look, which only made Carly more mad. "We should've discussed whether or not it's a good idea for Skye to get a sworn statement. Are you sure it's a good idea?"

"I'm positive," Landon said with the bravado Carly had come to both love and hate. "A detective from Houston PD is going to show up this afternoon, and God only knows what kind of questions he'll ask. You can damn well be certain he's going to write up a report, and we need to make sure whatever it says, Mandy is on record stating she never saw Trevor be violent or even threaten Jocelyn."

"Yes, but I'd like a little time to do some due diligence on Mandy to see if she's a credible witness. Plus it would've been nice to consider whether there's anything else we should have Skye include in the statement."

"You heard Skye, she needs to get back to Dallas. This is the nature of the game—we don't always get a chance to reflect. Sometimes you just have to act."

Carly resisted pointing out that her own recent urge to act had nearly resulted in disaster. Instead she referenced her personal affront. "It would just be nice if you would ask me or at least confer with me before you make a decision."

"Like the way you marched in Jane's office with your own personal strategy for winning the case?"

"Are you ever going to let that go?"

"I already have, but I don't appreciate being lectured about being a team player from someone who would clearly rather work on everything all by herself."

Carly digested Landon's words, unable to come up with a quick retort—further evidence that she wasn't great coming up with ideas on the fly. Frustrating, but that just wasn't her skill. Her forte was examining a case from every angle, analyzing all the issues, and distilling a decision from careful consideration. Landon's point-and-shoot style wasn't hers, but she could acknowledge its benefits. Why couldn't Landon recognize her way had merits too?

"It's going to be a long drive home if you don't speak to me the whole way," Landon said.

"Maybe we should do something besides talk about work for a while."

Landon raised her eyebrows and grinned. "What exactly did you have in mind?"

Carly play slapped Landon's arm. "Don't even. Didn't you say you needed to stop by your apartment?" Instantly sorry she'd brought up something so personal, she quickly added. "And I'm starving. Maybe we could grab a late lunch before we head back?"

"We can do both. Are you okay grabbing something to go? We

can take it back to my place and eat there while I check on a couple of things and pack some clothes."

Alarm bells rang in Carly's head. Sharing a meal at Landon's had the potential to stoke the feelings she'd had ever since Landon had shown up on her doorstep after the grand jury fiasco, but she couldn't think of a rational reason to say no. "Sounds good."

CHAPTER FIFTEEN

Landon unlocked the front door of her apartment and prayed any mess inside was confined to the bedroom. Memories of her last morning here were filled with visions of a feisty redhead and frantically packing for Dallas, and piles of clothes were stacked everywhere. But the kitchen and dining room should be fine since they were the least used rooms in the house.

They'd made a quick stop at Torchy's to pick up some of the best tacos in Austin. Carly had balked a bit when Landon insisted on ordering, but had acquiesced, which was good because Landon was hell-bent on satisfying at least one of her cravings today.

Which brought up the question of why she was craving Carly at all. They could not be more different, and Carly routinely drove her crazy with her rigid ways, but she sensed that underneath the laced-up outer shell was a wild woman struggling to get out. *And you think you're the one to coax her to the surface?* Maybe.

She needed a minute to clear her head, so she handed the bags to Carly. "If you'll take these into the dining room, I'll grab some plates and drinks. Topo Chico okay?"

"I have no idea what that is, but since I'm already trusting you for sustenance, I see no reason not to trust you to quench my thirst."

Damn, that feeling again. Why did Carly's simplest statements turn her on? Landon walked to the kitchen and counted to ten, but the feelings kept coming. She'd made a habit of dating women who weren't necessarily high in the IQ department. Doing so kept her from having to talk in depth about her work, her family's business, current events, or anything beyond getting undressed and which positions gave them the most pleasure. But now, all of a sudden, she was turned on by sheer intelligence. Who knew smart could be so damn sexy?

She opened the fridge and searched the contents, hoping to cool off in the process.

"If you don't find something in there soon, I can't promise there will be anything left to eat."

Landon turned, and Carly was standing directly behind her wearing a sexy smile. Well, it was just a smile, but everything about Carly seemed sexy from the way she stood with one hand on her hip, to the way she cocked her head when she was making a joke. Landon quickly grabbled two bottles of Topo Chico sparkling water and used the bottle opener on the counter to open them. She thrust one at Carly. "Try this."

Carly raised her eyebrows and tipped the bottle to her lips. Full, red, sexy lips. Holy hotness. Landon could barely watch, but she couldn't look away as Carly took a long pull and held the fizzy liquid in her mouth for a moment before swallowing.

"Oh my God, that's amazing." Carly held the bottle up and examined the label. "Mineral water." She read a bit more. "There's really nothing else in this?"

Landon tore her gaze away from the sexy lips. "Uh, no. I sometimes squeeze a lime in, but as you can see," she pointed to a wrinkled green object in the fridge, "I think this piece of fruit has seen better days."

"It doesn't need it." Carly tilted her bottle. "Aren't you going to drink yours?"

"Uh, yeah, sure." Landon reached back and grabbed her bottle, grateful to have something to do with her hands. "Hungry?"

"Starving."

Did she hear an undercurrent reflecting her own desire or was she imagining it? Hell, they hadn't eaten all day, of course Carly was hungry. Landon grabbed the Torchy's bag and led the way to her kitchen counter. "Not super fancy, but this is the dining counter. Not to be confused with the kitchen counter, which is what it doubles as when I'm cooking."

"Do you cook a lot?"

"Hardly ever. Ian is the only one with the chef gene, although I'm not sure where he got it. My mother's cooking skills consist of signing off on the household menu and occasionally strolling through the kitchen to make sure everyone is earning their keep." Landon could hear the bitter edge in her voice and wished she hadn't shared that last part. Seeking to add a little levity, she added, "My food skills are limited to picking good restaurants."

"So far, you're batting a thousand." Carly took another bite of her taco and wiped the edge of her mouth with a napkin. "I'm not big on cooking either, which usually means I throw together a salad or a bowl of cereal for dinner. If I keep hanging out with you, I'll need to be fitted for a new wardrobe."

"Oh please, you're beautiful and you'd be just as gorgeous with an extra ten or twenty pounds." The words tumbled out, and Landon didn't even try to reel them back in. She'd spoken the truth and what was the harm in that? She froze for a moment, meeting Carly's curious stare with a smile before grabbing a taco and shoving it in her mouth, more to keep from saying anything else embarrassing than because she was hungry.

They spent the next few moments in companionable silence, eating their food. Landon snuck a couple of sidelong glances at Carly, musing at how far they'd come from their rocky start.

"Do you think he did it?" Carly asked.

"What?"

"Trevor? Do you think he killed those women?"

"I don't know. I try not to think about it. Kinda gets in the way of the job. How about you?"

Carly nodded. "I try too, but I can't help but wonder. Seems a little crazy for someone so high profile to risk losing everything, but it's not like it hasn't happened before. Hello, O.J.?"

"Why did you ask?"

"Just a conversation I had with Jane. I get the impression she thinks he's guilty."

"And you care what she thinks because?"

"Well, for one, she has the power to decide my future. Our future."

"Is that so?" Carly's words stoked rebellion. "That's a pretty broad statement. She has the power to decide which one of us becomes a partner. At this firm. This year. Beyond that our futures are pretty much our own to decide."

"I don't know about you, but becoming a partner at this firm is what I've been working toward. It is my future, and I care a lot. What does your future hold?"

"I want this partnership as much as you do," Landon said, not quite believing her own words. She leaned close. "But my future's bigger than a job. I want everything."

Carly's breath hitched. "Everything, huh?"

"You bet." She'd said the words without thinking, but now that she had, she knew they were true. She did want more, but she wasn't sure what the more was. A wife? Family? She'd always assumed those things would happen, but she hadn't spent a lot of time thinking or planning for a future that involved other people. Until now. Sitting here in her apartment with Carly, sharing a meal, she could envision something more, and the mental image of what it would be like to kiss those lips supplanted all other thoughts. She reached for Carly's empty plate, and noted a faraway look in her eyes. "What are you thinking right now?"

Carly pushed the plate toward Landon. "Why?"

"Don't parse the question, just answer it."

"We have a lot of work to do."

"You were thinking about work?" Landon didn't believe her, but she wasn't surprised at the lie. Since the moment they'd met, Carly had focused on the job, corralling Landon's usual tendencies to get distracted. But Carly was fast becoming the distraction.

"No."

Landon's head shot up. "No?"

"I wasn't thinking about work," Carly said in a low voice. "But I should've been."

The roller-coaster admission left Landon uncertain. She wanted to say that should've beens were the enemy of pleasure, and life was too short not to indulge now and then. But words, even those, were an impediment to what she really wanted, and they would only break the spell. Before she could think herself out of it, she pulled Carly toward her and kissed her softly.

❖

At the touch of Landon's lips to hers, Carly placed a hand on Landon's chest. But instead of obeying the command of her brain, telling her to push Landon away, Carly wound her fingers in Landon's shirt and yanked her closer. She took her time, luxuriating in the firm press of flesh, and when Landon's tongue slipped through her lips, she matched her stroke for stroke, sending waves of arousal through her body.

When they finally broke for air, Landon's breath was jagged. "Best. Kiss. Ever."

Carly nodded but stopped short of asking if she meant it. The kiss was definitely her number one, but she imagined Landon had way more experience kissing tons of other girls, so her assessment was kind of incredible. Instead of asking for affirmation, she asked for what she really wanted. "Can we do it again?"

Landon barely waited for her to finish the words before she captured her bottom lip and ran her tongue lightly along the surface, teasing with delicious delay. Carly moaned and sagged against her touch.

"You like?" Landon murmured.

"You are very observant."

"It's one of my main skills."

"But not your best one," Carly said, pulling Landon close. "What are we doing here?" she whispered, more to herself than Landon.

"I don't know about you, but I've been wanting to do this for a while now. And by this, I mean…"

Landon finished her sentence with another searing kiss, and Carly melted into the slow, lingering strokes of Landon's tongue tangling with hers. She couldn't remember the last time she'd been kissed like this. Hell, when Landon touched her, she couldn't remember her own name. She ran her arms up Landon's side and stepped closer, letting Landon's hands pull her in and then wander over her body, stroking her neck, her breasts, and then dipping low to the waistline of her skirt. She was dangerously close to shucking off her clothes right here, next to the kitchen counter, when the sound of a phone buzzing broke through her haze.

"Ignore it," Landon whispered, her voice breathy and full of promise.

"But what if—"

Landon's lips cut off the rest of her feeble protest, and Carly nipped back at her, hungry for the connection.

A loud ringtone burst through their haze. "Tell me you have a spontaneous speaker system," Carly said against Landon's lips.

"I wish." Landon leaned back, her eyes full of regret.

"Is that 'The Imperial March' from *Star Wars*?"

"Uh, yeah. It's my ringtone for Jane."

"Better not let her hear it." Carly ran a finger down Landon's chest. "Now it's my turn to tell you to ignore it."

The ominous notes of the tune started up again.

"Tell me," Landon said.

"Ignore it."

"I will."

The tune stopped for a moment, but then started up again. Carly shot a look at the coffee table where the phone rattled against the wood with each ring. She wanted to ignore it, she really did, but she was certain now that the buzzing she'd heard earlier was Jane as well, and Jane was probably wondering why she wasn't able to reach either one of her two top attorneys who were allegedly in the car together, headed back to Dallas. She looked back at Landon, who greeted her with a gentle smile.

"I'm sorry," Carly said as she slipped out of Landon's arms and walked the short distance to her own phone. She scrolled through her missed calls, surprised to see Trevor's number along with Jane's. She'd never even heard the first call. She'd been too mesmerized by Landon's touch. She still was, but she had a job to do, and nowhere in the job description was long, slow kisses one of her assigned tasks.

Carly checked her text messages, but all she had were a string of "call mes" and "where are yous" from Trevor. It didn't bode well that neither one of them had been compelled to send any sort of detail about why in the hell they were so eager to reach them. She held up her phone. "I've got lots of calls, but no intel here. How about you?"

"Same. You want to call or should I?"

"Trevor called me. I'll call him back while you call Jane." Carly was already punching his number when notifications from CNN, Bloomberg, Huffpost, and more started cascading down her screen. "Hold up. Are you seeing what I'm seeing?"

Landon crossed the room, phone in hand. They stood shoulder

to shoulder and read the latest news. The Dallas County grand jury had indicted Trevor, and within moments after the announcement, the NFL commissioner had held a press conference calling on the Dallas Cowboys to terminate his contract.

"Someone must've tipped him off about the true bill," Landon said. "No way the commissioner could've put together a press conference that fast."

Carly merely nodded, but all she could think about was how many news alerts they'd missed during their little make-out session, and how mixed up her feelings were about whether, given the chance, she'd go back and do things differently.

"Are you okay?"

Carly looked up into Landon's dreamy eyes. It would be so incredibly easy to fall back into the haze that had swept them up in its spell just moments ago. She took a deep breath. She couldn't, wouldn't, change what had happened, but she could and would guard against letting it happen again. "I'm good, but we've got some work to do. Ready to hit the road?"

Landon checked the right lane and pulled over just in time to make the exit to the office. They'd spent most of the three-hour car ride on the phone, together and separately, and even though Carly was sitting only inches away, it felt like they were on different planets.

Carly seemed completely unaffected by what had happened at her apartment, while Landon had been hard-pressed to think of anything else. She'd thought kissing Carly would satisfy an itch, but now she ached all over. Several times during the ride, she'd considering pulling over and reaching for Carly again, but she could feel the wall Carly had erected between them the moment the job reached back into their world with its firm demands and tangled allegiances. She wished she could shut it down as easily as Carly had. She'd have to work on that.

In the meantime, they had to deal with a nervous client, an irate agent, an anxious football team management, and a commissioner with something to prove. Two of the four were waiting at the office, and Jane had made it clear they were to come straight there for a strategy session. The office was less than a mile away, and if she didn't take advantage now, there would be no time to talk to Carly about what happened between them. She'd faced angry prosecutors, grumpy judges, and unsympathetic juries, and never backed down, so why was she so reticent when it came to talking about a kiss with a woman she'd nearly undressed?

Because you don't usually talk to them.

It was a hard truth but a fair assessment. Since she'd been tossed aside after chasing a girl to Austin, she'd allowed plenty of women in her bed, but not in her heart, which meant her dating conversations usually started with things like "What do you want for dinner" and ended with "What do you like between the sheets?" She hadn't cared about the lack of depth, or at least she hadn't thought she cared. Until now. Working with and against Carly had stoked something besides the challenge of their rivalry. She'd gotten a glimpse of what it could be like to spend time with someone and actually get to know them before collapsing into each other's arms.

Time was running out. Landon pulled into the lot and barely got the key out of the ignition before Carly had the door open. It was now or never. "Wait a minute. Please."

"They're waiting for us."

"I know, but they've been waiting a while, another minute won't hurt."

Carly took her hand off the door and turned to face her. "I know what you're going to say."

"You do, do you?"

"The kissing, back at your place, it was nice."

"Nice?"

"Fine." Carly's smile didn't reach her eyes. "It was hot, steamy, amazing, but it can't happen again."

This was it, her opening. Her chance to argue the other side and win, but when Landon opened her mouth, all she could think to say was, "Why not?"

Carly looked down and fiddled with the door handle. "It just doesn't make sense. We're working together, but whatever the outcome of this trial, one of us is going to win and one is going to lose. Let's not complicate things by having the contest get personal."

Landon listened to the sterile delivery, barely able to believe that a few hours earlier Carly had melted into her arms. Had she completely misread the situation or was Carly a complete ice princess, able to turn her feelings off and on whenever she wanted? Clearly, she and Carly didn't want the same thing. When it came to now or never, she supposed she had her answer. Never.

CHAPTER SIXTEEN

Two months later

Carly hugged a sweater around her shoulders and shivered at the sound of the wind whipping outside her window. Dallas was having one of its rare runs of cold weather, but she was reluctant to turn on the heater since the temperatures were expected to be back up in the seventies in a few days. It didn't really matter what the weather app said, she'd been feeling cold inside for a while now.

She looked up from her work at the sound of a knock on her door. It was nine a.m. on the Sunday after Thanksgiving and she wasn't expecting anyone. She'd been up since six, prepping for Trevor's trial that was set to begin first thing tomorrow morning. This afternoon, she'd have to brave the outside world for another meeting with the rest of the team at the office, but she wasn't quite ready for human interaction.

When she looked out the door viewer she saw Mr. Jasper raising his hand to knock again. No doubt he knew she was inside, and he wouldn't go away until she answered. She cracked the door and stuck her head out. "Hi, Mr. Jasper, do you need something?"

"Not me, no." He held up a medium-sized square box. "This came for you yesterday, but the delivery guy left it in front of my door. Sorry I'm just now getting it to you. I was at my sister's for the holiday." He stood up tall and tried to peer over her shoulder. "Did you have a nice Thanksgiving?"

"Yes, thanks." She was thankful he'd been out of town and therefore hadn't tracked the fact she hadn't left her apartment and no one had come to visit her. All she wanted now was for him to go away, but she felt a stab of guilt for not knowing that he had a sister or that he'd been away. She glanced back at her dining room table, piled up with work. "I'd invite you in, but I'm working on a case and the files are spread all over the place. Maybe after the trial we can catch up."

He nodded. "That football player, right? Trial starts tomorrow?"

She shouldn't be surprised he knew. Everyone in Dallas was following the lead-up to Trevor's day in court as well as the team's playoff chances if Trevor was found not guilty and able to get back on the field before the regular season ended. "That's the one." She decided to take advantage of his touch on the pulse of the public. "What do you think our chances are?"

"Oh, I don't know. He seems like a good guy, but two dead girlfriends? Hard to ignore the facts."

Carly wanted to scream that he probably didn't know any of the facts, only the snippets he'd read in the paper, but since she wouldn't impress the jury by yelling at them, she practiced a calm, rational demeanor. "I know the prosecutor has tried her case in the papers, but we have facts of our own to introduce. We're just saving them for a jury. You'll hear all about it soon enough."

"I hope so. Would be nice to see the team have a good showing for once."

"We'll do everything we can to get Trevor back where he belongs."

"I should let you get back to it, then." He started to back away and then stopped. "There was a woman came by the other day, day before Thanksgiving. She stood at your door for a bit, but then she left. Didn't look like she knocked."

Carly perked up. "What did she look like?" Could it have been Landon? She hadn't seen Landon outside of the office since their trip to Austin, but the very idea she might have come by aroused all kinds of feelings.

"Not sure. Medium height and build. Had a hat on. One of these knit things with a ball on the end."

"A beanie?"

"Not sure what they're called, but her hair was all tucked up in it. She wasn't carrying anything, and she had gloves on. Leather, I think."

Carly resisted the urge to interrogate Mr. Jasper with questions about exactly what date and time the woman had come by. "Maybe she had the wrong address and figured it out before she knocked."

"Maybe," he allowed. "Whatever happened to that woman who came around before? She seemed very nice."

She wasn't fooled by his feigned innocence. He was talking about Landon, and apparently his curiosity was strong enough for him to reveal he'd been keeping tabs. What if it was Landon who'd come by this week? She'd be surprised if it was since they hadn't seen each other outside the office since their trip to Austin to meet with Mandy Hauser. Every interaction she'd had with Landon since had been purely business. No casual drop-ins to each other's offices, no foodie lunches, and definitely no kissing or touching of any kind.

The personal distance was exactly what she'd said she wanted, so she had little room for regret, but in the moments between projects while getting ready for Trevor's trial, she had plenty of misgivings. Not so much about getting involved with Landon in the first place, but of how abruptly she'd chosen to cut things off. But she hadn't had a choice. Had she? No way could she juggle the mountain of trial prep and its implications for her career with the smoldering draw of Landon's lips on hers. Her job was all she had, and Landon was a distraction designed to make her chuck everything she'd worked toward.

"She is nice, but she's just a colleague. She won't be coming back here again."

"That's too bad. You could use someone nice to keep you company."

After he left, she dove back into working on the voir dire questions for the jury panel, but the words swam on the page, and her attention was fractured. She blamed the distraction on her lack of sleep, but every nerve ending in her body knew her thoughts were focused not on the case, but on the attorney who'd be trying it with her. How was she going to make it through the next two weeks of trial with Landon sitting next to her, leaning in close to discuss strategy and working together to make decisions? She had no idea, but she had approximately twenty-four hours to figure it out.

❖

Landon was pushing the food around on her plate when her brother's voice boomed in her ear.

"If you don't like it just say so." Ian slumped into the chair next to her. "God knows the critic from the *Morning News* won't hold back, why should you?"

"I'm sorry. I'm sure everything is wonderful, but I'm just not hungry."

"Said no one at Sunday brunch ever." Ian snatched a piece of the maple-crusted bacon off her plate and held it like a cigar. "I was counting on you to tell me you can't live without this bacon. Have you seriously not even tried a bite?"

She'd been sitting in the back room at the Salt Block, surrounded by gourmet comfort food and witness files for the last few hours. Ian had paraded several new dishes into the room, but for the first time in her life, Landon didn't have an appetite for his amazing creations. She didn't have an appetite for much of anything and hadn't for a while. She'd attributed her malaise to the impending trial, but she knew this wasn't the same performance anxiety she usually experienced before a trial. She'd been a litigator long enough to know that once she was in the swing of things in front of a jury, excitement would outpace anxiety, and exhilaration would take over. No, her melancholy was a result of the solid wall Carly had erected between them. They still spoke, but it was all about the case. Their conversations always took place at the office, and each one was stiff and formal. At this point, Landon would take the more antagonistic exchanges they'd shared when they first met over the dry, apathetic interactions of the last couple of months.

Ian waved the bacon in her face. "Eat me. Please eat me," he said in a singsong voice.

"Stop it," she said, unable to suppress a grin at his antics. She grabbed it out of his hand and tore off a bite with her teeth. The bacon was crisp and rich, and salty sweet, and she couldn't hold back a slight moan. "Sweet and savory. I give it a ten on the brunch meter. I'm tasting a bit of smoke on the finish. Hickory?"

"Applewood. I thought it would go well with the maple."

"It does." She took another bite. Maybe she was hungry after all.

"So, you want to tell me what's wrong?"

"Nothing's wrong."

"You turned me down for Thanksgiving dinner, and now you're

barely eating bacon of all things. Something's definitely wrong, but if you don't want to tell me, that's cool."

She'd grabbed a plate from the hotel buffet on Thanksgiving Day and taken it back to her room. She assumed the food was good, but she'd barely eaten any of it. It had been a crummy day, but better than joining her mom and dad for lunch at Ian's and facing her father's probing questions about the case. "Really, it's nothing. Trial starts tomorrow. It's a big day." She kept her gaze trained on the bacon because he knew her well enough to see the lie in her eyes.

"Uh-huh." He folded his arms and nodded knowingly. "What are his chances?"

She flipped her palm up and down. "They have a decent case, but no smoking gun. Could go either way. I think it'll boil down to the kind of jury we get."

"What kind of evidence do you have?"

"Honestly? Not much. First off, it's not our job to present evidence, and even if it was, it's hard to prove a negative. He doesn't have a rock-solid alibi for the time of death, but their evidence is all circumstantial. No one saw him kill Vanessa Meyers or Jocelyn Aubrey, and there's no physical evidence to tie him to either crime scene other than fibers from a rope that's a pretty common brand."

"The rope thing sounds not great. Are you going to go all CSI on them?"

"Someone's been watching too much TV, but yes. Juries expect pretty sophisticated evidence from the prosecutor nowadays. The fact that Trevor had some rope in his garage that's the same brand doesn't prove anything on its own. Hell, you probably have some of the same brand at your house." Landon heard her voice rise and she took it down a notch. "Sorry about that. I might be a little passionate about the issue. I will admit, to you, the rope fibers will be more problematic if they manage to get in evidence that Jocelyn Aubrey was strangled with the same brand. The prosecutor will argue there are too many coincidences to deny Trevor's involvement in both cases." Landon gave silent thanks Carly was the one assigned to cross-examine the crime scene analyst and the motion to suppress the evidence gathered at the other crime scene.

"Is that all they have?"

"No, but the rest of the evidence is weak and incidental." Landon shifted into litigator mode. "Yes, Trevor dated Vanessa and Jocelyn. Yes, both woman were killed, but to say he's the killer because he was the only thing they had in common is a far cry from beyond a reasonable doubt."

"I see your point. Is there really no other connection between the two?"

"Nothing else other than the manner of death."

He swiped another piece of bacon. "But tell me more about the trial itself. Are you trying the case on your own?"

Exactly the topic Landon didn't want to discuss. She tried to shortcut the conversation. "No, Jane will be there."

"What about Carly? Wasn't she working on it too? You haven't mentioned her much in a while."

She hadn't mentioned her at all, and he knew that. Once Jane had successfully lobbied Judge Grafton for a quick trial date, she'd divvied up the work. Jane would pick the jury and handle the reputation witnesses, but she was leaving the rest to Landon and Carly. Landon would give the opening statement and cross-examine law enforcement, and Carly would cross the forensic witnesses and present closing argument for the defense. She and Carly had worked together on several pretrial motions, but their collaboration had consisted of sending drafts back and forth by email with little face-to-face time despite the fact their offices were only several feet apart. Jane had remarked several times on how seamlessly they seemed to be working together. If she only knew.

"There hasn't been anything to mention."

"Oh," he said, obviously surprised. "Both times I saw you together, I got a vibe there was something brewing."

"Maybe there was, but there isn't now." She admitted more than she'd intended to and prayed he'd let it go at that.

"What did she do?"

Landon sighed. She so didn't want to get into this with him, but Ian wouldn't simply let it go without some sort of explanation. "I think I misread the signals. She just wasn't that into me."

"Hmm." He frowned like there was something more he wanted to say. "If you want to talk about it, you know where to find me."

"Right here, Mr. Workaholic."

"You're one to talk."

Landon deflected the commentary by glancing at her phone. She needed to get a move on if she was going to make it to the office on time. She started shoving her papers into her briefcase. "I need to go. Rain check on another serving of that bacon?"

"Anytime, sis."

She was barely out of her seat when he scooped her up in a big hug. She allowed him to hold her for a moment, at first for his sake, and then because she actually needed the warmth and comfort of his strong embrace. "Love you," she mumbled.

"Love you too," he said and then leaned in closer. "You'll find the one. She's out there waiting for you. I promise."

"Thanks, bro." She eased out of his arms and started for the door.

"And for the record," he said.

"Yes?"

"I don't think you misread the signals."

She didn't reply, but he was right. The problem was what was she going to do about it?

❖

When Carly walked into the office, her hopes of grabbing a cup of tea and hiding out for a bit were quickly dashed. Jane, Landon, Trevor, Shelby, and several of the first-year associates were gathered in the glass-paneled large conference room, and based on the raised voices and exaggerated gestures, the discussion was heated.

She stopped in the doorway, but Trevor waved her in. "Hey, Carly, I'm so glad you're here. Maybe you can explain this." He pointed at the empty chair on his left, and she slipped into the seat, ignoring Shelby, who sat on his other side wearing pursed lips and what Carly had come to refer to as resting bitch face. Shelby's surly attitude didn't bother her since it didn't seem to have any impact on what Trevor thought about her. The good thing was she was as far from Landon as possible, and Carly would rather risk Shelby's annoyance than the lingering lure of Landon Holt.

Mr. Jasper's words had eaten at her all the way to the office. She wasn't lonely and she didn't need a nice woman to fill some void. And even if she was lonely and did want company, Landon couldn't be that person. After this trial, one of two things was going to happen. Landon would be her boss or she'd get the partnership, which meant Landon would go back to Austin. Neither one of those scenarios was a good foundation for a relationship.

She turned her attention to Trevor. "Explain what?"

"Shelby seems to think they can't try me here in Dallas for Jocelyn's murder, but you've been preparing to deal with evidence about it, so I assume it's going to come up."

It never ceased to amaze Carly how often defendants in a case simply didn't get all the angles, no matter how many times she explained them. She knew for a fact Jane and Landon had reviewed this very issue with Trevor last week. She shot a look at Jane, who nodded for her to take point, and then she looked around for a pad of paper. Like a mind reader, Landon pushed a legal pad and pen down the table toward her. As Carly said "thanks," she locked eyes with Landon. The look was long and intense, but Carly couldn't discern the message, choosing to believe it was only empathy for having to explain this subject again.

She drew three boxes on the pad, one centered over the other two. She wrote *Guilt/Innocence* in the box on top. "The guilt/innocence phase is the first part of the trial. The prosecutor won't be allowed to bring up Jocelyn's case during this phase for several reasons." She scrawled shorthand notes as she talked. "The most important ones for our purposes are that Dallas County doesn't have jurisdiction to charge you with a crime that happened somewhere else, and the rules of evidence don't allow the prosecution to use evidence of an uncharged crime to bolster their case. It would be like saying the more cases you're accused of, the more likely it is you're guilty. Got it?"

Trevor nodded slowly and pointed at the other boxes. "So what are those?"

Carly circled the word *Innocence*, drew an arrow to one of the boxes below, and wrote the word *Freedom*. "If the jury finds you not guilty, then you're free to go. A Houston DA could charge you with Jocelyn's murder, but you can bet they will consider what happened here in Dallas before they decide to pursue charges." She looked at Trevor as she said the words, but she was acutely conscious Landon was staring in her direction. Avoiding her gaze, Carly dropped her head, circled the word *Guilty*, and drew a line to the remaining empty box on the paper. She hesitated just a second, and then wrote *Punishment*.

"If the jury finds you guilty, then they will decide your punishment."

"Can't the judge decide?" Shelby asked.

Landon spoke up. "It's up to Trevor, but we have to decide whether to go to the judge or jury for punishment before the trial begins."

Carly turned to Trevor. "It's okay if you want to discuss the decision again, but we're all in agreement that it would be a bad idea to have Judge Grafton decide your punishment. She's a fair judge, but she's looking at a contested primary after the first of the year, and her fellow Democrats will eat her alive if she's perceived as going easy on a convicted murderer in a domestic violence case. If the jury finds you guilty, she's likely to give you the maximum to show she's strong on women's issues."

Trevor reached over and placed his hand on hers. "I trust you."

Carly shifted with discomfort but stopped just short of pushing his hand away. She got it. His entire life was on the line, and he was desperate to connect with the person who had answers, and she just happened to be that person. It should be Jane offering advice and explanations to their client, but this was another of the partnership tests, and she struggled to get through it. She squeezed his hand with what she hoped was an encouraging gesture and then extracted it gently under the guise of pulling the legal pad back toward her. Out of the corner of her eye, she saw Landon telegraph sympathy with a small sigh. Carly resisted the temptation to look too long in Landon's direction, and wrote the words *Aggravating Factors* next to the box labeled *Punishment*.

"If you're convicted, then we move to the punishment phase. We can call witnesses to provide mitigating evidence—to show why you should receive a sentence on the lower end of the scale—and the prosecution can present evidence to support aggravating factors. They will use that opportunity to say you killed or at least threatened Jocelyn." She paused to let her words sink in. "I understand that it feels weird to be planning to win at the same time as we're planning to lose, but if the jury finds you guilty, it's likely the sentencing phase could start the next day, and it's for your benefit that we need to be prepared."

"Contingencies. I get it." Trevor nodded vigorously. "You have to be ready to change course if the game isn't going your way."

"Exactly," Carly said, wishing she'd had the foresight to couch her words in gamespeak to begin with. "We have to be ready to run every play in the book." She delivered the words with a straight face, but she wanted to groan at the idea of equating the chess-like maneuvers of legal strategy with a game where the entire goal was to run a ball down a field.

They spent the rest of their session answering general questions about what to expect from jury selection and more general details about the trial. Carly was only too happy to let Jane and Landon take the lead on the rest, and when the meeting was finally over, she was the first one out of her chair.

"Carly?"

She turned back to face Trevor, who was fixated on her while everyone else was packing up their files. "Yes?"

"I imagine things are going to get pretty crazy starting tomorrow. I just wanted to say thank you for everything. No matter what happens, I know you have my back."

Her first instinct was to nod and get the hell out. Two more weeks. Once she was a partner in this firm, she wouldn't have to put on an act anymore. She could be her usual no-nonsense self and let her legal work speak for itself. In the meantime, she'd play whatever role necessary in order to get the job. "I do have your back, Trevor. We'll get through this together." She reached for his hand and gave it a tight squeeze. To her surprise, he pulled her into a hug. Over his shoulder, she locked looks with Shelby, whose eyes narrowed as the hug lingered on.

Finally, Carly slipped out of Trevor's arms. She avoided Shelby's hard stare and walked briskly toward her office. She could hear footfalls behind her, but she was desperate for a few moments alone after the intensity of the meeting. When she was almost at her door, she risked a look back. Landon stood a few feet away, leaning against the wall, staring in her direction with a hopeful expression. Carly glanced at her office door, wishing she could will herself to the other side. Instead she stood, rooted to the floor. "Yes?"

"You were great in there." Landon stepped closer as she said the words. "I couldn't have done better."

The air was thin and it got thinner as Landon came closer. Carly had been careful to avoid being alone with Landon since they'd returned from Austin, but the proximity threatened her resolve. "Just doing my job."

"About that, can we talk?"

Carly didn't know a way out. This was the first time Landon had approached her in a while. "About the case?"

Landon paused briefly before answering. "Sure. About the case."

Carly waved Landon into her office and shut the door behind them. She walked around behind her desk, the heavy wooden furniture a barrier to keep her from giving in to what she wanted. Landon settled in the chair across from her but didn't say anything. The silence was loud.

"You wanted to talk about the case?"

"This isn't working." Landon leaned forward. "I kissed you, and you kissed me back. I thought it was pretty amazing, and based on your reaction, I thought you felt the same. I'm willing to accept I was wrong, but I can't sit next to you for the next two weeks and make decisions with you in a murder case unless we clear the air between us."

"Oh, thank God." Carly breathed deep, trying to ignore the sharp shot of arousal she'd felt when Landon said the kiss was amazing. It had been amazing, and that was the problem. Amazing was distracting. Amazing kisses led to crappy litigation. Maybe when the case was over, there would be time for amazing. The thought barely formed before she remembered what would really happen when the case was over. One of them would win, and one of them would lose. One of them would stay, and one of them would go. But no matter what happened, kisses— amazing or not—weren't in their future.

Landon stood. "So we're good?"

"We're good." They were anything but good, but they were at least at a place where Carly could focus on the trial and nothing else. She watched Landon walk out of the room and stifled the urge to call her back. She'd gotten what she'd convinced herself she wanted. Why did it suddenly feel like she'd lost so much more?

CHAPTER SEVENTEEN

Landon looked out over the sea of faces in the courtroom. She sat between Jane and Carly at the defense counsel table, facing the gallery where the jury panel was assembled. Trevor was seated on the other side of Carly, but his presence was superfluous at this point since this part of the process was pure legal hocus-pocus. Shelby had angled to be present in the room, but Jane had gently informed her that there wasn't room for visitors during jury selection and she'd have to wait outside.

Judge Grafton had ordered double the usual number of jurors for a felony case, which was a good thing since a bunch of them were saying anything they could think of to get out of serving on a high-profile case. Hardly anyone could claim an excuse for not being available the length of the trial, since it wasn't expected to last more than two weeks. Texas was quick to justice in criminal trials. But plenty of the potential jurors labored under the assumption they could simply state that they loved or hated football and get tossed from the panel. Grafton had spent the morning dispelling them of that notion before she'd turned the questioning, or voir dire, over to the attorneys.

The prosecutor, Donna Wilhelm, hadn't been particularly impressive. She was an old-school workhorse when it came to questioning the panel, and she didn't employ any fancy tricks or attempts to sell the panel on the merits of the case. She merely went through her checklist of questions and did her best to get the jurors to open up and talk about their feelings.

Jane on the other hand, was a master. She managed to get most of the panel to engage in debate and conversation with each other, an expert move to keep them from feeling like they were being interrogated. By the time she was done, Landon and Carly had amassed pages of notes on almost everyone in the room.

Judge Grafton explained to the jurors they would be taking a short recess and they should plan to be back outside the courtroom in thirty minutes. It was a guess since there was no telling how long the rest of the process would take.

Landon, along with Jane, Carly, and the other attorneys, stood while the bailiff escorted the last panel member from the courtroom.

"Counsel," Judge Grafton said. "Does anyone have any challenges for cause?"

Donna spoke first. "Yes, Judge. Jurors number seven and twenty both expressed doubts they could be impartial based on their strong and abiding love of all things related to the Dallas Cowboys. Number seven even had his car custom painted to match the team's colors."

"That's crazy. Neither one of them said they couldn't be impartial."

Landon felt a hand on her arm and looked back at Carly sending cautionary signals with her eyebrows. "Respectfully, Your Honor, neither one of those professed fans definitely stated they couldn't be impartial when you questioned them further."

Grafton nodded. "It's true, Ms. Wilhelm, both jurors said they could set aside their fandom and decide this case on the merits. Absent any evidence to the contrary, I'm going to take them at their word. Anything else?"

Donna shook her head, but Landon spied Carly whispering in Jane's ear.

"Just one more, Your Honor," Jane said. "Juror number six listed on her questionnaire that she has been or knows someone who has been the victim of domestic abuse, but when I asked the same question during voir dire, the juror didn't raise her hand. Out of respect, we didn't pursue the matter in front of the entire panel, but we'd like the opportunity to ask her some questions."

"Very well." Judge Grafton signaled to the bailiff and asked him to bring juror number six back into the courtroom.

While they were waiting, Jane made a few notes and thanked Carly for making the catch. "Last thing we need is a sleeper on the jury." Carly shrugged off the compliment, but Landon took note. She was going to have to step up her game.

The rear door opened, and the bailiff entered with a petite African American woman who looked like she'd rather be anywhere else. Judge Grafton waved her up to the bench, and both sets of attorneys gathered around. "I noticed on your questionnaire that you checked yes to question eight," Grafton said, motioning for the bailiff to hand the juror a copy of the document. "The attorneys may have some questions for you about your response. Ms. Sturges?"

To Landon's surprise, Jane stepped back. "Ms. Pachett is going to take the lead on this."

Carly's eyes widened, and for a second it looked like she wanted to dash out the door, but when it became clear Jane wasn't kidding, she moved forward. "Just a couple of questions, Your Honor." She turned to face the juror. "Mrs. Franklin, were you referring to yourself or another person when you answered yes to the question about domestic abuse?"

"It was my sister," Mrs. Franklin replied, her voice barely above a whisper.

"And are you personally acquainted with the facts..." Carly stuttered and stopped, and she cleared her throat. "Tell us what happened to your sister."

"Her boyfriend beat her bad enough to send her to the hospital. He lost a bet on the Super Bowl last year."

"I'm sorry to hear that. Is she okay now?" Carly asked.

"Bruises are gone and bones are healed, but she'll never be okay again."

"And I imagine since you're her sister, you helped care for her while she was healing."

"I did."

"And how did what happened to her affect you?"

Mrs. Franklin looked confused for a moment, like no one had ever thought to ask her about her feelings. "Truth be told, it scared me. Vida is a strong woman, but she was no match for that man's anger."

"Do you think what happened to her would prevent you from keeping an open mind about this case?"

Mrs. Franklin nodded slowly. "It might." The nodding got more vigorous. "Yes, I think it would."

Donna rolled her eyes, and Landon could tell Donna thought Mrs. Franklin had just figured out the get out of jury duty pass. "That's all from me, Judge," Carly said.

"Mrs. Franklin, is there a reason you didn't raise your hand earlier when I asked, or when these other attorneys asked about this very issue?" Donna asked.

"I didn't want to make a big deal out of it. The judge had just told us how important jury duty is, and I wanted to do my part."

Donna smiled. "I understand. It sounds like you're willing to follow whatever instructions Judge Grafton gives, is that right?"

"Yes, ma'am."

"So if she tells you to put aside your personal experience and decide this case based only on what you hear in the courtroom during trial and nothing else, you will follow that instruction?"

"Of course." Mrs. Franklin looked at the judge as if for approval.

"Thank you for your honesty," Donna said. "Judge, the state has no issues with Mrs. Franklin's ability to serve on this jury."

Smooth, Landon thought. She watched Carly closely to see how she would respond. "Your Honor, I have just one more question." Grafton nodded, and Carly moved one step closer to Franklin. "I have no doubt you would make a diligent and fair juror under normal circumstances, but it's my job to make sure that my client starts this trial with a level playing field. Now I know the prosecutor and the judge have told you that if you are on the jury you will have to follow the judge's instructions to set aside any personal feelings you might have and decide this case only on the facts, but that's when you're already on the jury. But if you think there's any chance what happened to your sister might impair your ability to be fair, now is the time to tell us."

Mrs. Franklin's eyes welled with tears, and Landon thought she might start weeping right there in the courtroom, but she didn't. She did say, "Lord help me, I don't think I can be fair to that man."

The judge thanked her for her honesty and dismissed her from the courtroom. Donna barely waited until the doors shut behind her before starting in on Carly. "What was that?" She turned back to the bench. "Judge, she was clearly leading that woman into a way out of jury duty."

"Respectfully, Your Honor, that couldn't be further from the truth," Carly said, offended at the accusation. "We all had a right to know more, to dig a little deeper. Mrs. Franklin had already demonstrated that she was willing to serve or she would have made a bigger deal out of her experience during our questioning of the panel. Ms. Wilhelm's just lucky she didn't bring it up then, or I bet we'd have even more jurors digging through past experiences for a way out. But being willing to serve doesn't mean you get a free pass to sit in judgment when other factors point to an inability to set aside prejudice."

"I'm inclined to agree with you, Ms. Pachett." Grafton picked up her pen and made a note. "I'm removing juror number six for cause. She'll be dismissed when the rest of the panel goes. Is thirty minutes long enough for you to make your picks?"

They all agreed, and Judge Grafton and her court reporter left through the door behind the bench. The moment the door shut behind them, Donna motioned to her trial partner, Ed Barnes. "We'll take the jury room," she said. Without waiting for an answer, they took off toward the door in the front of the courtroom, by the jury box.

"Where are we supposed to go?" Landon asked.

"We usually stay in the courtroom," Carly said. "This won't take long." She sat back down at the defense table and spread out her notes. "Let's start with the first row."

Landon looked around, not keen on discussing which jurors they were going to strike in front of courthouse personnel, but the courtroom was fairly empty with the exception of the bailiff, who was busy helping other attorneys on the docket locate prisoners in the holdover. She slid into the seat next to Carly and set her notes on the table. Jane and Trevor sat on the end.

Everyone called it "picking" a jury, but the people they "picked" were the ones they wanted to eliminate. Each side could strike ten jurors, but they did so blind, which meant they could foreseeably strike the same jurors as their opponents, effectively wasting a strike. It happened, but not a lot. Most of the time, they tried to anticipate which jurors the other side would want and strike those. The common result was that they wound up with a jury comprised of individuals neither side had engaged with much during voir dire, and therefore, didn't know much about. The whole process was a gamble, but Landon had learned to trust her gut.

Carly's method looked a lot more intense. She was hunched over a cram-packed, color-coded chart full of symbols and abbreviations. Landon squinted as she tried to decipher the information. If a bus hit Carly, they'd be hard-pressed to figure out anything about her method.

Carly looked up from her hieroglyphics and smiled. "Don't try to understand, just trust that I know what I'm doing." She pointed at the first square. "Juror number one. Mr. Bailey. No ties to law enforcement. A once in a while sports fan. He's an engineer and his wife's a CPA—both professions high on facts and low on emotion. He'll want solid evidence from the prosecution, not wishy-washy emotions. Answered no to all the questions about whether he knows anyone who's been the victim of domestic abuse which probably means no one confides in him or he tends not to believe such stories. Didn't have a lot to say. I say he's a keeper for us."

"Wow," Trevor said. "You got all that from what went on in here? I could barely keep up with what everyone was saying, it went so fast."

Landon was impressed too, but she tempered her response. She was more of a feelings than facts person when it came to jury selection, but she couldn't argue with Carly's logic. What she could do was assert her own acumen before Carly stole the show. "I agree, but at this rate, we're not going to finish in time. How about we all write down the ten jurors we'd each strike, and see which ones we have in common, and then discuss the rest?"

After a few minutes of tallying their individual responses, they managed to agree on a list of ten strikes. Carly filled out the strike list and handed it to the bailiff with five minutes to spare. Landon decided to make a quick run to the restroom. When she walked through the double doors at the back of the courtroom, she ran into Shelby, who was pressed up against the window, looking into the courtroom.

"Hi, Shelby."

"Hey. Can I go in now? I know you said there wouldn't be room, but it's practically empty in there now."

"The jurors will be back in a few minutes. We're almost done with this part. When opening statements start, you can grab a seat. I'll make sure and save you one in the first row."

"You're a sweetheart." Shelby pointed back toward the courtroom. "Do you know what they're talking about?"

Landon followed her gesture and peered through the window. Trevor and Carly were sitting super close with their heads together, both looking down at the table. Landon assumed they were both reading something, but in a different environment, it looked like two young lovers, snuggling close. She made a mental note to mention how it looked to Carly, but she knew her reaction was about more than just appearances. She felt a stab of jealousy at their closeness, and not because they might be talking about the case without her, but because she wanted to be sitting where Trevor was. "Probably talking about the case. We'll start opening statements after lunch."

"You're doing that part, right?"

"Yes." Landon was still sore about it. She thought she was much better suited for closing since that was the more on the fly part of the trial, tying up all the loose ends that had come up during testimony into a pretty package designed to sway the jury to their side. She'd argued the same to Jane.

"Carly would be perfect for opening. She makes intricate outlines and she's excellent at delivering facts."

"And you're not?"

"I think my skills would be wasted on opening."

"And I think it's a good idea to mix things up a bit. If each of you only plays to your strengths, how am I supposed to judge how flexible you can be?"

Landon had started to say a high-profile case wasn't the right venue for "mixing things up," but she risked Jane kicking one of them off the case if she pushed too hard. She'd deliver the most incredible opening statement ever, but she didn't have to be happy about it.

"How long?"

Landon stared at Shelby, certain she'd missed a piece of the conversation. "What?"

"How long until things get started?"

"Probably another forty-five minutes. The judge will call the panel back in, and they'll seat the jury and swear them in. The prosecutor will read the Indictment, and the judge will ask for Trevor's plea." Landon looked at her watch. "She'll probably break for lunch, and we'll start back up with opening statements after."

"Do you need Trevor at lunch?"

"No." Landon hoped she hadn't answered too emphatically, but having a client tag along during trial breaks got tiring real fast. "If you need to talk to him, that would be a perfect time." Several jurors walked past them on their way back into the courtroom. "I should get back in there. Wait out here. We shouldn't be too long."

Jane and Carly had already switched the chairs back so they were facing the front of the courtroom, but they were standing in front of the table, and they would remain there while the jury panel filed in. Trevor and Jane had moved to the side and were engaged in a whispered conversation, so Landon took the opportunity to talk to Carly. "Great job on Mrs. Franklin."

"Thanks. Of course, who knows how many other Mrs. Franklins there were in the panel who weren't honest with us."

"True, but we can only do what we can do." Landon considered her next words carefully. "Hey, so I was just in the back of the room and happened to look up and see you talking to Trevor." She cleared her throat. Now that she'd started talking, she wondered if she was making a big deal out of nothing. "If I were a stranger, seeing you two for the first time, I might think there was something going on."

Carly's expression was puzzled at first, but then she snorted a laugh. "You're kidding, right?"

"Uh, not really, no. Like I said, I know you didn't mean anything by it, but you were sitting awfully close and you were smiling..." As she played the words back in her head, she realized how lame she sounded, and judging by the fierce look on Carly's face, she felt the same. She didn't have to wait long to find out.

"If I want advice on how to act during trial, I'll ask for it, but you can be sure I won't be asking you. You've been flirting with Shelby Cross since the moment you met her. For all I know you're kissing up to her so she'll put in a good word with Jane. I wasn't flirting with Trevor, but if I was, I'd be justified in trying to level the playing field."

"Is that so?"

"Yes."

The mass of jurors started to file into the room, bringing an abrupt end to their rift. Landon stored up all kinds of possible comebacks, but she was wasting valuable brain space she'd need to deliver an edge-of-your-seat opening designed to capture the hearts and minds of the jury from the first moments of trial. Carly might not believe she'd been trying to be helpful, but at this point all bets were off. Landon had two goals—win this trial and become partner—but she'd have to find a way to stop wanting Carly or she'd lose both.

❖

"The evidence will show that Trevor Kincade had both the opportunity to kill Vanessa Meyers and the motive to do so."

Carly suppressed the urge to count how many times Donna's trial partner Ed had used the phrase, "the evidence will show." It was classic opening statement language if you were in law school doing a mock trial, but there were so many other ways to stick to the facts without reminding the jury every few seconds that you were bound by them.

Ed droned on for a while before finally taking his seat. As boring as he'd been, Carly's stomach was in knots after the one-sided recitation of the strikes against Trevor. She always felt this way in trial, which was one of the reasons she preferred the no drama landscape of appellate work where instead of anxious clients and fact hungry jurors, it was just her, the law, and the paper record.

She glanced over at Landon, who had avoided her during lunch under the guise of going over her notes. When Ed finished, it would be up to Landon to divert the jury's attention back to their side, and Carly could see her morphing into litigator mode. Landon looked every bit the high-powered lawyer in a sharply tailored navy suit with a crisp white shirt, and Carly experienced a surge of pride they were on the same side.

Landon waited until Ed had taken his seat before standing and striding over to the jury box. She thanked them for their service and launched right into her opening. "What Mr. Barnes just described to you is horrifying." Landon walked the few steps to the witness stand, where Ed had conveniently left a framed eleven-by-seventeen photo of Vanessa Meyers, looking happy and very much alive. Landon paused for a moment in front of the photo and then lifted it from the easel. She held the portrait in front of the jurors. "What happened to Vanessa Meyers was a tragedy, and that tragedy has lingered since her death, altering forever the lives of the family and loved ones she left behind.

"You heard Mr. Barnes recite a litany of things he promised the evidence would show. As you can imagine, we have a different list, and I will share it with you." As Landon spoke, she walked over to the side of the jury box and gently propped the photo of Vanessa out of sight. Without missing a beat, she returned to the defense table and placed a hand on Trevor's shoulder. "But first I'd like to talk to you about something I bet you all can relate to. Getting blamed for something you didn't do. Whether it's big or small, we have a story that starts off with 'they said I did something, but they were mistaken.' You can all relate to that, right?" She nodded and at least half of the jury nodded with her. "Maybe you were in the wrong place at the wrong time. Perhaps you had a reputation in college for being the party guy or girl—a preconception you could never seem to shake. Can you imagine if those preconceptions were magnified on an enormous scale, and no matter who you really were, everyone defined you by what they thought was the truth without taking the time to figure out you aren't the kind of person who could do the thing you've been accused of doing?"

Landon continued in this vein, setting the tone for reasonable doubt before moving on to challenge Eddie's litany of evidence. By the time she sat back down, Carly was captivated and could tell by their rapt attention, the jury was as well. Judge Grafton looked at the clock on the wall and asked Donna who they planned to call as their first witness. When Donna replied she planned to call the lead detective on the case, Leon Royal, the judge nodded in thought.

"It's almost five, and the State's witness will likely be on the stand for a while. I'm calling a recess until tomorrow morning and we'll start fresh then." She spent a few minutes explaining to the jurors that they were not allowed to talk to anyone about the case or read or watch any news coverage. Carly stood with the rest of the attorneys as the jurors filed out of the room.

"Is it a good thing that she cut things short today?" Trevor whispered in her ear as the last juror filed out of the room.

"It doesn't mean anything, really," Carly replied. "Royal's testimony will probably run longer than anyone else, and it's easier to do it all in one day than figure out the best place to break it up."

"Are you busy tonight?"

"What?" His question had caught her off guard. Carly scrambled for a response. "We'll probably spend most nights during the trial preparing for the next day."

"But I thought Landon was going to cross-examine the detective? I was hoping we could talk, maybe over dinner. Nothing big, but it would help alleviate my stress to get a play-by-play of how you think things will go."

Carly spotted Jane, who was standing behind Trevor, mouthing "say yes." Not what she wanted to hear. Trevor was a nice guy, but she had more important work to do than babysit a worried client, not to mention she was getting an inappropriate vibe from all the extra attention he'd been sending her way. Then again, if babysitting Trevor was the path to partnership, maybe it was a small price to pay. "Okay."

"Sounds good. I'll text you for the address and pick you up at seven."

"Trevor, we should get going." Shelby tugged him out of the courtroom with Jane close behind.

Carly watched them go, lingering behind with Landon. "I think I'll wait here a minute and let them hog the press. Great job on the opening, by the way."

"Thanks. That was the easy part. Now we just have to wait and hear what the witnesses say when they get on the stand." Landon pointed to where Jane, Shelby, and Trevor were exiting the courtroom. "What was that all about?"

"What?"

"Are you really having dinner with Trevor?"

Landon's tone made it clear she thought it was a bad idea. Carly agreed and had already started thinking of ways to get out of it but wasn't about to say so in the face of Landon's patronizing attitude. "He wants to talk about the case and feels comfortable with me."

"As long as that's all he's feeling."

Landon muttered the words, barely loud enough for Carly to hear. "I thought we agreed to get along?"

"We did. During trial. But you cozying up to the client after hours is a whole new ball game."

"Are you trying to be clever?" Carly steamed at Landon's characterization and wondered if she was imagining the undercurrent of jealously in Landon's tone. Was she jealous of her relationship with Trevor or the advantage it gave her on the job? Whatever the source, Carly was determined not to let it distract her. "I guess you thought agreeing to get along meant I was going to roll over and let you have this partnership. I can't help it if our mutual client decided to bond with me, but you can bet I'm not going to tank my chance at the prize by blowing him off. If Trevor does wind up taking the stand, which of us do you think Jane is going to pick to take the lead? Why don't you focus on your own trial prep and let me handle mine?"

Carly didn't wait for an answer before stalking out of the courtroom. She stopped before she hit the doors and arranged her expression into a look that she hoped conveyed confidence in case she ran into jurors, the press, or any law enforcement scheduled to testify the next day. She should be wearing the game face twenty-four seven during this trial. Why was it just a few words from Landon always seemed to crumble her defenses?

CHAPTER EIGHTEEN

Landon watched Carly go, torn between wanting to chase after her and wanting to restore her own dignity. She took her time, gathering the rest of the files, but before she left the courtroom, Landon walked over to where she'd left the photo of Vanessa Meyers and turned it over.

Vanessa was pretty, not bombshell beautiful, but definitely attractive. Tall, slender, with brunette waves of hair and deep chocolate brown eyes, she would catch anyone's attention. But there were plenty of other women who looked like her, which was exactly what had been bugging Landon since the moment she'd seen the picture propped up on the easel in the witness box.

"Hey, Landon, everything okay?"

She turned to see Skye standing a few feet behind her. "Yes... Maybe." She motioned Skye over to where she'd assembled the files and handed her a stack. "Help me find the file on Jocelyn Aubrey. It's one of these." She flipped through her bunch, wishing she'd been more organized, but she'd focused all her attention the day before on preparing her opening statement and her cross-examination of Detective Royal.

Skye handed her a file. "Here you go. What're you looking for?"

Landon scanned the contents, growing increasingly frustrated. Finally, she found the slip of paper at the back of the file. She hadn't really needed it as evidence, but she'd had Skye get it from Mandy anyway. She picked it up and shoved it at Skye. "Who does she look like?"

Skye studied the color photo on the piece of paper, and then looked over at the photo of Vanessa that Landon had been studying. "He definitely has a type. Pretty, brunette, kind of all-American."

"And who else do we know that fits this description?" She jabbed a finger at the photo in Skye's hand, willing her to see.

It didn't take long. "You're right. There's definitely a resemblance. Do you think that's why he's always deferring to Carly like she's the lead attorney?"

"I think his attention goes beyond lawyering. He asked Carly to dinner tonight. Carly tried to pass it off like he just wanted to talk about trial prep, but…" Landon glanced around. The courtroom was empty, and the bailiff was in the holdover closing out the jail roster for the day, but she couldn't risk speaking her fears out loud.

"How about I help you carry this stuff to your car?" Skye asked, reading her mind.

Landon led the way, moving briskly through the courthouse. When they finally reached her car, she opened the trunk and shoved the files inside, and she and Skye sat in the front seat to finish their conversation.

"You're worried about Trevor's interest in Carly?" Skye asked.

"I don't know. Yes. Maybe. Feel free to tell me I'm overreacting," Landon said. She watched Skye's face for some signal that she was worrying over nothing, but all she got was typical cop poker face. "You're not helping."

"I'm thinking. My gut tells me there's something off about Trevor, but I can't put my finger on it. He doesn't exhibit a lot of the classic signs of a domestic abuser, but two dead bodies are pretty hard to dismiss."

"You're not making me feel better."

"Something going on between you two?" Skye asked.

Landon's first impulse was to feign ignorance, but if she wanted Skye's help, she should level with her, but considering the way things kept exploding between them, she didn't really know what to say. "All I know is that Jane has Carly and me competing for a partnership slot, and I think Carly agreed to have dinner with Trevor so she can get a leg up in the competition. I'd just hate for her to get hurt. That's not the way I want to win."

"Uh-huh." Skye narrowed her eyes, but she didn't pick apart Landon's explanation. "Would it make you feel better if I scouted out their date? Just make sure nothing weird is going on?"

Landon considered the offer. Carly would be pissed if she thought Landon was having her followed. She'd think it was because Landon was trying to gain an advantage. She probably wouldn't speak to her for days, but the thought of something happening to Carly because she didn't speak up was too horrible to conceive. She made the only decision any rational woman who had a completely irrational crush on her rival would do. "Yes, please."

❖

Carly stopped at the office long enough to dump some files and pick up new ones before taking off to her apartment. She didn't see Landon while she was there and was annoyed that she cared enough to wonder where Landon was and what she was doing. How dare Landon act like her dinner with Trevor was a date. Did Landon really think she would stoop so low as to flirt with the client to gain an advantage?

Of course, she'd thought the same thing about Landon several times when she'd seen her engaged in whispered conversations with Shelby Cross. Maybe it was just that Jane's whole idea of pitting them against each other when they were supposed to be working toward the same goal was stupid. There might only be one partnership, but making the legal work a zero-sum game wasn't logical and it certainly wasn't in Trevor's best interest.

Trevor. She never should've agreed to go to dinner with him. He only had one of two goals in mind: having an actual date or taking the opportunity to pepper her with questions about the case. She had no interest in either, and if they were seen alone in public together, the press would speculate that he'd moved on to his next catch. But she didn't want to meet him at her place and no way was she going to his house because she'd never get away. She should've told him no to begin with and avoided this silly mental exercise about how to escape her client.

What would Landon do, besides making the right decision in the first place? The answer came quickly. Landon would pick up the phone, call Trevor, and tell him the truth, or some version of it designed to leave Trevor feeling good about himself and supportive of her decision not to join him for dinner.

Carly waited until she got home to make the call. The phone rang five times and she was about to hang up when a woman's voice came on the line. "Hello?"

Carly held the phone out and stared at the screen to make sure she'd dialed Trevor's cell. She had. "Hi, I'm trying to reach Trevor Kincade."

"Who is this?"

Not a lot of words, but enough for Carly to figure out exactly who she was talking to. "Shelby, is that you? It's Carly." She hoped hearing her name wouldn't drive Shelby to hang up.

"Hello, Carly. Can I help you with something?"

"Actually, I thought I was calling Trevor's number. Is he there?" She knew she'd dialed the correct number, but Shelby's micromanaging was starting to get on her nerves.

"He's busy right now, but I'll let him know you called."

Enough of this mean girl shit. Carly put some steel behind her response. "Actually, I need to talk to him now. It's important."

"Yeah, okay. I'll get him."

Carly heard footsteps and muffled voices. A few moments later, Trevor's voice greeted her. "Hey, Carly. Did you decide where you want to have dinner?"

A small part of her wanted to keep her dinner date with him just to piss Shelby off, but she fought the urge. "About that. There were a ton of press at the courthouse today, and I don't think it's a good idea for us to be seen together or for me to be seen coming over to your house in a way that might be misconstrued." She rushed on, hoping to keep him from coming up with some solution. "I want to answer all your questions. How about we have lunch together tomorrow? Detective Royal will be in the middle of testifying and I'm sure you'll have a ton of questions. I'll be all yours then." She grimaced at her last words. She was walking the line between lawyer and perceived fangirl.

"I'm pretty disappointed, but if you absolutely promise about tomorrow."

"I promise."

"And what about after the trial? No one will be watching then, and we can do anything we want, right?"

There it was—proof she hadn't imagined that Trevor's interest was personal, not professional. Carly wondered if she was imagining the creepy undercurrent or if she'd induced it. Hating herself for it, she took the easy way out and hoped that by the time the trial was over, he'd have moved on. "You bet."

Happy to have the evening free to prepare for trial, Carly spread her witness files out on the dining room table and plunged in. Detective Royal would be on the stand for the better part of the day, but there was a good chance Donna would have time left to bring in the medical examiner, and Carly wanted to be sure she was prepared.

If there was any way to knock him off his presumed time of death, she had to find it. Trevor had been in town at the time the neighbor heard arguing, although he hadn't been spotted around the house that day, but he'd ridden with a few other team members to College Station that week. They'd stayed overnight and met with an alumni group for a school fundraiser. She needed to create enough uncertainty about the time of death to give the jury a reason to doubt Trevor's involvement.

After an hour of scouring the file for the dozenth time, her stomach growled, reminding her the only thing she'd eaten since breakfast had been a PowerBar. She didn't have to look in the fridge to know there was no food, and she pulled up the Uber Eats app on her phone and ordered all her favorites from Royal Thai. Seeing the Uber logo made her think of Landon and the day they'd gone to the game. Except for running into Shelby and Landon's father, everything about that day had been perfect—meeting Ian, making nachos, sharing the entire experience with Landon. It had all seemed so easy, so normal, and so not what she was used to.

And then the kiss happened. Stoked by days of anticipation and loads of resistance, it had been perfection. If Jane hadn't called demanding they come back to the office, she and Landon would have been undressed and in Landon's bed within moments of that soul-shattering kiss. Just thinking about Landon, naked, slick, and ready, sent waves of arousal coursing through her, but the vision stopped there. What would have happened if they had succumbed to their attraction? How would they be able to continue this race to the top if reaching the summit meant leaving the other one behind?

Funny how just a taste of what it was like to have a social life, to focus on something besides work and a promotion, had such a powerful pull. She'd convinced herself she'd done the right thing by pushing Landon away, but the memory of how she'd felt in Landon's arms shadowed every thought and threatened to derail her still.

❖

Landon answered her cell on the first ring when she saw Skye's name flash across the screen. "Hey, what's the story?"

"Not much to report. Trevor must've picked her up before I could get over there. Her car's in the parking lot of her complex, but I don't know where they went. I made the rounds of his usual haunts, but he's not there. I called his house, but the woman who answered the phone—I think it was Shelby—said he wasn't home."

"What do you mean? You don't know where they went?" Landon tried not to sound as exasperated as she felt, but she wasn't succeeding.

"They had a pretty big head start. I'm good, but I'm not magic."

"Sorry. I know."

"I could knock on her door. Maybe they decided to bail and she stayed in."

Landon rolled the idea around in her head. Carly would know something was up if Skye knocked on her door. Even if Carly wasn't home, her nosy neighbor would probably report she'd been there. She tried to come up with a plausible reason for Skye to drop by, but everything she thought of could be handled with a simple phone call. Unless…

"No. Don't go over there, but if you get any news about Trevor, shoot me a text."

"Will do."

Landon walked over to the mirror and did a quick appraisal. She'd shed her suit the minute she'd walked through the door of the condo and put on her favorite pair of old jeans and a UT sweatshirt—perfect clothes considering her big plans for the evening had centered around takeout and trial prep. She considered changing, but the super-casual attire would be part of her cover. Before she could rethink her hastily made plan, she shoved her phone in her pocket, scooped up her keys, and headed out the door.

Light shone through the window of Carly's apartment, but that didn't necessarily mean she was home. As she approached the door, she spotted a young guy in jeans, sneakers, and a hoodie approaching Carly's door. He stopped to check a piece of paper, and then raised his hand to knock.

"Hey," she called out to him in a loud whisper. When he turned toward her, she crooked a finger, motioning him over, thinking fast. "Is that my order?"

"You Carly Pachett?"

"Yep," she said without hesitating. She reached for the cash in her pocket. "How much?"

He looked at the cash like he was trying to make up his mind about something, then he shook his head. "Says it was charged to the credit card on file."

"Cool." Landon reached for the bag and pressed a twenty-dollar bill into his hand, hoping the tip was big enough to smooth over any trouble he might get in for giving the food to the wrong person. "Have a good night." She waited until he was out of sight before stepping closer to the door. Hoping she wasn't making a huge mistake, she knocked and held up the bag to the door viewer.

The door swung open and Carly said, "Thanks for getting here so fast. I was about to starve to—"

Her words skidded to a halt, and Landon held the bag out toward her. "Peace offering?"

Carly shook her head slowly. "I don't think you get how peace offerings work. I believe that's the dinner I already paid to have delivered to me. Not sure how you got your hands on it, but it's not going to make up for you being an ass at the courthouse."

Landon leaned against the doorframe. "I get it. And I apologize for being an ass, but I would like to make peace, and there's something important I want to talk to you about." She glanced back at the nosy neighbor's door. "Can I come in?"

"He's not home," Carly said. "You can say whatever you have to say right here."

Landon shifted from one foot to the other. She didn't know how Carly was going to react to her theory about Trevor, and she wasn't interested in being yelled at in front of Carly's other neighbors. "Please?"

Carly waved her in with a sigh, but she didn't offer her a seat. Landon fished around for the right way to voice her suspicions about

Trevor. "I'm sorry I made a scene at the courthouse. I have no business telling you what you can and cannot do, but when Trevor asked you out, I—"

"You were right."

"Pardon me?" Landon genuinely wondered if she'd heard Carly correctly.

"You were right. I was about to go against my better instincts and have dinner with Trevor because I thought keeping the client happy might buy me some mileage in this partnership race, but I decided against it. It wouldn't do for him to be seen with a woman alone while he stands accused of killing his girlfriend, even if that woman is one of his lawyers. Besides, I have no interest in spending my personal time with Trevor Kincade."

Landon wanted to ask Carly who she did have interest in spending her personal time with but refrained. "And he was okay with that?"

"He was the perfect gentleman."

Suddenly, Landon's suspicions about Trevor setting his sights on Carly as his next victim seemed silly. More likely than not, fueled by jealousy, she'd let her imagination run away from her. "I'm glad."

"Are you hungry?"

"Starving."

"Good, because I ordered enough for six. Never let me loose with a menu when I haven't eaten all day."

"Duly noted." She followed Carly to the table. "Looks like we're having trial with a side of Thai. The first part doesn't sound too appetizing, but whatever's in this bag is making my mouth water." The smell of food wasn't the only thing whetting her appetite. Carly was wearing tights that hugged her well-toned legs and an oversized T-shirt that hung off one shoulder. Her hair was wild, like she'd been running her hands through it, and all Landon could think about was doing the same.

"Don't just stand there," Carly said. "Grab a couple of plates out of the cabinet on the far left, and I'll get these files out of the way."

"We could talk about the case over food if you want," Landon said, hoping Carly wouldn't take her up on it. She reached into the cabinet and selected two midnight blue dinner plates. "Where's the silverware?"

"Not a chopstick person?"

"Not when I'm really hungry."

Carly grinned. "Me neither. And I don't know about you, but I could use a little break from the Trevor Kincade show."

Landon walked the plates over to the table and wondered if she should press the point or just let Carly's comment go. She decided on the latter and started opening the boxes of food. "This looks like pad kee mow. What are these?"

"Crab Rangoon. Best I've ever had with the exception of a restaurant I know in Palm Springs."

"Palm Springs, huh? I thought you weren't big on travel?"

"Bar conference. After two days of hotel food, I wandered onto the strip to find something besides the obligatory chicken breast on rice and found this Thai place called Peppers. I didn't have time to see anything else on the trip, but by the time I flew back to Dallas, the waiter knew my name and favorite order. I feel a little guilty for never having gone back."

"I love Palm Springs." Landon stopped shy of offering to take Carly there and show her something besides the Thai restaurant. Instead she dipped a piece of Rangoon in the sweet chili sauce and took a bite. "Holy Hannah, this is incredible."

"I know, right?"

Carly reached over and brushed the corner of Landon's mouth with her fingertip. "Don't want to waste the sauce," Carly said, her voice low and sexy. "It's liquid gold."

Landon stared as Carly slowly licked the sauce from her finger—a simple act that elicited deliciously complicated layers of arousal. Landon was mesmerized, and her hunger for anything other than Carly completely disappeared. She stood and closed the distance between them, sweeping Carly into her arms. She ran her hands through Carly's hair and tilted her head back. Carly's eyes were hazy with desire, and Landon was emboldened. She bent and kissed Carly's full lips, and her body thrummed with anticipation as Carly pulled her closer.

After the first hungry kiss, Landon asked, "Where's your bedroom?"

Carly answered by taking her hand and leading her out of the room, down the hall, and through a doorway into an immaculate, picture-perfect bedroom, complete with a canopy bed made up with a designer duvet and matching accent pillows, perfectly placed. Carly turned back toward her, trepidation filling her eyes. "Should we be doing this?" They shouldn't. What they were about to do would cause problems between them and problems for how they would work the case, but in this moment Landon didn't care about consequences. Every nerve ending in her body was on high alert and she was on the brink of discovering a side of Carly she knew existed but hadn't seen—reckless, sensual, willing to surrender to emotion—not the buttoned-up woman who kept her bedroom looking like a display at a high-end boutique. Landon was consumed by the desire to strip Carly out of her clothes and spend the next few hours making a mess out of this perfectly appointed bedroom. She couldn't, wouldn't, walk away from this chance to see, touch, make love to this Carly. Whatever happened after…well, she would deal with that later.

CHAPTER NINETEEN

"If you want to stop, I'll stop," Landon said. "But the only thing I want right now is you."

Carly closed her eyes. If she couldn't see Landon, would she still be tempted? She didn't have to wait long for the answer. Blind to Landon's sexy body and hopeful expression, the rest of Carly's body told her what she needed to know. The thrill of anticipation sent shock waves to her center and she felt the wet, hot heat of arousal between her legs. There was only one answer she could possibly give, and she gave it quickly before either of them could change their minds. "I want you. Now."

Carly barely had the words out before Landon placed a hand behind her neck and pulled her in for another searing kiss. As Landon's tongue pressed past her lips, Carly skimmed her hands up under Landon's sweatshirt and shivered as her fingers traced circles around Landon's bare breasts.

Landon arched into her touch. "You're killing me."

"You're one to talk."

Landon slid her fingers into the waistband of Carly's tights. "Too many…" She dipped her hand lower, cupping Carly's butt, her voice husky and low. "Clothes."

Carly answered by tugging her shirt over her head. Landon stepped back and smiled, slow and sexy, and then she pulled her own shirt off and tossed it to the floor. Without breaking eye contact, Landon unbuttoned her jeans and eased them slowly down her legs. Carly could barely breathe as she watched the slow striptease, her body an inferno of desire.

When Landon was completely naked, she held out a hand to Carly and led her to the bed. Carly tried not to flinch as Landon bunched the duvet off to the side and ripped the bedsheets from their well-tucked corners, but she feared she hadn't completely hidden her irrational angst at seeing her bedroom in disarray. Before she could give it another thought, Landon's arms circled her waist, her ragged breath a warm whisper trailing down Carly's neck.

"We can make it up again later, but we need to be able to move around for what I have planned." She turned Carly in her arms until they were face-to-face. "Trust me?"

Habit nearly propelled her to back away at the loaded question, but old instinct gave way to new revelation, and her certainty was instant and strong. In this moment, in Landon's arms, she had no fear of what the future might bring. Carly laced her fingers behind Landon's neck and tugged her close. "I do."

Landon kissed her again and eased her onto the bed, nestling her head on the pile of pillows, and then bending down to remove her black tights and underwear, casting them to the floor. Carly reached down and skimmed the palms of her hands along Landon's taut nipples as Landon stretched out over her, shuddering at Carly's touch. "I'm so turned on right now."

"So am I," Carly said, her body humming with excitement.

Landon settled on top of her and dipped her head to Carly's breasts, taking a nipple into her mouth. Carly's back arched to meet Landon's tongue as Landon's thigh slid through her slick, wet sex. Carly groaned as Landon nipped and sucked at one nipple while increasing the building pressure between her legs. "Please don't stop," she gasped.

"Not a chance," Landon murmured against her skin. She shifted slightly and kissed a trail from Carly's chest to the apex of her thighs.

Carly felt featherlight fingers touching her folds followed by the long, slow glide of Landon's tongue, dipping and licking again and again. The intensity of Landon's touch was consuming, and when Landon's lips brushed against her clit, her head rolled back. Lost in the pleasure of Landon's touch, she had no idea how much time passed before she surrendered to the waves of pleasure surging through her, barely recognizing the cries she heard as her own.

Satisfied that Carly was spent, Landon gently eased out from between her legs and tucked Carly into her arms. Carly rolled to face her.

"Um, that was…I can't even…"

Landon grinned. "Tell me how you really feel."

"Words. Are hard." Carly nipped at her shoulder. "I'm like Jell-O right now. I can't remember the last time I felt this way."

Landon grinned. "I happen to like Jell-O."

"Nobody likes Jell-O."

"Not true. I'm the one who steals it from the refrigerator when I'm visiting someone in the hospital."

"Somehow I believe you."

"You should totally believe me. I speak only the truth."

Carly stretched her hand across Landon's abdomen. "Okay, Truth Teller, tell me this. If I reach lower, will you be as wet as I am?"

Landon's body twitched with anticipation at the idea of Carly taking charge. "Some things you have to find out for yourself." A second later, she moaned as Carly slowly drew a finger along the inside of one thigh and then teased her way to the other.

"I bet you're really wet now," Carly whispered in her ear.

"You have no idea."

Carly rolled over until she was on top and their eyes met for a brief second before Carly bent and took one of Landon's nipples into her mouth, circling the hard point with her tongue, over and over, sending charged pulses directly to her aching clit. By the time Carly moved to the other nipple, Landon was certain she was going to come without Carly applying an ounce of pressure between her legs, but a long, slow stroke around her clit left her gasping for more. She bucked against Carly's hand, begging for release.

Carly lifted her head and smiled, slow and sexy. "I love touching you."

"You're kind of incredible at it." Landon breathed deep. "More, please."

"Absolutely." Carly inched down until she was between Landon's legs and retraced the route her fingers had traveled, but this time with her tongue. Landon thrashed beneath her touch, wanting desperately to prolong the connection at the same time she ached for release. When the orgasm surged through her, the pinnacle of pleasure brought with it a moment of clarity. When it came to Carly, she had no choice but to give in.

❖

Landon reached out and connected with empty space. She slowly opened her eyes. It was still dark, but she hadn't dreamed that she was in Carly's bed. Naked and very much spent. The question was, where was Carly?

"Hey, sleepyhead."

Landon tracked the sound to the other side of the room where Carly was sitting in front of a small desk, already dressed for court.

"Hey, workaholic. What time is it and what are you doing?"

Carly came over and sat next to her on the bed. "Too jazzed to sleep. I was making a few notes for Royal's testimony this morning. You'll thank me when you're trying to cross-examine him on two hours' sleep."

"Jazzed, huh? Is that what you call it when you're running on the excess energy created by multiple orgasms?"

Carly leaned forward and pulled her into a kiss. "I think you could use some excess energy of your own. Should we meet back here tonight? There's leftover Thai food, and you know…"

Landon pushed the sheet back and motioned to the space beside her. "What about right now?"

"I wish, but we need to get moving or we're going to be late." Carly traced a finger along Landon's thigh. "I'm guessing you might want to change before we head to court. Take your time getting ready. I'll go by the office, pick up your files, and meet you at the courthouse."

Landon looked around for her clothes and spotted them folded neatly on an ottoman. "I suppose it might cause a ruckus if I showed up in jeans and a sweatshirt." She started to swing her legs out of the bed, but Carly pressed a hand to her chest before she could stand.

"Just so you know, if I had my way," Carly said, "you'd stay naked all day long."

Carly's words sparked instant arousal, and Landon wanted to say to hell with the trial, the partnership, and anything else that wasn't Carly naked in bed with her. The idea both excited and frightened her.

She wanted all the things, but she couldn't have everything, could she? "How is this going to work?"

"I don't have a clue, but we don't have to figure it out right now." Carly reached for her hand and pulled her out of bed and into her arms. "Let's just enjoy this for now."

"That sounds like something I would say. Funny advice coming from the woman who likes to have everything planned out."

"I'm taking a page from the Landon Holt seize the day philosophy. I have to tell you, so far it's a good fit."

Thirty minutes later, Landon was back at the condo, reliving the memory of her night with Carly under a punishingly powerful hot shower. When she emerged, she downed two cups of coffee and a bagel she'd snagged from the hotel buffet while she reviewed her notes, but memories of her night with Carly pushed around the edges of her thoughts, distracting her. Everything about last night had been amazing. She'd connected with Carly so seamlessly, it was like a perfect blend of new and familiar. How was she going to sit next to Carly all day and not touch her?

She was gathering her things to head to the courthouse when her phone rang. She didn't recognize the number and almost let it go to voice mail, but Skye had been pursuing some of Trevor's old girlfriends and she supposed it was possible Skye had given out her number. "Landon Holt."

"I was hoping you'd answer."

Landon held the phone away from her ear and stared at it with distaste as if doing so would change who was on the other end. "Hello, Dad. I'm very busy right now and need to get to the courthouse."

"I won't keep you. I only wanted to wish you good luck. You won't need it. The papers say your opening statement was riveting." She heard paper rustling, and then he said, "'A perfect counterpoint to the prosecutor's workmanlike recitation of the facts. Defense attorney Landon Holt offered a prosaic balance at the beginning of the trial, sure to keep the jurors receptive to hearing all the evidence before making up their minds.'"

Wow. She'd been so busy thinking of Carly and preparing for today's testimony, she hadn't thought to check the paper for press coverage of the trial. She played it down for him. "Seems like a bit of an exaggeration, but I'll take it."

"I think there are good things in store for you. Your brother says you're up for a partnership?"

"Yes. Things are looking good." Landon wondered what angle he was working. Surely he didn't call her out of the blue just to give her an attagirl.

"I think you have a good shot."

"Thanks. I do too." Landon felt a twinge of guilt at the acknowledgment. She did want the partnership, but did she want to advance at the expense of losing Carly? This morning's euphoria was fading fast in the face of reality. Things were feeling so completely upside down. "Dad, did you need anything else? I have to go."

"I did want to talk to you about some other things, but it can wait until your trial is over. Knock 'em dead."

Not the best way to cheer on someone representing a client accused of murder, but she let it pass and took a moment to ponder what had just happened. George Holt didn't make casual phone calls or casual conversation. He wanted something and today's contact had been a setup of some kind, but a tiny part of her that still yearned for parental approval couldn't help but wish he had reached out for purely altruistic reasons.

Her first instinct was to call Carly and tell her about the call, but Carly would be getting ready for court, which was exactly what she should be doing. She'd talk to Ian about it later. Right now, she needed every ounce of focus she could muster to keep her attention on the testimony of Detective Royal and off of the gorgeous, captivating woman who'd kept her up all night.

CHAPTER TWENTY

Carly tossed her briefcase on her desk and checked the clock on her phone, pleased to see she had plenty of time to spare. She wondered what Landon was doing right now. In the shower? Getting dressed? It had been incredibly difficult watching her leave this morning, but she wouldn't have been able to concentrate on anything else if Landon had stuck around.

She'd never expected them to wind up in bed, but now she knew she'd wanted it as much as she'd wanted anything in her entire life. What was it about Landon that made her want to step outside the mold of her no-nonsense life? Whatever it was, the feeling was a powerful force that had left her super charged and ready for whatever today might bring.

She bumped into Keith on her way to Jane's office.

"How's the trial going?"

"Hard to tell." She practiced new Carly and gave him a big smile. "We've barely gotten started. You should come down and watch some of the testimony."

He held up the newspaper in his hand. "Looks like Landon's killing it."

Carly flashed to a memory of Landon standing in front of the jury box, the jurors captivated by her delivery, and immediately fast-forwarded to a vision of Landon's naked body stretched out over her, every bit as captivating as she'd been in the courtroom. Probably more so. "Yes, she's definitely skilled." Carly suppressed a grin at the understatement.

"Do you think she's going to get the partnership?"

The question struck Carly by surprise. It hadn't occurred to her that Jane or Mark would have shared the details about the competition with anyone else in the office, let alone the town gossip. She tamped down her annoyance and brushed off his comment with a simple, "She's definitely partnership material." She made some excuse about needing to talk to Jane and walked away, but the encounter had left her a little off-kilter. From the time Landon had kissed her last night until just now, she'd managed to push any thoughts about the partnership to the far corners of her mind while she let her heart out to play. But that might have been a mistake.

No, nothing about last night had been a mistake. She'd never felt the way Landon made her feel. Appreciated, adored, incredible, and she was certain it had been real. Her only apprehension was what to do with all these feelings about Landon, but she'd decided she would take it one day at a time. Today she would sit next to Landon at trial and do everything she could to win this case for Trevor, but tonight the only competition would be who could get their clothes off faster. When the trial was over, they could face what came next, but until then, she would bask in this feeling and enjoy every moment with Landon that she could.

Rhonda the gatekeeper wasn't at her desk, and Jane's door was partially open. She raised her hand to knock, but the sound of voices from within stilled her hand.

"As soon as this trial is over, I'll make it happen."

"I'm holding you to it. Mark says you're interested in taking on transactional work, and we have plenty to send your way, but I'm sure you know there are bigger, better equipped firms we could use."

Carly started to turn and go, but Jane's next words rooted her in place.

"How long have you known me? Landon deserves the promotion, although I had planned to wait another year to make it happen."

"I want her here in Dallas. To stay. I have plans for her future, and it's been way too long since this silly estrangement started. You bring my daughter back to me and you'll see your billable hours double. I promise you that."

"And I promise you Landon Holt will be a partner at Sturges and Lloyd by Christmas."

Carly froze at the declaration, but before she could digest the words, the sound of movement from inside Jane's office sent her scrambling. Lightning fast, she was back behind her desk, certain no one had spotted her lurking, when George Holt walked past her door with Jane by his side.

She stared at their backs while struggling to process what she'd just heard. There was nothing to struggle about. Jane's statement had been crystal clear. She'd already decided Landon would be the next partner at Sturges and Lloyd, and apparently, the whole "let's see who does the best job in trial" exercise was a complete farce. All her hard work, not just on this case, but on every single matter that had been handled by the firm, and Carly's only reward was a bunch of broken promises. The betrayal by her employer stung, but knowing Landon had used her father's influence to gain an advantage cut deep.

You don't know if Landon knows anything about this. She didn't, but it hardly seemed likely George Holt would just show up on his own to advocate for his daughter, not after the acrimony Carly had witnessed between them at the Cowboys game. She closed her eyes and replayed the events of the last twenty-four hours. Landon had overreacted about her dinner with Trevor and the possible implications on their race for partnership, but then she'd been a playful, tender lover completely devoted to delivering pleasure. Had Landon been able to be so relaxed and at ease about the shift in their relationship because she knew she had the partnership in the bag? Carly hated to think it could be true, but she couldn't deny the very real possibility she'd been played.

There was only one way to find out. She'd ask Landon straight out. She looked at the time. She needed to get to the courthouse, and now wasn't the time to confront Landon or she'd risk rattling her before Royal's testimony. She would wait until tonight. Landon would tell her the truth or anything—everything—personal between them was over.

What if she tells you she knew all along that Daddy Dearest was buying her the partnership? Are you willing to deny your feelings and show her the door?

The idea of ending what had developed between them flooded Carly with sadness, but survival mechanisms weren't designed to make her feel good, they were designed to keep her safe. And where Landon Holt was concerned, Carly's heart was anything but safe.

❖

Detective Royal tapped the wooden railing of the witness stand and tilted his head back. Donna's question to him hadn't been particularly difficult, but Landon noted that he employed the finger-tapping, head-rolling maneuver every time he wanted the jury to think he was a thoughtful guy, taking caution not to jump to conclusions about the case. She couldn't wait to get her hands on him.

"Detective, I'm showing you what has been marked as Exhibit A27. Without telling the jury what it says, please give us a description of this document." Donna's trial partner, Ed, leaned over and shoved a copy of the exhibit at Landon. She picked it up and skimmed the lines. At first glance it appeared to be a straightforward inventory of the evidence collected at the crime scene, a copy of which was already in her file. Landon started to set it off to the side, but then something caught her eye. Canine hairs.

She leaned over to Carly and scrawled on a piece of paper. *Pull the original report.* She almost underscored the note with a smiley face just to get Carly to show some emotion, but refrained. From the moment Carly had shown up at the courthouse, Landon had sensed a shift in her mood from the sexy, playful woman she'd made love to all night. Surrounded by press, other lawyers, and their client, she hadn't had a chance to ask Carly what was wrong. It was entirely possible she was imagining the whole thing and this was just Carly's game face, but for now she needed to keep her attention on the drama unfolding in the courtroom.

Carly slid the report over and Landon lined up the copies side by side. Her instinct had been right. Dog hairs weren't listed on the original report. She turned her attention back to Donna's exchange with Royal.

"This is a comprehensive list of the evidence gathered at the crime scene," he said.

"Did you assist in the preparation of this list?"

"I did."

"And does it represent a full and complete list of all the evidence gathered by either you, your partner, or other law enforcement professionals working the case?"

"It does."

Donna turned to Judge Grafton. "Your Honor, the state offers

Exhibit A27 into evidence at this time." Judge Grafton looked at Landon. "Any objection?"

Landon scooped up both reports and stood even though such formality wasn't customary in state court. She was walking a minefield here and she needed every advantage. "Sidebar, Your Honor?"

Judge Grafton waved them forward. Landon was the first one there with Carly and Jane close behind. Donna and Ed walked slowly forward, engaged in a frantic whispered conversation. When all five attorneys were huddled to the side of the bench, Judge Grafton turned her microphone in the opposite direction of the group. "What is it?" her brisk tone a signal she wasn't a fan of delaying the proceeding.

Landon handed over both reports. "One of these is the exhibit that the state just handed to us, but the other one is the report of the crime scene evidence that was provided to us in pretrial discovery." She pointed to a line on the exhibit. "This line isn't on the first report. Before we can properly assess whether we have an objection to admitting the report into evidence, I'd like to know why we were provided a different version of this report than the one that state is trying to get into evidence today, and whether the difference matters."

Grafton held the reports up and skimmed each page before turning to Donna. "Ms. Wilhelm, why the difference?"

Donna cleared her throat and glanced over at Ed before speaking. "The item that Ms. Holt pointed out on the trial exhibit came to light just last week. It was my understanding that a new version of the report was provided to defense counsel days ago, but I've just learned that it was not." She reached a hand out to Ed, who handed her a clipped stack of paper. "It has also come to my attention that this lab report, which is related to the item on the list of evidence, was not provided to defense counsel. I promise you this was an innocent mistake—careless, but not malicious."

Landon stared at the papers in her hand, only able to make out the words "DNA report" and "canine hair" through the blur of anger marring her careful preparation. "Judge, the mistake may be innocent, but the consequences aren't. How are we supposed to cross-examine this witness or any other, on lab reports we've never seen, let alone been able to share with an expert of our own?"

The judge sighed. "I have a feeling this is going to take more than a few minutes to sort out. Go have a seat." Once they were back at their respective counsel tables, she addressed the jury. "From time to time throughout the trial, I may need to meet with the attorneys outside of your presence to address some administrative issues. If the meeting will take longer than a few minutes, the bailiff will take you back to the jury room where you can relax until it's time to reconvene. This is one of those times. I promise we'll do everything we can to make the process go as efficiently as possible, but for now, please go with the bailiff."

The attorneys stood as the jurors filed out of the room, and Landon could hear Trevor whispering to Carly, asking what was going on, but Carly's response was cut off by the judge telling them to be seated.

"Ms. Wilhelm, would you like to make a proffer as to what exactly these new reports contain and how it matters to your case?"

The sour expression on Donna's face told Landon she'd rather chew nails than reveal her strategy, but she really didn't have a choice at this point. "Detective Royal will testify that the crime scene techs accidentally bagged together two sets of hair gathered at the scene, one from the victim and one from a previously unknown source. The mistake was discovered at the lab."

"What's the significance?"

"The second set of hairs were determined to be from a dog. A second look at fibers gathered from the scene revealed several strands of canine hair. The strands were sent for analysis and they are a match for the defendant's French bulldog."

Landon's head shot up. "What?"

"You have something to say?" Judge Grafton didn't look pleased at the outburst.

"Yes, Judge. If I could have a moment." Without waiting for permission, Landon started digging through her files.

Carly tapped her on the shoulder and whispered, "If you're looking for the search warrant, here it is."

Of course, Carly had read her mind. After things between them had seemed out of sync since they'd arrived at the courthouse, Landon was relieved. "Thanks."

"I already checked," Carly said. "They didn't ask for permission to take a DNA swab from the dog."

"Can they get a swab without a warrant?"

Carly shrugged. "I don't know. Can't say that I've ever had this one come up."

Landon glanced up at the bench where Judge Grafton frowned to show her impatience. "Let me see if I can buy us some time." She stood. "Judge, may I take the witness on voir dire? Just a few questions."

"Go ahead."

"Detective, I'm holding a lab report that purports to show a probable match between hairs that were improperly classified as belonging to Ms. Meyers and which the state failed to produce to the defense until today, and Mr. Kincade's dog. My question to you is, what is the basis of the comparison?"

"I'm not sure I follow you." He didn't meet her eyes and she was certain he knew exactly where she was going with her question.

"Well, how did the lab get DNA from Mr. Kincade's dog to compare with these random other hairs?"

He looked at Donna as if seeking permission to reveal his source, and she nodded. "We did a buccal swab on the dog."

"And when and where did you do this?"

"Last week. At the dog park."

"I assume my client wasn't there at the time?"

"I didn't see him. There was some guy watching the dog, but he was playing with other dogs and wasn't on a leash."

So that's how it was going to go. Landon leaned over to Trevor and whispered, "Were you there?"

He shook his head. "That was Blake, Dijon's dog walker. He takes him to the park sometimes to socialize."

Landon sat for a second, gathering her thoughts, when Carly scrawled on the pad in between them. *Ask for a mistrial. Then ask for more time to research legality of search and admissibility of evidence.* Landon nodded. "Your Honor, the defense requests a mistrial. The prosecutor claims this was an innocent mistake, but key evidence has been withheld and there are serious questions about the legality of how that evidence was obtained."

Donna shot out of her chair. "A mistrial would be completely inappropriate. Yes, we should have shared this evidence with the defense before today, but frankly, we haven't had it very long. If they need time to examine the evidence, we have no objections to a brief recess."

Grafton steepled her fingers, her forehead furrowed. "We've barely begun, and I'm sure this is not the last skirmish that will threaten to derail the process, but I'm not inclined to grant a mistrial, although if this late production of evidence starts to become a habit, I'll entertain a new motion. Ms. Holt, I'm giving you and your team the rest of the day. You'll be allowed to supplement the witness list if you identify any experts or fact witnesses to rebut the evidence. If you decide to file any evidentiary motions, I want them on my desk an hour before the jury files in tomorrow morning. Understood?"

"Yes, Your Honor." Landon hadn't expected the request for the mistrial to be granted, but she'd had to make the motion in order to preserve the record, and it'd been worth a shot. The takeaway bonus was she would get to spend the day with Carly, sorting through this new evidence.

Judge Grafton brought the jury back in and gave them some vague excuse for why they were being dismissed for the rest of the day. She issued a stern warning about how they were still subject to all the rules she'd outlined earlier, and everyone stood while they filed back out of the room again. Once the last juror had cleared the door and Grafton adjourned, Landon leaned over to Carly and whispered, "Looking forward to working with you the rest of the day."

Carly opened her mouth to speak, but Trevor appeared between them with Shelby right beside him. "What's going on? Are they saying Dijon was at Vanessa's house? I never took him over there. She was a freak about her white carpeting. Carly, can you fix this?"

Landon stared at him, blown away by his cluelessness while Jane took control. "Why don't we all have a seat in the workroom and talk things over?" Jane said. She started walking toward the back of the courtroom and Landon followed but not before catching Carly shooting daggers at Jane's back. Something must have happened at the office this morning that had gotten Carly in a bad mood. She made a mental note to ask Carly about it when they were alone.

The five of them crowded into the small room and stood because there were only two chairs and a desk with a bum fourth leg. Jane explained to Shelby and Trevor that the prosecutors were prepared to present evidence that Dijon's hairs were found on Vanessa's clothing at the crime scene.

"But that doesn't mean anything," Shelby said. "She probably picked them up when she was at Trevor's or they were on his clothes when he went to see her."

"Except under his agreement with the NFL, he wasn't to have any contact with her while the suspension action was pending," Carly said.

Shelby rolled her eyes. "Like he could stop that b—" She paused and seemed to realize where she was. "If she wanted to come over and see him, he couldn't stop her."

"Did she?" Carly asked, turning to Trevor. "If she did, you'll need to remember dates and times, and someone else will need to be able to testify that she did because we haven't decided if you'll be taking the stand."

"I don't remember," Trevor said.

"Of course, he'll be taking the stand," Shelby said. "He didn't do anything and he has nothing to hide."

"That's not your decision to make," Carly snapped.

Landon watched the back and forth between the two of them. It was out of character for Carly to be so confrontational with Shelby, but she was right.

"Let's take a breath," Jane said. "Landon, you've had a chance to glance at the report. Any questions for Trevor before we cut him loose for the day?"

"Just one. How long have you had Dijon?"

"About eight months," Trevor said and looked to Shelby for confirmation.

Shelby nodded. "He bought him from a breeder here in Dallas. Do you need the name of the breeder?"

"We'll let you know if we do. Thanks."

Jane closed the file. "Okay then. We'll all be at the office working if you need us."

Shelby started toward the door while she was still talking with Trevor in tow. Carly jumped in before they cleared the door. "I think we should split up the work. I can research and develop a line of questioning for the lab tech about the canine DNA, and Landon can take on the search issues. And, Jane, if it's okay with you, I'd like to work from home. I've got an article on my computer there about this very topic."

Landon muddled through Carly's words, looking for a hidden meaning. Did Carly expect her to go with her? Was work at home code for work a little, play a little? Carly's expression gave her no clues and she wasn't making eye contact. Landon decided to wait until they were alone to ask.

She didn't have to wait long. Jane told them she needed to make some calls and would check in later, and was out the door. Carly was close behind, barely giving Landon a glance.

"Hey, wait up," Landon said, reaching for Carly's arm.

Carly took a step away. "We've got a lot of work to do."

"I know that, but is there some reason we can't work together?"

"Maybe because when we work toward the same goal, it's a losing proposition."

Landon tried for some levity to break the icy mood. "Does really hot sex make you speak in riddles? Because I can get down with that, it's just unexpected is all." She smiled, but Carly didn't smile back.

"When's the last time you spoke with your father?"

"What? Why are you asking about him?"

"Just answer."

"Actually, we spoke this morning. I was going to tell you about it, but then we got here and things started ramping up and there wasn't a chance. You wouldn't believe it. We actually had a nice conversation. He—"

Carly held up a hand. "I don't need to hear all the specifics. It's bad enough you didn't tell me yourself."

"Tell you what?"

"That your dear old dad already got you the partnership. Bought and paid for courtesy of Holt Industries."

"Wait a minute." Landon's brain shifted into slow motion. "He did what?"

"It doesn't matter. None of this matters." Carly took another step toward the door. "This is how the world works. I'm going home to work now. Please leave me alone outside of the office, and then don't talk to me unless it has to do with the case."

And she was gone, leaving Landon staring at the door, wondering what the hell had just happened.

CHAPTER TWENTY-ONE

The minute Carly opened the door of her apartment, memories flooded back. It had been a mistake to come back here to work when everywhere she turned something reminded her of Landon and last night—the receipt from Royal Thai, Landon's coffee cup in the sink, and her scent lingering on the bedsheets. But working at the office with Landon two doors down would have been even worse. All she had to do was steer clear of Landon until this trial was over, and then her time at Sturges and Lloyd would be done.

She would survive. She was smart and capable and lots of firms would be lucky to have her. But she was beginning to realize she'd been simply surviving her entire life. Now that she'd had a glimpse of how rich her life could be with someone to share her hopes and dreams, someone who thought she was desirable for something more than her sharp brain, settling for survival was a tough blow.

Maybe someday, she'd look for something more—something to fill her heart as well as her mind—but right now the bruises of Landon's betrayal were too fresh. Since her brain was in demand, she went into autopilot. She quickly changed into jeans and a sweater and settled in at her computer to look for the article she'd seen in a past issue of the NACDL magazine about search warrants and pet DNA. There were two issues: whether the police had unlawfully obtained the DNA sample from Dijon, and whether the science was reliable enough for the expert from the lab to state whether the hair from the scene belonged to Dijon. What a bunch of jerks, dragging a guy's pet into this mess.

She skimmed the article and then signed onto Lexis and started researching case law. The subject was a black hole, and when she heard a knock on her door and looked up from the computer, she was surprised to see that she'd been at it for a couple of hours. She willed whoever was outside her door to go away, but the knocking persisted. Certain it was Mr. Jasper wondering what she was doing home in the middle of a workday, she walked to the door, fully prepared to shoo him away, but when she looked through the viewer, she saw Shelby standing outside.

She opened the door. "Shelby? Is everything okay?"

Shelby's eyes darted around and she was obviously distraught. "No. It's Trevor. He's panicked and won't talk to anyone but you. I'm seriously worried. He's been trying to reach you, but you haven't answered any of his calls."

Carly bit her lip. She hadn't turned her phone ringer back on after leaving court. No wonder she'd gotten completely immersed in her research. "Sorry about that. I've been working on the case. We have a tight deadline to get some motions filed. Can you tell Trevor I'll call him as soon as I'm done?"

Shelby sighed. "I don't think it will keep that long. He's talking about going on one of those talk radio shows and making his case. He's very upset and there's no telling what he'll say. I've tried to talk him out of it, but I think you're the only one he'll listen to. He respects you."

Carly looked back at her computer and ran through a list of work she still had to do. As if sensing her reluctance, Shelby said, "I know I haven't always been nice to you, but Trevor thinks you're the best. I wouldn't be here if it wasn't important."

She'd have to stay up most of the night, but if she left now, she could still get the work done by morning. "Okay. I just need to save my work. Is he at home? I can meet you there."

"Oh no. I'll take you. It's the least I can do since it's so last minute. I can fill you in on the way."

Carly hesitated, loath to get stuck at Trevor's, but she could always Uber home if necessary, and surely he'd understand she needed to get back home to prepare for trial. "Yeah, okay. Why don't you come in and wait while I grab my jacket?"

"That's okay. I have to make a phone call. I'll be in the car. It's the Corvette parked by the curb."

Shelby walked away and Carly retrieved her keys, phone, and jacket. Satisfied she didn't need anything else, she locked up and started walking to the parking lot. She'd barely made it two steps before Mr. Jasper's door opened.

"Hey, Mr. Jasper," she said but didn't stop walking.

"How's the trial going?"

"Good. I'll tell you all about it later, but I have to get to a meeting. Have a good evening." She heard him tell her to have a good day too as she strode away, and she resisted the urge to tell him good days were behind her for a while. At least until she got over Landon.

Landon stood in front of Jane's desk, unable to believe what she was hearing.

"I guess there's no point in pretending it's not true," Jane said. "Yes, you're getting the partnership, but for obvious reasons we'd appreciate it if you don't tell anyone until after the trial. We'll make a formal announcement at the holiday party."

"'Obvious reasons'?" Landon's voice rose, but she didn't bother trying to dial back her anger. Everything had unraveled after she'd left the courthouse. Her first call had been to her father, who'd conveniently been out of the office. Next, she'd called Ian, who'd told her he knew nothing about their father's maneuverings. She believed him, but it didn't ease the sting that came with knowing her father thought he had to purchase her success. She'd deal with Dad later, but for now all her fury was focused on Jane. "Let me guess," Landon said. "You're scared if word gets out you didn't award this partnership based on merit, you'll chase off one of the smartest lawyers you've probably ever hired while simultaneously pissing off your big celebrity client."

"Oh, I don't think Carly will leave us. She's a top-notch appellate lawyer, but she doesn't possess the rainmaker qualities necessary to be a good partner. You have a big enough personality to draw in the new business we need to grow into a full-service firm, handling more than simply criminal defense. We can hire some brainiac first-year associates to do research."

Landon could read between the lines. Her so-called big personality was really just her connection to Holt Industries and the business her father could throw their way. "Thanks for implying I'm not intelligent enough to make it on my smarts alone."

"That's not what I meant. I didn't think you were so thin-skinned. Come on, Landon, you know how this works. We're only successful if we can continue to attract new clients. Most criminal defense cases are one-offs, but if we can expand the practice to include transactional work, there's no limit to how big we can grow."

"You sound like my father," Landon said, and the words triggered a realization. "You wanted me to give the opening statement because you needed to close the deal with my father and show him you were willing to put me front and center. He acted so proud of me when he called this morning—your strategy was on the money."

"I'm sure he was proud of you, but what's important right now is that we focus on Trevor's case. Win or lose, the press from this trial is going to bring us a lot more business from athletes. If you want, you can have it all. Frankly, I find these guys who're wrapped up in sports rather boring."

Landon shook her head. What should've been a major milestone in her career was now marred forever. "Why the charade?"

Jane shrugged. "Like you said, the client likes Carly. I promised your father I'd promote you before the end of the year, but we needed to make sure Carly would stick around to keep Trevor from looking elsewhere. She'll be fine, and if she chooses to stick around, maybe you can find a way to make it up to her."

Landon chose to ignore the implication. "She won't because I'm going to make damn sure she knows how you played her."

"You'll do no such thing. What happens at the partnership level remains confidential. You'll learn soon enough the importance of not upsetting the rank and file with details that don't concern them."

"Actually, I won't. You'll have to figure out some other way to get my father's business, because as soon as this trial is over, I'm done with this firm. I quit."

Landon stormed out of Jane's office before she could respond. She needed to hole up in her office and work on her motions, but there was no way she'd be able to concentrate with Jane down the hall, plotting her next scheme. Instead Landon packed up her files, stuffed her laptop in a bag, and left the office. When she got behind the wheel of her car, she took a few deep breaths and pondered her next move. What she wanted to do was see Carly and tell her what had happened, but Carly's words echoed. *Leave me alone outside of the office.* Carly deserved to know what happened, but she also deserved to have her wishes respected.

Landon started the car and drove to Ian's restaurant. She wasn't the least bit hungry, but she needed to vent and Ian was the only person who could truly understand. The drive was quick and she was through the doors in less than fifteen minutes. Ian was standing at the bar, and when he spotted her, he ran over and swept her into a tight hug. After a minute of brotherly squeezing, she squirmed out of his grasp. "Let go or you're going to make me cry."

"And that wouldn't be the end of the world. Maybe you need a good cry."

"Maybe I need to punch someone in the face."

"Maybe. In the meantime, how about lunch?" Ian waved a hand and Beckett, the waiter, materialized at his side. "I'll be in the back room with my sister. Bring us one of each of the specials and a half carafe of the new red."

"I have work to do," Landon protested.

"Fuel first. Come on." He led the way back to the room where she and Carly had shared dinner several months before. As she stepped into the room, her heart ached at the idea she might never share another evening, or anything else, with Carly again.

"You look like someone stole your last piece of candy," Ian said. "Sit and tell me everything."

Landon slid into the nearest chair and gave him the rundown, starting with the made-up race for partner and ending with Jane's admission that the entire thing had been a fake-out. When she was finished, she put her head between her hands. "Everything is so messed up."

"I talked to Dad."

She raised her head. "He denied it, didn't he?"

"Not even. He was proud of his little chess game. Jane's been after him for ages to get his business, and in his mind, he played her like a pawn, getting his daughter to move back to Dallas and work for the family business. I let him have it when he said he knew what was best for you."

"Well, the joke's on him because I just quit."

"Holy shit, really?"

"Oh yeah, there's no way I'm going to work for him, even indirectly, but it's not just that. His little game with Jane really fucked with Carly. Apparently, she never intended to make Carly partner but was just stringing her along because she didn't want her looking elsewhere before this trial was over."

"That's rough. You really like Carly, don't you?"

"*Like* is an understatement." Like didn't begin to cover the flush of heat she felt when she remembered last night in Carly's bed, but it wasn't just the incredible sex they'd shared. A ton of other feelings— affection, happiness, genuine respect, all tumbled through her whenever she thought about Carly, and she didn't want to imagine a life without her in it even if she didn't want to say the words out loud just yet.

Ian nodded with a knowing smile. "I knew it."

"You didn't know jack shit. Hell, I just realized it myself. I don't want to lose her over this, but she's really angry and basically told me to get lost."

"People say things in the heat of the moment. Give her some time."

He might be right, but Landon couldn't bear the idea of sitting next to Carly for the duration of this trial with a sea of hurt between them. And when the trial was over? What would happen then? "I can't wait."

"Then you need some kind of grand gesture."

"I quit my job. That was kind of a big deal."

Ian shook his head. "No, the gesture needs to be personal. Something that will warm her heart and make her fall in love with you."

"Like a flash mob? Oh, I don't think Carly's a grand gesture kind of girl."

"Yeah, I didn't get that impression either, but flash mob wasn't what I had in mind. You need to tell her what happened and how you feel. No ducking it, just say it outright. Go see her and lay it on the line. Take a risk, sis."

"Easy for you to say."

"What have you got to lose? You've already quit your job, and it's not like you've ever let yourself feel this way before. Go big or go home. If you fall on your face, you can have Beckett's job because he should've been in here at least fifteen minutes ago with our food."

They both laughed and Landon felt the tightness in her chest release. Before she did anything else today, she would find Carly and tell her how she felt.

CHAPTER TWENTY-TWO

I thought we were going to Trevor's," Carly said as they zoomed past the exit she would've taken for Trevor's place. Shelby had been quiet as she navigated traffic on the tollway, and Carly's few attempts at conversation hadn't yielded much of the promised information Shelby had used to lure her into this urgent meeting.

"Trevor sent a text saying he wants us to meet him at a friend's place." Shelby kept her eyes trained on the highway as she talked. "Less likelihood of reporters being around."

The reasoning made sense, but Carly hadn't seen Shelby on her phone during the ride. She supposed Shelby could've received a text from him before she'd gotten into the car. Carly wrote off her unease to the odd circumstance that put her in a car with this woman who'd expressed clear hostility from the day they'd met. "You were going to fill me in."

"What?"

"About Trevor and how he's doing. You said you were going to talk to me about it in the car."

Shelby's hands tensed on the wheel. "Yes, of course. He's very upset. None of this is going the way it was planned. He never should've been charged. He couldn't have killed those girls."

Carly replayed Shelby's words in her head. Her cadence was stilted, but there was something else off about her wording that struck Carly as odd. She decided to try to get her to say more so she could sort it out. "It's a little too early in the process to think it's all going downhill. Yes, there's some evidence we hadn't anticipated, but I was researching ways to keep the jury from hearing it when you came by."

She let the implication hang that she'd still be working if Shelby hadn't interrupted.

"There shouldn't have been any evidence."

Shelby uttered the statement with a growl, and Carly was certain this time she wasn't imagining that Shelby knew more than she was saying. Was Trevor really guilty? Had he confessed to Shelby? Was that why he was so upset? Had she been summoned to help him figure out a way to turn himself in? She treaded carefully. "Trevor seems like a great guy. I'm sure he wouldn't hurt anyone on purpose."

Shelby frowned and her voice rose. "Trevor would never hurt anyone." She dropped her voice back to a normal, conversational tone. "You shouldn't fawn over him the way you do. It's embarrassing."

Carly was disconcerted by the abrupt change in subject, but strangely relieved that Shelby had finally said how she really felt instead of implying it. "I promise you I have no interest in Trevor except as his attorney."

"Uh-huh." Shelby appeared distracted and then quickly changed lanes, narrowly missing the car to their left. "He likes to make everyone feel special, but he doesn't realize how he leads women on. I almost feel sorry for them. Almost."

It was pretty clear Shelby was lumping her in with "these women." Carly started to protest again, but decided not to bother. What Shelby believed wasn't her concern, but at the next opportunity, she was going to make it perfectly clear to Trevor that the only relationship they would ever have would be a professional one. Funny, that seemed to be her mantra today. She remembered Landon's face when they parted at the courthouse. Landon had appeared genuinely surprised when Carly confronted her about her father, but Carly wasn't sure it made a difference even if Landon hadn't known in advance. Could she be with Landon knowing that Landon's family name and influential connections would always have the power to rob her of what she'd worked so hard to earn? She'd never trusted anyone that much.

But if Landon hadn't been involved in her father's scheme, why shouldn't she trust her? Carly remembered Landon's reaction to her father at the Cowboys game. No way had Landon faked the animosity between them, and although it was possible they'd repaired their relationship in the two months she and Landon were barely speaking, did she really believe Landon—sweet, gentle Landon, who'd been so attentive to her last night—would be capable of conniving with her father to buy her way into the partnership? Surely she hadn't misjudged Landon so incredibly.

Shelby swerved into another abrupt lane change, and Carly looked up at the road. They were still headed north on the tollway, but they were outside the loop and headed into the suburbs. "Will we be there soon?"

"Soon enough. You'll see."

Shelby's deceptively simple statement was delivered with exaggerated emphasis, and for the first time since she'd gotten in the car, Carly felt truly uneasy. Deciding she might feel better if she let someone know where she was, she reached into her bag and pulled out her phone. A text notification rolled down from the top of the screen. It was from Landon. *I promise I didn't know.* Carly started to type a response, but all the things she had to say were more than her thumbs could handle. She switched over to her contact list, located Skye's number, and dialed.

"What are you doing?"

"Just making a quick call."

Carly had the phone halfway up to her ear and could hear Skye saying hello, but before she could respond, Shelby reached between the seats and yanked a gun out of the console. "Hang up."

Carly's insides froze and she struggled to remain calm. "Shelby, I'm just making a call." Carly spoke louder than normal, hoping Skye could hear her.

"Don't say another word." Shelby pointed the gun directly at her. "Hang up. Now. Or else." She brandished the gun to show Carly what "or else" meant.

Carly's heart raced as she quickly ran through her options. No one knew where she was, and her only lifeline was the phone in her hand and its connection to Skye. She needed to get away from Shelby and fast, but with the car speeding down the tollway, that wasn't going to happen anytime soon.

"Now!" Shelby shouted.

Carly jumped like she was scared—not a stretch—and tossed the phone onto the rear floorboard, praying she hadn't disconnected the call and there was some small chance Skye could still hear her. "I'm sorry. You frightened me. Why do you have a gun?"

Shelby's lips curled into a feral smile. "I don't like to use them, but they do come in handy for getting people to do what you want."

Carly decided her best bet at this point was to get Shelby to disclose where they were going in case Skye could hear them because Shelby clearly had something nefarious planned. "You don't need to threaten me to get me to come with you. Is the place we're going near the training facility? I've never been inside, but I remember seeing it once from the tollway."

Shelby laughed. "Quit pretending you have any interest in football. I can tell by the way your eyes glaze over whenever anyone talks about the game that you aren't a fan. You can bet Trevor sees through your little act."

"I've tried to take an interest, but I'll admit I've never been much of a fan in the past." Carly hesitated, and then decided to press her luck. "I hear the facility is gorgeous."

"We're not going there, and Trevor's not there anyway. Thanks to your inability to get his case dismissed, he's not allowed to train with the team. I don't know what he sees in you."

"Nothing, Shelby. He sees nothing. How many times do I have to tell you there is nothing going on between Trevor and me? When we see him, I'm sure he'll clear this up."

Shelby laughed, an awkward snorting sound. "If you think I'm taking you to him, then you're as stupid as all the other girls. Trevor doesn't know anything about all of this," she waved the gun again for emphasis, "and he never will. It's my job to protect him."

Carly's gut clenched as the pieces started to fall into place. How could she have missed the subtle clues? The way Shelby always hung by Trevor's side, her overt jealousy every time Trevor turned to her instead of Shelby for advice, her insistence on knowing every detail of his case.

Moments passed in awkward silence while Carly debated whether she should provoke more confessions from Shelby or hope for the best whenever they arrived at their destination. The urge to take action finally won out. "You're in love with him, aren't you?"

Shelby smiled. "Of course I am. He needs me. He's always needed me."

Shelby delivered the statement in a soft, tender, and totally creepy manner considering the implication. Carly had to know more. "Were there others besides Jocelyn and Vanessa?"

"They were the only ones who pushed back. Everyone else backed off after very little effort, but those two were stubborn, kept insisting Trevor cared about them, loved them even. They didn't have a clue, but no way could I let them stick around. Vanessa tried to ruin his career with her stupid claims of harassment."

"You sent the emails," Carly said. "Didn't you realize that Trevor would be blamed?"

"Don't be stupid. Those women needed to believe Trevor did it, but I made sure there was no real proof. You know that yourself since you got his suspension lifted. Thanks for that, by the way. If you'd only managed to keep from falling for him, then you wouldn't be here right now."

Carly struggled to process the roller coaster of information. Her first instinct was to insist there was only one person she'd fallen for during the course of this case, and it wasn't Trevor Kincade, but she had no desire to share her intimate feelings with the crazy lady holding a gun on her.

Landon. Now Carly wished she'd called Landon instead of Skye, if for no other reason than to have one final connection with her before she died, because it was pretty clear this wasn't going to end well. Hoping that Skye could hear her and that she'd pass the details of this conversation along, Carly risked a cryptic statement. "You're wrong, you know. I *am* falling for someone, but it's not Trevor. In fact, she and I made love just last night."

"You're lying!"

Shelby's shouted words were punctuated by the screech of tires, and Carly looked out the windshield in time to see them barely miss rear-ending the car directly ahead. As Carly tried to catch her breath, she realized they were about two hundred feet from the tollbooths and all the traffic around them was stopped.

"What the hell's going on?" Shelby was no longer yelling, but her words were sharp and angry, and she waved the gun carelessly in the air.

Carly ran through her options. She could either wait and hope someone saved her or try to save herself. Banking on a little of both, she waited until Shelby leaned her head out the driver's side window, to get a better look at the traffic snafu, and then eased her door open, shouting to cover the sound of her action. "Red Corvette. The tollbooth on Arapaho. She has a gun!" Carly pushed the car door open with both hands and tumbled out of the car onto the concrete roadway as the sound of gunfire cracked through the air.

Landon sensed the eyes of the shopkeeper trained on her back. He probably wasn't trying to rush her, but because the store was empty, she was getting all his attention, which only made her less able to make up her mind. Red roses seemed clichéd, but they were the only thing she could think of to accompany the bold statement she was about to make. She glanced at a cluster of bird-of-paradise. Funky, edgy, but too many sharp edges. The gerbera daisies were colorful and pretty, but definitely not grand gesture material. Roses it was.

"I'll take two dozen of the red roses."

"Two dozen?" The look on the florist's face made Landon want to ditch the whole idea and become a hermit. "Too much, huh? It's the first time. I mean the first time I've given her flowers. I need it to be big, but not so big that she gets scared away, but big enough to send a message. You know what I mean."

He nodded sagely. "Roses are the right choice, but I'd stick with a single dozen. Two can be a bit overwhelming. I can layer in some pretty greenery, but it's best to let the roses stand on their own. Do you need a vase or would you like them wrapped or in a box?"

She stared at him, willing him to read her mind, which was completely blank. She'd sent flowers before, but it was always via an order placed on the internet. She'd never walked into a florist for a full-on interrogation, and she was completely unprepared.

Apparently reading her dilemma, he said, "How about I use my best judgment? I only have one more question."

Landon braced for it. "Okay."

"Are these for a particular special occasion?"

What do you call it when you've angered the woman you've fallen for and she's not speaking to you outside of work, but you want to show her that you think she might be the one and so you're trying to come up with a grand gesture worthy of getting her to forgive you? "Let's just say I hope these are the first of many bouquets to come."

"Got it." He smiled and shooed her away. "I'll have this ready in a few minutes."

Landon wandered around the store and pulled out her phone. Carly hadn't responded to her text, and Landon resisted the urge to send another for fear she'd chase her away before she had a chance to say whatever it was she intended to say—she was still working that part out. She hoped the flowers would do some of the talking, but she needed to have a plan before she went marching over to Carly's, roses in hand.

Was it too soon? She'd felt this way only once before, years ago, but she'd given too freely only to have her love bartered away by her father, who viewed every human interaction as a potential business transaction. Carly, as business-oriented as she was, would never have chosen opportunity over affection, but without even knowing how Landon felt about Carly, her father had managed to mess things up again, employing whatever measures necessary to achieve the bottom line he desired without a single thought to what she cared about or needed.

Landon paid for the roses and drove to Carly's apartment. It was time for all her experience persuading juries to pay off.

There wasn't much traffic in the middle of the day, so she made it to Carly's complex in a few minutes. She parked in the lot, got out of the car, and cradled the bundle of roses in the crook of her arm. Her breath quickened as she reached Carly's door, but before she could raise her hand to knock, she heard the door across the way open and a voice call out.

"She's not home."

The neighbor. Of course. Landon fixed a smile on her face and turned toward him, deciding to use his spy skills to her advantage. "Do you happen to know when she'll be back?"

He stepped outside his apartment and stuck out his hand. "We met before. I'm Eugene Jasper, and you're…"

"Landon. Landon Holt." She shook his hand and prompted him about Carly. "Did she mention when she might get home?"

"She didn't say. Those are beautiful flowers. You get them at McShan's? I always get my flowers there. They only sell what's fresh, even have their own greenhouse. I tried another place—had a coupon—but the flowers looked like they'd been picked the week before and left lying on the counter. Fresh-cut flowers means fresh, if you know what I mean."

Landon let the bundle of roses drop to her side. Mission Carly had taken a wrong turn. What was she supposed to do now? Wait on Carly's doorstep while Mr. Jasper regaled her with stories or wander around town looking for Carly like Prince Charming with the lost glass slipper?

She should go back to work. As much as she loathed the idea of seeing Jane again, they had to be back in trial in the morning and she needed to be prepared. As soon as Mr. Jasper took a breath, she'd let him know she had to get back to the office. Like magic, her phone rang, saving her from having to wait. She didn't recognize the number but answering meant freedom from another story about a flower buying experience gone wrong. She punched the answer button. "Landon Holt."

"Landon, it's Skye. I don't have long, so listen close. Shelby Cross has two cars, a Denali and a Corvette. Do you know which one she usually drives?"

"What kind of question is that?"

"Come on, Landon, answer the question."

Landon's breath quickened at Skye's urgent tone. "I've only ever seen her drive the 'Vette. Candy apple red. Tell me why you're asking."

"She's got Carly and she's driving up north with her. Carly's in trouble. Shelby basically admitted she was the one who killed Vanessa and Jocelyn."

Landon dropped the roses and grabbed onto the phone with both hands like it was her only connection to Carly. "Where are you?"

"I'm on my way to the Uptown substation. One of my brothers is stationed there."

Landon did quick mental calculations. "I'm at Carly's apartment. It's like two blocks away. I'll meet you there."

"Roger that." Skye clicked off the line and Landon stood staring into her phone, trying to make sense of what she'd just heard.

"Is everything okay?"

Landon looked up from her phone at Mr. Jasper. "I don't know."

Then remembering that he'd seen Carly leave, she asked, "Was anyone with Carly when she left? Tell me everything you remember."

He pointed to the parking lot. "Yes, a woman came to the door. About your size and build. She had on a hat that covered her hair, so I couldn't tell you what color it was."

Landon resisted the urge to squeeze him to make him talk faster. "Did you see what kind of car they drove away in?"

"Matter of fact I did. Remember distinctly because it was parked in the fire lane, and I was going to report it to the property manager, but then when I saw Carly get in, I figured no sense getting her in trouble. She's always been very nice to me, and I'm sure she didn't mean to break the rules."

Landon sorted through his rambling words and latched onto a single detail. "You said you were going to report it. Did you happen to write down the plate number?"

"I did indeed." He pulled a small spiral-bound pad out of his pocket that Landon imagined he used to record lots of neighborhood infractions and flipped to a page near the back. "Here you go," he said, handing it over.

Landon's hand shook as she read the detailed description of the make and model of the car along with the license number. "Can I take this?" She didn't wait for an answer before she ripped out the page, shoved the notebook into his hand, and ran to her car.

Five minutes later, she burst through the doors of the police substation and shouted at the uniformed officer behind the counter. "Skye Keaton. Is she here?"

"Landon!"

She turned to see Skye standing on the other side of the room next to a police officer who could've been her twin. Landon jogged over to her. "I've got the license plate for Shelby's car." She held up the notebook page so Skye could see Mr. Jasper's notes.

"It's okay. We have it. We just weren't sure which car she was in." She pointed to the officer. "This is my brother Sean. Come on."

Sean used a password to open a door behind the counter and led them into a conference room. When they entered the room, Landon saw a Hispanic man dressed in jeans and a tweed sports coat seated at the table. He was speaking softly into a landline phone. Landon spotted a cell phone on the table with a digital recorder sitting next to it. Skye slid into the seat beside the man and handed him the paper. The man covered the handset of the phone with his palm. "Just highway sounds since you left the room."

"What's going on?" Landon asked.

Skye placed a finger over her lips and whispered. "I'll tell you everything I know, but you have to stay calm." She pointed at the cell phone on the table. "Carly called me when she realized she was in trouble, and Shelby pulled a gun on her and told Carly to hang up the phone. I guess Carly pretended to hang up but didn't actually do it because we've been able to hear everything they've been saying."

"Can't they hear us?"

"We've got the phone muted, and we're recording the whole thing with this." Skye pointed at the recorder.

Landon's knees buckled and she reached out to keep from falling. Skye grabbed her arm. "Have a seat." She pointed to the man on the other phone. "This is Detective Castillo. He's in touch with DPS. Carly managed to drop some clues and mentioned they are on the tollway. If that's where they are, DPS will find them."

"And what if they're not?"

Suddenly, the sound of Carly's voice crackled through the line. "...*am* falling for someone, but it's not Trevor. In fact, she and I made love just last night."

Landon gripped the armrest, desperate to call out to Carly, to tell her to be safe, that help was on the way. Next, she heard Shelby call Carly a liar followed by the sound of screeching tires.

"Do you think they've been pulled over?" She whispered the question to Skye, hoping the answer was yes and this nightmare would be over soon.

Skye's reply was cut off by the sound of Carly yelling, "Red Corvette. The tollbooth on Arapaho. She has a gun!" Landon braced for Shelby's reply, but nothing could've prepared her for the sharp crack of gunfire flooding the air, muted only by the sound of her own voice, yelling, "Noooo!"

CHAPTER TWENTY-THREE

Carly shivered in the back seat of the patrol car. The blanket the state trooper had wrapped her in was having no effect. He looked at her in the rearview mirror. "We'll be at the station in just a minute. Are you sure you don't want to go to the hospital?"

"Positive." Everything had happened at once. When she'd jumped out of Shelby's car, gunshots and sirens filled the air. She'd barely hit the ground when traffic around her started to move, and next thing she knew Shelby's car was surrounded by state troopers with guns drawn. While one of them negotiated with Shelby on a bullhorn, another two belly-crawled across the roadway and escorted her to the car she was in, then whisked her away from the scene. Other than a little road rash, she wasn't hurt, just shaken up and wanting answers, and so far, no one had been able to give her any.

Instinctively, she reached for her phone, only to remember it was in the back seat of Shelby's car. She started to ask the trooper if she could borrow his, but true to his word, they arrived at the station in record time. He told her to wait a minute, that he'd open her door, but she ignored him. She needed a phone and she needed it now. "I'll meet you inside," she called out on her way into the building. She marched up to the uniformed woman behind the desk. "I'm with Trooper Laramie. Do you have a phone I could use?"

The woman pointed to a desk with a phone in the waiting area. Carly made a beeline for it. She picked up the handset. She should call Skye first to let her know she was okay, but there was only one person's voice Carly needed to hear above all else.

"Carly!"

Carly stared at the handset. She hadn't dialed yet, but Landon's voice was loud and clear. She turned and Landon and Skye were walking toward her, but before she could reply, Landon was at her side, holding her in her arms.

"I was so scared. I thought she shot you." Landon leaned back and looked her up and down. "Are you hurt? Tell me you're not hurt."

"I'm not." Carly pulled her close. "Shelby's still there. They have her surrounded."

"It's over. She surrendered. Actually, I think she just ran out of bullets, but she's in custody. Thanks to you. If you hadn't thought to call Skye, then…" Landon shook her head, tears welling in her eyes.

"Don't," Carly said. "I'm fine. Barely a scratch. But I need something."

"Anything."

"Get me out of here. Please, take me home."

Landon hugged her close and whispered, "On it."

"Excuse me."

They both turned to Trooper Laramie standing behind them. "Ma'am, we need to get your statement now."

Landon stepped in front of Carly. "Ms. Pachett will be happy to give you a statement, but she's been through a harrowing ordeal and I'm going to take her home now." Landon handed him a card. "Call me later on my cell, and we'll set up a time to talk. Tomorrow."

He studied Landon's card and frowned. "We really need to get her statement while it's fresh in her mind."

"Oh, today is going to be fresh in my mind for a very long time," Carly said.

Skye walked over to join them. "Trooper, I know you're just doing your job, but the Dallas Uptown substation has a tape recording of the whole incident. Ms. Pachett's an attorney. If she gives you her word she'll talk to you tomorrow, you can count on it."

The trooper looked at the three of them. "Okay, tomorrow it is." He pointed at Landon. "I'll call you first thing in the morning."

Carly followed Landon and Skye to Skye's SUV, and climbed into the back seat. Landon paused before getting in the car, and Carly reached out a hand. "Please ride back here with me. Skye won't mind."

Skye answered with a knowing smile in the rearview mirror. Landon settled into the back seat and pulled Carly into her arms. Carly tilted her head back and looked up into Landon's eyes. "I have so much to tell you."

"Me too," Landon said.

"I should've said this before now, but I was scared, but now I'm scared not to say it because anything could happen. I'm sure Skye is a perfectly capable driver, but after what just happened, I'm seizing all the moments."

Landon grinned. "Seize away."

"I love you." Carly stared into Landon's eyes, hoping the sudden proclamation wouldn't send her running. "I think I've been falling in love with you since the first day you took me to eat barbecue. I started to realize then how dry and boring my life had become and how I've been missing out on all the good stuff. You make me want to live life to its fullest, and that doesn't mean a partnership at a law firm. The only partnership I want is one with you."

Carly watched Landon's face for her reaction, but she was unprepared when Landon started laughing. "What's so damn funny?"

"I quit the firm today. And I marched right out of there and bought a bunch of roses. I was headed to your house to tell you basically the same thing you just told me." Landon grinned again. "That stupid partnership doesn't add anything to my life if you're not in it. If you don't mind having a lover who's an unemployed lawyer, I'm all yours."

Carly answered by pulling Landon into a deep, blistering kiss. When they broke for air, she placed a hand against Landon's chest. "Nothing would make me happier."

❖

The next morning, Landon sat propped up on her elbow, watching Carly sleep, debating whether to wake her. By now, Jane and Judge Grafton knew what had happened yesterday and neither one of them could fault Carly for staying at home, especially since she and Skye could provide the details necessary to support a motion to dismiss or at least continue Trevor's case until everything could be sorted out.

"Are you going to stare at me all day?" Carly said, her eyes still closed. "Because if you are, you're going to have to follow me to the shower. We've got to get to the courthouse soon."

"Is that an invitation?"

Carly opened her eyes and smiled. "Maybe, but only if you promise to be good. I don't want to be late."

"Oh, I promise to be good all right." Landon pretended to be offended when Carly play slapped her. "Okay, okay, I get it. Sometimes a shower is just a shower." She shifted to a more serious tone. "Are you sure you want to go? Everyone would understand if you need a day."

Carly sat up against the pillows and tugged Landon into her arms. "I'm positive. Besides, I have my very own letter of resignation to deliver."

"Babe, you don't have to quit. Jane will probably give you the partnership now. Besides, you deserve it."

"I know I deserve it. I deserve it every bit as much as you do, but I don't want it anymore. Not with Sturges and Lloyd. There'll be something else out there for me. Something new and fresh. Besides, I have a pretty nice nest egg after five years of making good money and essentially living like a hermit."

Landon hadn't thought past her own resignation to what the future held other than being with Carly. "You don't have to worry. I have a sizable trust fund I've never tapped into."

"I thought you didn't want anything to do with your family's money."

"I didn't have a good enough reason before, but you know I think after everything that's happened, I actually earned my share. Besides, while you were sleeping, I had this crazy idea." Landon spent the next few minutes telling Carly her plan. "Don't tell me what you think now. Think it over, okay?"

Carly rolled on top of her and lowered her head for a long, lingering kiss. Landon moaned with want, wishing neither one of them had to get out of bed. When Carly slowly pulled back, she was wearing a big grin. "When I'm around you, thinking is not my strong suit," she said.

"Right back at you." Landon ran her hands up Carly's side. "To be continued."

"Most definitely."

❖

The courthouse lobby was crammed with reporters, and Carly ducked her head and tried to ignore the flurry of questions directed her way.

"When did you learn Shelby Cross was the killer?"

"Are you going to represent her?"

"Is it true she tried to shoot you and you overpowered her?"

Landon ushered her through the crowd, placing her body between Carly and the shouting press. When they finally reached the courtroom, it was packed, but much more quiet and subdued. Carly nodded at Jane and took her regular seat next to Trevor. He leaned close and whispered, "Are you okay?"

"She's fine," Landon interjected. "But she doesn't want to talk about it."

Carly gave him a sympathetic look but didn't bother trying to smooth things over. She didn't blame Trevor for what happened, but there was a part of her that wondered if in all the years he'd known Shelby, he should've noticed something off about her and the way he was the sole focus of her life. She supposed his stardom had led him to expect no less from the people in his orbit, but if he had paid attention, Vanessa and Jocelyn might still be alive.

Donna walked over to their table and handed Jane a stapled set of papers. "DPD searched Shelby's house last night." She shook her head. "You wouldn't believe what they found. An entire shrine to your client, along with enough evidence to definitely tie her to this case and the one in Houston." She pointed at the papers. "I filed that motion this morning, and I've asked the judge to rule on it before we go any further. I don't think you'll have any objection."

Carly looked at the papers in Jane's hand and saw that the motion was styled Motion to Dismiss in the matter of the *State of Texas vs. Trevor Kincade*. A rare move in the middle of a trial. The evidence against Shelby must've been rock solid.

"All rise."

Judge Grafton took the bench, and a few minutes later it was all over. She granted the state's motion, dismissed the jury, and told Trevor he was free to go. Carly watched him open his arms as if to hug her and then veer off at the last minute to hug Jane instead. She looked over her shoulder and saw Landon standing directly behind her, staring at Trevor.

"He's harmless, you know."

"He might be, but I'd rather he keep his hands to himself."

Carly whispered in Landon's ear. "Yours are the only hands I want on me." As she said the words, she started plotting the fastest way to get out of the courthouse and back in bed.

Jane's voice snapped her back to reality. "Carly, Landon, I was hoping we could have a moment to talk."

Carly looked at Landon who shrugged. "I suppose we can hear what she has to say."

"Okay." Carly looked at her watch. "We have somewhere to be, but we can give you five minutes."

Jane looked offended, but she quickly smothered her annoyance with a fake smile. "Mark and I had a long talk last night. You've both done such good work on this case, we decided we couldn't choose between you. We're making you both partners of Sturges and Lloyd. Effective immediately."

Carly choked back a laugh. "Is that so?"

"Yes, it's true."

"Landon, what do you think about this *generous* offer?" Carly asked, purposely not looking at her for fear she'd lose it.

"I think I'll take a pass. Besides, I already quit."

"And you know, I was planning to quit this morning," Carly said. "So, that's a hard pass for me too."

"What?" Jane appeared flummoxed.

"We appreciate that you came here with a plan to make us both partners, but we've got plans of our own." Carly reached down and took Landon's hand in hers. "Big plans." Carly didn't wait for a response. Instead she walked hand in hand with her lover out of the courtroom and toward a future they would share together.

EPILOGUE

Two months later

Landon stopped one of the cater waiters carrying food pans and surveyed the contents. "Are those fritters?"

He nodded. "With pimento cheese and a pepper jelly drizzle."

"Be still my heart."

Carly grabbed her from behind. "Do *not* give your heart away to a bunch of fritters."

Landon turned in Carly's arms and smiled. "Not to worry. My heart's all yours."

"I think we might have too much food. Have you seen how many pans are already in the kitchen and Ian keeps sending more."

"The proper response is 'my heart's all yours too.'" Landon gave Carly a light, quick kiss, hoping to distract her from obsessing over the party preparations.

"It is. I promise. I'm just worried. What if no one comes?"

Ah, so that was it. Landon reached into her pocket and pulled out a ragged slip of paper. She'd been carrying it with her since the morning Trevor Kincade's case had been dismissed. She set it on the nearest table and smoothed it out. "This," she pointed at the words *Pachett and Holt, Attorneys at Law*, "is going to be the very best law firm in Dallas. With the winning combination of Pachett's supersonic brain and Holt's ability to charm retainers out of even the stingiest of clients, they are destined for greatness." She reached for Carly's hand. "And it all starts tonight. With lots of food."

"Don't forget the drinks." Ian appeared next to them holding a fancy glass beverage dispenser filled with a light blue concoction. "A special recipe just for you. I'm calling this the Not Guilty."

"I'll drink to that," Landon said.

"So will I." Carly squeezed Landon's hand and watched Ian walk back to the kitchen. They'd all worked hard to bring the grand opening of their law firm to fruition. "I'm going to take a page from your book and envision a wildly successful night."

"Make that a wildly successful *lifetime* and you're on." Landon reached into her pocket and pulled out a small red leather box. "I was going to wait until Valentine's Day, but I'm not very good at waiting when I know exactly what I want, and I want you to be my partner in everything life has to offer for the rest of our lives. Carly Pachett, will you marry me?"

She held her breath while she waited for Carly's response, but she didn't have to wait long.

"There is absolutely nothing I'd rather do more. Yes. A thousand times yes!"

About the Author

Carsen Taite's goal as an author is to spin tales with plot lines as interesting as the cases she encountered in her career as a criminal defense lawyer. She is the award-winning author of numerous novels of romance and romantic intrigue, including the Luca Bennett Bounty Hunter series and the Lone Star Law series.

Books Available From Bold Strokes Books

Captive by Donna K. Ford. To escape a human trafficking ring, Greyson Cooper and Olivia Danner become players in a game of deceit and violence. Will their love stand a chance? (978-1-63555-215-7)

Crossing the Line by CF Frizzell. The Mob discovers a nemesis within its ranks, and in the ultimate retaliation, draws Stick McLaughlin from anonymity by threatening everything she holds dear. (978-1-63555-161-7)

Love's Verdict by Carsen Taite. Attorneys Landon Holt and Carly Pachett want the exact same thing: the only open partnership spot at their prestigious criminal defense firm. But will they compromise their careers for love? (978-1-63555-042-9)

Precipice of Doubt by Mardi Alexander & Laurie Eichler. Can Cole Jameson resist her attraction to her boss, veterinarian Jodi Bowman, or will she risk a workplace romance and her heart? (978-1-63555-128-0)

Savage Horizons by CJ Birch. Captain Jordan Kellow's feelings for Lt. Ali Ash have her past and future colliding, setting in motion a series of events that strands her crew in an unknown galaxy thousands of light years from home. (978-1-63555-250-8)

Secrets of the Last Castle by A. Rose Mathieu. When Elizabeth Campbell represents a young man accused of murdering an elderly woman, her investigation leads to an abandoned plantation that reveals many dark Southern secrets. (978-1-63555-240-9)

Take Your Time by VK Powell. A neurotic parrot brings police officer Grace Booker and temporary veterinarian Dr. Dani Wingate together in the tiny town of Pine Cone, but their unexpected attraction keeps the sparks flying. (978-1-63555-130-3)

The Last Seduction by Ronica Black. When you allow true love to elude you once and you desperately regret it, are you brave enough to grab it when it comes around again? (978-1-63555-211-9)

The Shape of You by Georgia Beers. Rebecca McCall doesn't play it safe, but when sexy Spencer Thompson joins her workout class, their nonstop sparring forces her to face her ultimate challenge—a chance at love. (978-1-63555-217-1)

Exposed by MJ Williamz. The closet is no place to live if you want to find true love. (978-1-62639-989-1)

Force of Fire: Toujours a Vous by Ali Vali. Immortals Kendal and Piper welcome their new child and celebrate the defeat of an old enemy, but another ancient evil is about to awaken deep in the jungles of Costa Rica. (978-1-63555-047-4)

Landing Zone by Erin Dutton. Can a career veteran finally discover a love stronger than even her pride? (978-1-63555-199-0)

Love at Last Call by M. Ullrich. Is balancing business, friendship, and love more than any willing woman can handle? (978-1-63555-197-6)

Pleasure Cruise by Yolanda Wallace. Spencer Collins and Amy Donovan have few things in common, but a Caribbean cruise offers both women an unexpected chance to face one of their greatest fears: falling in love. (978-1-63555-219-5)

Running Off Radar by MB Austin. Maji's plans to win Rose back are interrupted when work intrudes, and duty calls her to help a SEAL team stop a Russian mobster from harvesting gold from the bottom of Sitka Sound. (978-1-63555-152-5)

Shadow of the Phoenix by Rebecca Harwell. In the final battle for the fate of Storm's Quarry, even Nadya's and Shay's powers may not be enough. (978-1-63555-181-5)

Take a Chance by D. Jackson Leigh. There's hardly a woman within fifty miles of Pine Cone that veterinarian Trip Beaumont can't charm, except for the irritating new cop, Jamie Grant, who keeps leaving parking tickets on her truck. (978-1-63555-118-1)

Death in Time by Robyn Nyx. Working in the past is hell on your future. (978-1-63555-053-5)

The Outcasts by Alexa Black. Spacebus driver Sue Jones is running from her past. When she crash-lands on a faraway world, the Outcast Kara might be her chance for redemption. (978-1-63555-242-3)

Alias by Cari Hunter. A car crash leaves a woman with no memory and no identity. Together with Detective Bronwen Pryce, she fights to uncover a truth that might just kill them both. (978-1-63555-221-8)

Hers to Protect by Nicole Disney. Ex–high school sweethearts Kaia and Adrienne will have to see past their differences and survive the vengeance of a brutal gang if they want to be together. (978-1-63555-229-4)

Perfect Little Worlds by Clifford Mae Henderson. Lucy can't hold the secret any longer. Twenty-six years ago, her sister did the unthinkable. (978-1-63555-164-8)

Room Service by Fiona Riley. Interior designer Olivia likes stability, but when work brings footloose Savannah into her world and into a new city every month, Olivia must decide if what makes her comfortable is what makes her happy. (978-1-63555-120-4)

Sparks Like Ours by Melissa Brayden. Professional surfers Gia Malone and Elle Britton can't deny their chemistry on and off the beach. But only one can win… (978-1-63555-016-0)

Take My Hand by Missouri Vaun. River Hemsworth arrives in Georgia intent on escaping quickly, but when she crashes her Mercedes into the Clip 'n Curl, sexy Clay Cahill ends up rescuing more than her car. (978-1-63555-104-4)

The Last Time I Saw Her by Kathleen Knowles. Lane Hudson only has twelve days to win back Alison's heart. That is, if she can gather the courage to try. (978-1-63555-067-2)

Wayworn Lovers by Gun Brooke. Will agoraphobic composer Giselle Bonnaire and Tierney Edwards, a wandering soul who can't remain in one place for long, trust in the passionate love destiny hands them? (978-1-62639-995-2)